Pride Publishing books by C F White

Responsible Adult
Misdemeanor
Hard Time
Reformed

St. Cross
Won't Feel a Thing
Won't Be Fooled Again

Pink Rock
Love & Tea Bags

I0542403

St. Cross

WON'T BE FOOLED AGAIN

C F WHITE

Won't Be Fooled Again
ISBN # 978-1-83943-825-7
©Copyright C F White 2019
Cover Art by Cherith Vaughan ©Copyright August 2019
Interior text design by Claire Siemaszkiewicz
Pride Publishing

WON'T BE
FOOLED AGAIN

Dedication

To Claire. *My* oldest friend.

Chapter One

Narrow Escape

The yellow toy candy egg that was perched on the shabby chest of drawers wobbled with every foot stomp from outside. It stared at him. *Mocked* him. Forced him back to a life he'd tried escaping.

Pacing the dishevelled bedroom in his fifth-floor flat, Callum scraped his hair back and tied it into a messy topknot. With nothing more than a pull-out bed and a wardrobe, the space was so small that his uneasy strides took him full circle. *This bloke cannot get here quick enough.*

He had to swat away the beads of sweat sprinkling his bottom lip with the ball of his thumb—his fingers were useless with trembling. He wiped his hands down his ripped jeans then rubbed his palms together, needing his hands back at full function. *Get a fucking grip. It'll all be over in a minute.* Adrenaline had him jumping on the spot and the crash of his heart pained his chest with every energetic leap.

Fuck. All. This. Shit.

Deep thuds from above and below pounded louder, like a herd of fucking elephants were marching down the communal stairway opposite his single occupancy. *Why can't these people use the damn fucking lifts?*

Catching his reflection in the smeared mirror hanging on the wardrobe by one rusty nail, Callum paused. Not for thought — more for context. He glanced away just as quickly. The clothes strewn about the room covered every inch of the grey tiled carpet and his fraying rucksack propped up by the door was ready and waiting for his swift exit. His stomach growled, which temporarily masked the heavy stomps from outside. At least after this, he'd have a bit of dough and could buy a decent meal. He'd had enough of the tinned crap from the food bank.

The candy egg caught his eye again. *Just one?* No one would know. Might take the edge off.

Fuck. He needed gloves. He ransacked the flat — every room, every drawer, every cupboard, under every discarded item of clothing — stopping in the living area for composure. He checked in his stone-washed-jeans pockets, a last resort. *Come on!* Snatching his bag, he then ripped open the zip with trembling fingers. He hung it upside down over the once-red fabric sofa that was now stained with varying amounts of he didn't want to know what. Nothing of interest fell out. Just the two throwaway phones. He checked the display on one, then switched it off, smacked it against his leg to release the SIM card and stamped on it with his steel-toe-capped boot.

The front door rattled on its hinges and Callum's heart leapt into his throat along with a sizeable amount of bile. He peered through to his bedroom just in time to witness the plastic egg falling from the chest of

8

drawers and being captured within the soft cotton of a tattered jumper. *Bollocks.* He couldn't touch it. He couldn't. Not without the damn gloves.

Bang, bang, bang. Knuckles rapped the front door, drilling through Callum's temple and whatever resolve he might still have had left. *Thank fuck.*

Pulling himself together, he trampled over the clutter to flick the latch up, making the clang ricochet off the oppressive walls. He nudged open the door just enough to fit his face through the gap.

An Indian man stared back at him, eyes wide. "Gotta get out, son. Fire."

"*What?*" Callum clung onto the door, unwilling to open it farther.

"Leave everything. It's spreading." The man, Callum suddenly recalled, lived three doors down from him in one of the larger flats. This was the longest conversation they'd ever had—Callum had become a bit of a recluse.

As his grip released, the door drifted open wider to reveal a horde of families rushing down the fire escape steps opposite. All panic-stricken. No forming an orderly queue. His neighbours halted up ahead by the stairwell—four young girls all clinging to their mum's skirt, glaring in frustration as the woman yelled something to him in her mother tongue.

The man responded to her in a quick-fire language that Callum couldn't decipher, then, with fear apparent in his dark eyes, gripped Callum's arm. "Please. Come."

"Wait." Callum held up a finger, when the sudden stench of thick smoke drifted to his nostrils. He coughed.

"Now!" The man yanked him again, but soon gave up when fog clouded around his family. He left, rushed to their aid and ushered them all down the stairs.

Callum's eyes streamed. He couldn't leave. He couldn't. Not yet. *Not now, for fuck's sake!* He looked through the flat to his bedroom, to his bag, his stuff, his life. The plastic toy egg —

Then he slammed the door shut behind him and lunged for the staircase.

Slapping a palm on the railing, he paused. Others bundled past him, bashing him in their hasty retreat. Callum's legs wouldn't move. He shut his stinging eyes for a moment, then, when he opened them, peered along the corridor to the flat at the end. The door was shut.

Shit.

Growling, Callum launched himself off the steps and ran the length of the corridor, landing with a balled fist at number fifty-nine. He banged, hard, coughing through the surrounding smoke and the rising heat enveloping him. *She could have left already?*

He'd never forgive himself if he didn't find out for sure.

Stepping back, he lifted his leg and lined up the outsole of his heavy-duty standard work boots at the door. He sucked in a deep breath that was clouded with bristling fumes, then slammed his sole, full force, onto the PVC. The pressure-pain ricocheted up his leg to his hip and the door flung open, ripping half the wood from the frame along with it.

Coughing, Callum bolted inside the flat. "Eve!" He held his sleeve up to his mouth as he stormed through the corridor.

The living area was vacant, no one inside. The kitchen opposite also empty. Farther still, he pushed open the door to the first bedroom. Neatly kept, not slept in. Not for years. Callum's heart sank through to his feet.

"Callum! What are you —" Eve's tight braids that had used to be wound into an on-the-top bun were left dangling over her shoulders as she emerged from the main bedroom. Her hair used to be solid black, but now there were speckles of ash white running through, serving Callum a dreaded reminder of how long it had been since he'd last seen her this close. But he couldn't think about that now. Or they'd both be dead and buried, like the past was supposed to be.

"Fire. We need to get out." Callum's mouth was dry, but he ignored the parch in his throat to grab her arm.

"What? Callum, no!" She resisted, yanking away from him. Her long night dress was only mildly covered by a towelled dressing gown that hung down to a cast on her left foot. He'd heard about her fall, but he hadn't had the guts to ask how she'd been doing. He hated himself for that. "Fires are contained to the flats. We stay put and secure the doors."

"*Everyone* is leaving." Callum's panicked voice elevated in urgency and he widened his eyes in plea.

The screech of a long and loud blast from the internal fire alarms burst through to the room and Eve staggered back.

"Your door's broken now, anyway!" Callum dug fingertips into the soft fibres of Eve's dressing gown as smoke trailed in through the open front door and down the corridor. "Auntie, please." The endearment fell from his tongue without conscious thought, even if he hadn't uttered the word in so long. He had no right to call her that. He didn't deserve it. Not anymore.

11

Eve bit her bottom lip, drawing troubled eyebrows in. She stared at Callum, her chest rising. And for a moment Callum thought this would be how it all ended. And wouldn't that make for a piece of fucking irony? Eventually, though, she nodded and allowed Callum to usher her out of the flat. She had to hobble, the cast on her foot making it difficult to walk, let alone rush. Callum stayed at her side, coughing through the rising fumes and taking all Eve's weight for her.

As they reached the stairwell, the smoke had thickened, distorting much of Callum's view and preventing any clean air from reaching his lungs. Grabbing Eve's wrist, he held her towelling sleeve to her mouth. "Breathe through that."

They tumbled down the first flight, awkwardly falling into each other or the wall, to stop at the separating landing. A little boy, no more than five or six, stood against the wall and wailed, calling for his mummy.

"That's Thomas!" Eve choked out the boy's name in urgency.

Callum didn't think. He rarely did. With a clenched jaw, he let Eve go and grabbed the boy to haul him up to rest on his hip. The boy wrapped thin, quivering arms around Callum's neck and clasped his hands together.

If this fire didn't kill Callum, strangulation would.

"Where is his mother?" Eve asked.

"Everyone left, Auntie." Callum tapped the boy's arm, attempting to loosen the kid's tight grip. It didn't work. Delving deep to find a courage he didn't know he had, he linked his arm through Eve's and hobbled them all the rest of the way down the stairs.

As they emerged into daylight, he set the boy to the ground but clung to his tiny, trembling hand. He wasn't sure it was any comfort to the snot-nosed kid, but, for some reason, it was to Callum.

"You're all right, yeah?" Callum wasn't sure if that was a question, or just hope vocalised.

The little kid didn't answer. Which was okay with Callum. He wouldn't have known what to do if he'd been given the negative anyway.

"Thomas!" A woman's petrified scream sounded up ahead. Her approaching voice was distorted by the other sounds that rippled Callum's skin. He could see her mouth moving, but no words were decipherable. Slipping down onto her knees, the panic-stricken woman snatched the boy to her chest. "Eve!" She stood. "Thank you! I lost him on the stairs. Are you okay?"

Eve shook her head, tears trailing down her cheeks as she slipped away from Callum and into the woman's outstretched hand.

"Let's get you to an ambulance."

Dazed, confused, Callum lost them all. Alone, he stumbled up the path and passed the fenced-off playground, where the one lone swing swaying in the breeze appeared as inviting as it ever had. Bashed, Callum was forced back to the present, his head a haze of cotton wool. Dozens of firemen decked out in full head gear rushed toward the entrance of the building.

Only once he'd reached the pedestrian walkway littered with onlookers did Callum stop and turn.

Flames sizzled from the fourth floor of the block and drifted upward, blurring the outline of the concrete. Gasps, cries and sobs stabbed Callum's eardrums, whilst flashing emergency lights, thick black smoke and bright orange sparks saturated his vision.

Involuntary retching pained his chest. He couldn't get a handle on himself. Bending double, he threw up into the gutter, his limited stomach contents now discarded down the drain for the rats to consume.

"You okay, mate?" A light tap to his back stopped the pitiful display.

Callum stood, tufts of hair falling from the band to irritate his eyes, but he could still see the concern flickering behind the fireman's shielded mask. "Yeah." He nodded and looked back up at his childhood home. "Lucky escape."

Never a truer statement.

Chapter Two

Tick, Tock

"How many times are you going to look up at that clock?"

Kez instinctively looked up at that clock. Then laughed and crunched through his mid-afternoon apple. "Sorry."

His supervisor, Lisa, at the opposite desk to his, gave a twisted smile before continuing her rampant typing. Kez sank lower behind his computer screen so his face would be masked by the separating border that was cluttered with reminders, along with a few motivating work-life-balance quotes ironically covered up by policy and procedure print-outs.

He'd memorised them all, the quotes *and* the policies, so he never did understand why he had to have them cluttering up the pinboard that could be put to better use. He also knew the core values of St. Cross Children's Hospital like the back of his hand. His real one, that was, the one he'd had from birth and not the prosthetic that the NHS had finally caved in and given him a couple of years ago, twenty-three years after having been born without a left forearm.

Drifting his gaze up to the back wall, he mentally counted the aggravating ticks.

"I can hear you looking at it." Lisa tapped pointy fingernails along her keypad as though drumming to her own beat.

At least that was something to home in on other than *tick tock, tick tock*.

"Maybe we need to take it down?" Kez suggested. "What's the point of a clock on the wall, anyway? It only reminds the patients of how late their appointment is."

"And why might you be staring at it, then?" Lisa peeped over the screen, her perfectly smoothed-out eyebrows trailing up her forehead and hiding beneath her thick dark fringe.

She was trying out this look to cover the lines she claimed to have developed overnight when she'd turned forty last month. As far as Kez was concerned, her brow was as smooth as his left arm, and that was covered in a light-brown plastic that stood in stark contrast to his darker skin tone. But it was the best he was gonna get on the NHS. The cheaper versions tended to favour white patients.

Catching her gaze, Kez smiled as sweetly as he could and a few deep-set wrinkles appeared through the locks of her hair. *Huh, they only appear when she frowns.*

For those working in the cardiology outpatients department of a busy children's hospital, frowning was a common occurrence. Especially when the admin staff were wishing they were elsewhere and the clinic was overrunning, as it so often did in the Rawlings-Khan practice. Both doctors were particularly thorough. A good thing for the patients being seen to, a not-so-good-thing for the secretaries who dealt with all the fallouts from those they were holding up. Or for Lisa, who had to ensure that her admin staff, aka Kez, didn't overwork like the doctors so often did.

"Why? To magically make it whizz around to five p.m." Kez had to be honest. Lying made him sweat.

Lisa tutted just as the *p-ding* of an inbound email burst from Kez's computer speakers and brought the conversation to an immediate standstill. When Kez darted his gaze to his inbox, he couldn't have prevented the spreading grin if his job had depended on it. And it kinda did.

Good morning, Kwesi! Are we still on for our meeting later? Kind regards, Dr. Rafferty Carmichael.

The little winky face after the name suggested this wasn't the usual professional meeting exchange. Throwing his apple core into the bin, Kez shuffled forward and tapped out his reply with speedy fingers.

Dear Dr. Carmichael, I have indeed scheduled our appointment into my calendar. Five p.m. cannot come around quick enough. This may be the first meeting I've ever looked forward to. Best wishes, Kez x

He wasn't sure about adding the kiss. Especially considering this was on his work account. But his fingers had done the talking and it had whooshed off before he could feel any guilt about it. This couldn't be the first email exchange that had overstepped the boundaries laid out in the policy notes stapled to his cubicle border. Not if the St. Cross rumour mill was to be believed.

Can't wait either. Meet you outside. Raff xx

Well, well, well. Two *kisses.* Kez's smile grew tenfold to pain his cheeks.

Gasping, Lisa peered higher over the barrier. "You have a hot date, don't you?"

Kez tried a flippant shrug, but guessed his curving lips would give him away. "Maybe."

"I knew it! You've been smiling all day, even when you were talking to Mrs. Marsh earlier. Come on, out with it. Who is it? Someone here?"

"He may be an employee of the hospital, yes."

"A doctor?"

Kez grinned.

"You, Mr. Zakari" — Lisa pointed the tip of her highlighter pen at him — "are a dark horse. And I seriously hope it's not Rawlings. There's enough going around about him as it is."

Kez laughed. "No, it's not Rawlings." He tilted his head. "Although, I wouldn't have minded before all the rumours."

"I'll bet. But we don't know they're true, so let's give the bloke the benefit of the doubt, yes?"

"Sure." Kez had to. He was Rawlings' secretary after all.

"So which doctor is it?" Lisa hummed. "The new one on Walrus Ward? Straight out of med school? Bit of a dish in tweed?"

"My lips are sealed on this one, I'm afraid. I'm hoping it actually works out, after the disastrous last one. You'd think a doctor, even one who's from Social

Sciences, would be able to tell that this was fake." Kez held up his left arm.

Lisa winced. "Oh, crap. What happened?"

"Took my shirt off and he miraculously had an urgent call to attend to."

"Oh, Kwesi. What an arsehole."

Kez shrugged. "Used to it. So, you'll understand why I won't be divulging the name of this one just yet."

"Fine. Don't tell me." Lisa huffed and tapped her nails across her keypad. "Well, you know what they say, right?"

"It's always the quiet ones?"

"Ain't that the truth?" Lisa peeped up from behind the barrier. "But no, I was referring to the time."

"Oh, right! It's good to be fashionably late?"

"Ha, no, but in this ward I'd say we'd win the London catwalk. You seriously do have this mystery date on your mind. I meant that time flies…"

"Yeah, when you're having *fun*?" Kez furrowed his brow, forming his own wrinkles.

Lisa chuckled. "Well, I mean the day goes quicker when you're busy. So…" She prodded the tip of her pen through an imaginary target in the air.

Said target was clearly Kez and his procrastination efforts. Shuffling his chair under the desk, he attempted to get his work mode back on. He really did need to concentrate when typing out Dr. Rawlings' notes. The consultant Kez serviced had practically illegible handwriting as it was, but having been the doctor's secretary for a couple of years now, Kez had learned to decipher most of it. The rest he highlighted, and if Lisa turned up a blank, then he had to do the embarrassing cross-check with the doctor himself, taking up too much of Rawlings' already precious time.

Squinting at the notes, he leaned forward, then huffed and bit off the lid to his pink highlighter.

"Kwesi!"

Kez swivelled in his chair. That demanding tone, along with his full name, meant business. *What have I fucked up this time?*

Kez blew the pen lid onto his desk. "Yes, Doctor?"

"We may have to cancel the rest of today's appointments." Dr. Rawlings swung the multicoloured stethoscope around his neck, then tucked his tight-fitting chequered shirt into his just-as-figure-hugging chinos.

Damn, that man is hot for a middle-aged bloke. Kez shook himself out. Not for the first time either. Whilst not technically his line manager — Lisa was the one who did his supervisions and annual reviews — the doctor was still his superior, and one of the most glorified paediatric cardiology consultants in the country. *Swoon much?*

And if the current rumours infecting the hospital's sterile walls were to be believed, Dr. Elliot Rawlings actually preferred men to the women who threw themselves at him more often than Kez was meant to notice. *What are the chances, eh?* Not that Kez had one, of course. Rumour mill also suggested that Rawlings had a type, and Kez wasn't it. The doctor was into blonds. *Who isn't these days?*

"You want me to send these ones home?" Kez lowered his voice so as not to alert the remaining patients who were crowding the waiting area, with the clinic already behind on the routine check-ups.

"Best do." The doctor nodded. "Or transfer the urgent ones to Dr. Khan. There's been an emergency call-out for doctors in the area. I'm on standby."

The doctor scurried off, his dress-shoes clomping on the varnished flooring. Kez didn't linger too long on the man's backside, he was almost certainly sure this time.

Instead, he exchanged uneasy looks with Lisa over the top of their desk barriers, silently conversing as to what this emergency call-out could be. She tapped nails across her keyboard, obviously in an attempt to check the latest management level notices that Kez's pay grade forbade him to see, when a shallow gasp from the cardiology waiting area caught his attention and prickled his skin.

He stood, scooted out from behind his desk and stepped toward the door that separated the administration area from the medical bays. The television, normally tuned into Cbeebies or some Disney film, had been switched to News 24. The bold white-type lettering trailing the screen sent instant gut-wrenching fear into Kez's normally iron stomach. His daily apple that, unfortunately, never kept the doctor away from him, curdled among that morning's breakfast efforts of honey-flavoured porridge oats.

FIRE IN MARLYTE ESTATE, BRANTON.

The parents still left in the waiting area all stared up at the screen. Their intense focus rendered the usually buzzing waiting area silent except for the odd burst of song from whichever plastic toy hadn't run out of batteries and was currently being put to full use by one of Dr. Rawlings' patients.

"A fire has broken out in a block of flats in Branton, East London." The news reporter motioned to the building she stood before with a well-practised solemn expression. "The flames spread quickly and emergency services have been called a full hour after the fire is suspected to have started. Residents declare the alarm system hadn't worked, with many having been alerted to the blaze by their neighbours."

The reporter swished a lock of hair away from her face and the wind blew the blonde strands straight back to stick to her glossy lips. Kez had no idea why he fixated on her and not what she stood in front of. *Perhaps so I don't have to look at it.*

"There have been no fatalities reported, but those with serious injuries have been taken to nearby hospitals, which are doing their best to cope with the overwhelming demand, pulling specialists out from other hospitals in the area."

Kez's fingers trembled, the tips frozen as he clamped them over his mouth.

"Residents of the Marlyte Estate in Branton have been granted access to nearby community centres, with church buildings opening their doors for those who have now suddenly found themselves homeless…"

Ice-cold blood surged through his entire body and Kez hurtled back to his desk, grabbed his keys and flung his jacket over his sedentary arm.

"Kez!" Lisa stood, hands on hips. "Where are you going?"

Kez didn't stop. He couldn't. He ran through the corridors, slaloming through the scrubs heading his way and ricocheting off moving beds, all in an attempt to get to the exit of the hospital.

Some things were more important than a job.

Or a hot date with a doctor.

* * * *

He would have thought he'd be used to hospitals, especially having worked in one for the best part of three years and being a regular outpatient due to his congenital defect, but the entrance to the Accident & Emergency department of Newham University Hospital in Plaistow didn't have the same welcoming vibe that Kez's home from home at St. Cross did. There, they covered up the atrocities that life threw at unsuspecting families with smiley, happy volunteers, brightly coloured furniture and inspiring murals painted on the walls.

Here, it was all business.

Overcrowded with patients demanding to be seen or to be shown where their loved ones were or to be told what was happening next, the hospital appeared more like a battleground. And there was something so very off-putting about adult patients in emergency wards. They screamed wounds and sickness and…*death*. The smell wasn't the same either, despite all NHS-led hospitals bulk buying the same sterilising solution for cleaning.

Kez felt for the staff on duty, but that was minor in comparison to his need to push through the mounds of people and give his best demanding clearing of his throat to the girl behind the counter. Whilst he didn't work an A&E clinic, he knew what irate patients who had been waiting for far longer than was deemed appropriate could be like. *Draining your very soul.* But he hadn't just abandoned his frontline post, rushed through the city of London via several modes of public transport and sprinted from the station to be told to wait.

"Hi, sorry, could you tell me if Eve Atta has been admitted?" He had no idea if his aunt had even been conscious on arrival and would use her English given name, or if they'd had to do a routine ID check that would show up her Ghanaian birth name. It was best to offer both, to help out the admin staff. Kez knew what it was like dealing with names that sometimes didn't match up to database records.

The girl responded to Kez's hopeful smile by nodding and checking through the patient listings. "Yes, cubical five. Waiting for a bed upstairs."

Kez gave his thanks and hurried through to the main cubicles, not even bothering to ask for permission. They could come find him later, but he suspected the security staff had enough on their plates, judging by the sudden outburst from the man with a nail pounded into his hand.

As Kez pulled apart the green curtain to bay five, he nearly gave the cleaners more work for their minimum wage by vomiting his curdled apple onto the sterile floor.

His aunt lay there on the fold-out bed, covered in her old dressing gown as if she were sleeping soundly at home, but she wasn't. Sleeping, that was. *Is she?* The oxygen mask covering her mouth made it difficult to decipher whether she was inhaling her own breaths, and the cast on her foot had slipped to the edge of the wafer-thin mattress as if it was too heavy for her to cope with.

"Auntie!" Kez rushed to her side and placed his clammy hand in hers.

Eve's eyes flickered open and she smiled through the mask. Pulling it down, she licked her dried lips and gripped Kez's fingers with warm skin. *That's a good a sign as any that she's okay, right?*

Right?

"Kwesi. Oh, Kwesi." Her normally husky voice was gritty and deep.

"Are you okay?" Bit of a stupid question considering, but what else could he say?

She nodded. "Yes. Lucky really. I wouldn't have left. They told us, stay put." She had to pause to cough. "But he rescued me."

"Who did?" Was this where she swooned over some young fireman? Kez held down the need to utter that some people get all the luck.

Eve swallowed, then pointed to the glass of water by the side of her bed. Kez handed it over and helped her drink, lowering to perch on the edge of the mattress. Eve looked weary, her skin ashy, and the scattered silver strands of hair fuzzed out from her usual tight braids that draped over her shoulders and down to her chest.

"Your Callum."

Kez jolted. He shook his head. It had been a while since he'd heard that name, especially coming from his Aunt Eve, and the prefix was a shock in itself.

"Callum?" Kez confirmed, just for the record.

Eve nodded, gesturing to the plastic cup once more. After taking a sip, she settled back against the metal headboard.

"He came to me, Kwesi. He carried me out. And a little boy."

Disbelief ran through Kez's frosty veins. "Callum?" He glanced around, half expecting the man to show up and corroborate her story. When he didn't, Kez laughed at himself for thinking that miracles might happen. "Where is he now?"

"I don't know. They whisked me off to here. I expect he didn't want to hang around for the authorities."

Kez had to laugh. Wouldn't that be the truth? Regardless, he didn't want to think about Callum. Not then. Not ever, really.

Trouble was, he'd been trying that for the better part of five years.

And failing miserably.

"What's happening to you?" Kez shifted his focus to the one person he could trust to always be there. At least he could rely on her. She hadn't left him. Thank God. *Apparently, thank Callum. Now there's some serious irony.*

"I'll stay here for a day or so. They'll be checking me over, no doubt."

"Then you'll come stay with me."

Eve smiled that beatific smile of hers but shook her head. "No need, darling. I've already agreed to stay with Grace, from the church. You have your own life now. Don't need this old dear cramping your style."

"Don't be daft. It's us, Auntie. Me and you. You look after me, I look after you. The way we always have. Family, remember?" *Family isn't all about flesh and blood.* That very thought caused an unexpected prickle that Kez couldn't shake off. He had to ask. "Did Callum's mum get out?"

Eve tilted her neck and reached out a hand to tap Kez's cheek. "She's been long gone, dear. Ever since he came back."

"Right." Kez frowned, shaking to roll the odd sense of guilt off his tense shoulders. He hadn't known that. And he'd used to have known everything there was to know about Callum's life. *Times change.* "You're coming home with me, though. No arguments."

"I have somewhere to go, darling. I am the fortunate one. There are so many who aren't."

Why was it his aunt could say so much with so few words? Like that time she'd thrown her traditional Catholic principles out of the window to declare that *'Karma would work its way and serve them all cold.'*

Turned out she was wrong though. Karma was a scorcher.

Chapter Three

Blast from the Past

The crying was getting on his nerves. But probably not more so than it was for the mother of the poor kid who hadn't stopped weeping since setting foot in the community centre. The tiny hall was overcrowded. And stuffy. And excruciatingly loud. Callum had found himself here, along with the other residents of the council-run housing who now had no home to go to, in a bit of a daze. Some of his neighbours had relatives, of course, and friends. And those people had come in droves, gathering the residents of Marlyte Estate and their limited belongings that they had sacrificed their lives to escape the fire with.

Callum had come with nothing. Not even the toy egg. And he doubted the owner of that would still be coming at the designated time to claim it back. If there was any silver lining in this utter catastrophe, it was that.

Sitting arms-folded on an uncomfortable plastic chair, he jiggled his knees and zoned in and out of the mass brawl surrounding the designated speaker for the council.

"I'm sorry, but we cannot allow anyone access to the building." The suited man at the front was doing his best to soothe the horde that surrounded him. He looked as bad as Callum felt. And just as young, too. The council had clearly sent their junior housing officer to deal with the aftermath. Callum felt sorry for him. "The fire is now under control and whilst many floors haven't been affected, we need to keep the entire building evacuated."

"But our things are in there!" a woman barked over the crowd, waggling an angry finger toward the officer. "Our clothes, our money, our possessions! Where are we meant to go?"

"I understand and we will keep disruption to an absolute minimum." The man stepped back and hit the desk behind him.

Callum stifled the need to snort. *Disruption to a minimum?* It was chaos.

"We have to deem the building structurally sound before anyone can go inside." The man held out his palms, calming the outcry from those who demanded they be let into their homes. "We have to ensure the safety of all our residences as well as determine the cause of the fire. Our forensic team will scan each and every room."

That jolted Callum from his slump. He swallowed. Hard. *Fuck.* Leaning forward, he scraped back his hair that had fallen from its knot, and hung his head. His fingers trembled and he couldn't settle his racing pulse, or the real threat that his insides were gonna burst free to be his outsides at any moment. If he couldn't get back in his flat, and he didn't have the egg on him, and the feds were in the Marlyte then...*fuck, fuck fuck*. He should leave. *Like, now.*

"We will be re-homing you all as soon as we can find you suitable accommodation." The man's voice cracked the more the crowd pushed forward.

Callum knew what that meant. It would be the families with young children re-homed first, followed by the elderly, then the most vulnerable after that. Callum — male, single, twenty-four and with no additional needs — would be too far down on their list to even bother with. If only he had mates to help him, keep him hidden, give him a place to sweat all this out.

He didn't, so there wasn't much point dwelling on his life choices now.

"Please, remain here," the council bloke rattled on despite the continued heckles and indicated the community hall surroundings. "We will get started on re-homing you as soon as we possibly can."

A portly woman in a bright polo top with the Rescue logo stitched on her ample bosom slapped down a mattress next to Callum's seat. That was obviously his bed for the foreseeable — on the floor, pushed up against the wall in a dingy, damp community hall. He had no idea what would be better. To stay where he was and at least rely on the food donations, *or to fend for myself on the streets?* At least he could resort to what he knew best out there, with a limited chance of being traced. Which was his biggest worry, if he was honest. He didn't think his plea of 'but I didn't start the fire' was going to go down well with his temporary employer when he had to claim that he'd left their meal ticket behind.

What a fucking mess.

The council man exited the community hall with the crowd parting into smaller groups — those resigned to a night within these walls and finding a clear spot, and those angry enough to keep demanding a better explanation from the charity workers. A baby's wail from the corner brought Callum to the realisation that there were bigger problems he could have than having to figure out whether he should stay, or go.

"Mr. Wright?"

Snapping to, Callum peered up. Mattress lady smiled down at him. He'd forgotten her name. He was shit at that sort of thing on a normal day. But he could be let off, considering he'd been a bit preoccupied when he'd entered. It was an educated guess that she was part of the rescue mission run by the homeless charity—not that Callum was particularly educated.

Scrubbing a hand over his face made the grime and grit entrenched in his skin scratch more than his calloused fingertips would have. *Shit. I'm fucking homeless now and all.* That had dawned on him a few hours too late. The baby had already figured that one out.

"It is Mr. Wright, right?"

Callum would have normally chuckled at that. It never got old, but he could hardly muster the enthusiasm to say the third 'right' in order to break the ice and form a bond. He'd become accustomed to being standoffish anyway.

"Yeah. Call me Callum, though." He hated formalities. It reminded him too much of the courtroom. Maybe she'd say her name again so he didn't have to resort to all that 'love' and 'darlin'' shit. She didn't look the sort to take too kindly to being patronised—least of all by him.

"Callum, we have a visitor for you, but we wanted to check with you first."

Callum's eyes widened and his throat closed up, finding it difficult to swallow. *Shit.* He couldn't have been found already? Those from the charity were running the community centre access, forming a desk at the door to prevent any strays and wanderers coming in, and he doubted that the two elderly women at the front would be any decent barrier for anyone wanting to get to him. *Is there a back exit? Window in the toilets?* He prevented himself from asking those questions out loud.

After a few shuffles from the groups of people still crammed up at the front, the man in question came into view. He caught Callum's eye, holding his gaze. Then, in the way that Callum had all but forgotten, held up a hand and waved. Awkwardly.

Callum's heart gave a sudden jolt, as if reminding him it was there. Every moment of every day that organ kept him alive without him even noticing. He'd never had a use for it before, other than to pump the essentials around his stone-cold body. Except now, his skin flushed. Callum didn't need a mirror to know that was true. He could feel it burning.

"Fuckin' 'ell." And he couldn't keep that under his breath either.

"Sorry." Charity lady placed a hand on his shoulder. "Could you just mind the language? We do have children here."

Callum tore his gaze from the man up front to acknowledge the woman with the three kids a few mattresses down — one of her offspring had boa-constricted him a few hours earlier — and he could see her torment through to her frail, quivering bones.

Yeah, there were definitely bigger problems he could have.

He tried an apologetic smile, but was unsure if he even had one. So he turned his attention back to the charity bird. "Yeah. Course. Soz."

"So, about your visitor." The woman nodded up ahead, reminding Callum that he hadn't just seen a ghost. "He says he's an old friend of yours."

Callum gazed over to the front desk again, and he might as well have been transported through a time tunnel. The swirling in his mushed stomach certainly made him feel as if he was being ripped through a black hole. *Well, today's been a headfuck all round.*

"Would you like me to bring him over?"

Callum stood — a miracle his legs had gotten him that far. His knees knocked together and he couldn't tell if the ridiculous trembling was due to the fear, the anticipation or something else entirely. Something that he'd ignored for so fucking long. Swallowing made his ears ring and temple pound. *This is so fucking stupid! You're Callum, and he's just —*

"Are you okay?" Charity woman slipped a hand on his shoulder. "You look a little peaky. You could be in shock. You've been through a terrible ordeal. Shall I get some help?"

Callum stared at her. Was he in shock? *Probably.* But not for the reasons that she might think. Shaking his head, he wiped his dust-ridden hands down his just as caked in dirt jeans. "I'm fine." He wasn't sure that was true, but what else could he say? That he'd just been slapped in the face by the past? It sounded so lame in comparison to what everyone here had been through a few hours previously.

With a deep breath, he urged his feet to walk forward. He might as well go face this. It wasn't as if he had anything better to do. On approach, he clenched his fists to the point his nails would leave crescent moon marks indented on his skin.

"Kez?" That came across as rather hostile, but what could the bloke expect? A *hug? A kiss? A 'thank fuck you're here'?*

Callum would offer any of those if he wasn't doused in five years' worth of doubt.

"Cal." Kez stood rigid, and tall. So very tall. Not in stature as such, more in presence. Overbearing presence. Perhaps it was because he hadn't stood in front of Callum for so long. Kez'd been a mere fleck in the distance. One that had walked away from him.

Unable to look him in the eye, Callum darted his gaze to something else. *Anything else.* Finding the sights all too much to take right then, he dragged his focus back to the concern flashing across Kez's flawless features. Callum breathed in, holding the air into his lungs to calm his thrashing heartbeat.

"You…you look, well, shit." Kez at least winced.

"Yeah?" Callum knew he did. Especially in comparison to the epic change of appearance in front of him. He couldn't blame it all on his current situation. But he would. "Ain't the only one."

Kez narrowed his eyes, and Callum waved a hand indicating the surroundings.

"Right, of course." Kez shook his head, biting down on his bottom lip.

Callum rammed his hands in his pockets. *Well, this is as awkward as fuck.* If Kez being here now was to find out if Callum had finally paid his dues — karma come to bite him on the arse good and proper this time — then he could fuck off. Callum didn't need it. He knew it had. And Callum was pretty sure that the world wasn't over fucking about with him yet. Especially if this visitor was here to be a witness to the ultimate 'what comes around.'

"You got somewhere to go?" Kez broke the awkward silence with a calming voice. "I mean, are they finding you somewhere?"

"Er..." Callum untucked one hand from his pocket and flapped it around at the centre. "Ain't five star, but apparently there's room service."

Kez breathed out a laugh, his sharp cheekbones protruding to enhance his boyish features. Callum focused on him, tracing the man against the one he had in his pained memories. After a brief moment of stillness, Callum flared his nostrils through his heady exhalation. He couldn't hold it back anymore. He had to ask.

"What you doin' here, Kez?"

"Auntie. She told me."

"Yeah?" Course she would have, and probably took delight in recounting that Callum had smashed down her door. *Once a thug, always a thug.* "She all right now?"

"Hospital. But she'll be out soon. She owes you a big thank you. So do I, for that matter."

"No worries. No big deal." Why was he downplaying it? Because it sure as hell *was* a big deal. A real big fucking deal. He'd just rescued the person who hated him the most in the goddamn fucking world. And the next person down on his list of aggravated acquaintances now stood in front of him. Thanking him.

Funny how the world works like that.

"Are you okay?" Kez tilted his head.

And there was that innocence sparkling behind dark brown eyes that penetrated through into Callum's soul. The soul he thought he'd left behind in that burning building. *Or should have. Whatever.*

"Why do you ask?" It was a valid question and Callum had no filter at the best of times.

"Why wouldn't I?"

There were so many reasons. *So. Many.* But Callum wasn't going to list them all here. Not in front of those who were in charge of the current roof over his head. He was already way down on their re-homing list. He'd be knocked off it completely. So he slammed his lips shut and shrugged.

"Look, Cal, if you want, you could...I mean, you don't have to, but, well, if you haven't got anywhere else, then..."

Kez's babbling gave Callum a moment to check the bloke over for any signs that this was a set-up. A really elaborate set-up. Whose side was Kez on? Who would know to send him? Who would know that Callum trusted this man beyond any reasonable doubt, regardless of their five years of separation, and would be willingly led wherever Kez would want to take him? *If I do, will I be cuffed on the curb or beaten to a pulp?*

Yeah, right. If anything, Kez roamed in different circles from the ones Callum did. He had for a long time. Ever since...

Nope, not going there.

Callum sighed, attempting to clear his mind and focus on what Kez was saying. He was still trying to find the right words and shuffled on his feet, scrubbing fingertips through his cropped hair. Callum smiled. Kez had always been a bit of a bumbling fool, uncomfortable in his skin, perhaps — had made him an easy target back in the day. But five years was a long time, and there was a different Kez in front of Callum right then. Callum wasn't sure the reverse could be true. Especially considering the current situation.

Kez was taller, stockier, *fitter*. Kez had been a scrawny kid. So had Callum, really, but that had been down to a lack of any decent nutrition and parental neglect. Things for Kez had been different. Now Kez seemed to fill out the light blue shirt, deeper blue tie and black suit trousers he wore. *Smart bastard.* Kez had always been smart. *Dress for the job you want, not the one you got.* That had been Kez's motto growing up, regardless of how that had fixed the target on his back. The statement seemed a tad ridiculous to Callum. He couldn't very well turn up on the building site decked out in a football kit.

He couldn't kick a ball for shit, either.

"Cal?" Kez's clipped tone snapped Callum from his reverie.

What had Kez been saying? Callum tried to focus on the present and not tumble down ye olde Memory Lane. Not only because the memories weren't all good ones—that had been his fault, of course, but he'd repented for that. *Apparently.* But he also couldn't stomach seeing the transition of the man in front him. That was when something else caught his attention and threw him off guard.

"You got two arms." Not very tactful, but when had Callum ever been?

Kez adjusted the cuff of his shirt to cover the protruding hand that had not been there the last time Callum had seen the bloke. Many changes. *Many, many changes.*

"Prosthetic. Got it a couple of years ago. Still getting used to it."

Callum nodded. "Right. Looks real."

"Like it to be darker, but beggers can't be choosers."

"So, is it, like bionic? Like Bucky? Squeeze a man dead in one grip?" He hoped not, as he would be first on Kez's list especially after such a flippant jibe that he wasn't sure he could get away with saying anymore. Shouldn't jokes only be shared amongst friends? What was he to Kez now then? *Barely even strangers anymore.*

"Not quite." Kez gave a shifty look at the women at the desk. *Guess jokes are off-limits then.* "You've grown your hair."

Callum slipped back the loose strands and tucked them back into the band. "Cheaper, innit? Grow it out and shave underneath. And you've cut off your braids."

Scraping his hand over his now closely cropped black waves, Kez nodded. "Yeah. Sorta did that for work."

"Right." Callum sniffed, squaring his shoulders in an attempt to cover how fucking confused he was at Kez being here at all. "Come here to swap fashion tips, did ya?"

"Not quite." Kez sighed, as if he was psyching himself up to say something else. Perhaps fighting with his inner self. "So, do you want get outta here?"

"And go where?" As much as he could use a pint, his dishevelled appearance might turn a few heads.

"My place. I got a one-bed flat in Stratford. By Westfield. Sofa's all yours if you want it."

"*Seriously?*" Callum's elevated tone was caught by the ladies at the front desk.

Kez smiled at them, all sweetness and light, just the right amount of eye contact and apologetic lip curl. The bastard could still do it. Tapping Callum's arm, he ushered him away from the desk and prying ears.

"Course. Cal, look, I know we had our differences, and it's been a long time —"

"Five years, Kez." *Five, long, soul-destroying years.*

"Yeah. Like I said, long time. But this...this puts all that into perspective. I mean, I owe you. For Eve. I'm pretty sure she would have stayed in that flat. Stickler for the rules, isn't she?"

Didn't Callum know it?

"Kinda meant you having a flat in Stratford," Callum replied, cutting off any chance of an emotional reunion. Today wasn't the day. He couldn't relive it. He never wanted to. He'd buried the past so deep that he'd made himself believe that Kez had been his imaginary childhood friend. But now the fella was here. In front of him. Offering him a way out of this hell hole. Callum squared his shoulders. "How d'you wrangle that outta the council?"

"Private let. Like I said, I've got a job."

"So that suit ain't just for my benefit then?"

There was that twinkle within the deep brown eyes. And that smile. *Damn.* Callum stepped back, sniffed and glanced around. More people were being led in, sobbing and comforted by that soft, welcoming bosom belonging to Charity woman. Children woke up and asked when they were going home. Two uniformed police officers were talking to the mum with the three kids hanging on to her like fragile limpets and the tears fell from her eyes into the knotted locks of her daughter's hair.

Shit. It's here. The street. Or risk it with Kez…

"Fuck it. Let's go." Without thinking of all the reasons why he really shouldn't, Callum leapt around the desk.

"Should you tell them where you're going?" Kez lifted his prosthetic to point at the ladies at the front desk. "Just in case they need to get in touch with you."

"Nah. They're all busy with the kids and elderly right now. I'll call the council tomorrow, give them your address."

Like fuck I will.

"Right. Cool."

Is it?

Guess I'll find out.

Chapter Four

Journey into the Known

The silence cut into Kez like a scalpel. Callum wasn't speaking. Neither was he. The whole journey from Branton Town Hall to Stratford felt as awkward as that time he'd caught his ex with his hands in Eve's savings jar when she'd invited them round after Sunday church. Drake had claimed ingnorance, of course. Said he'd knocked it over and was tucking the escaped notes back in. Kez had wanted to believe him. But that bus ride home had been filled with a stagnant air that had spoken volumes. Slightly different scenario now, but the apprehension ached the same.

He didn't know whether to small talk to fill the journey with mundane chit-chat. Nothing sprang to mind to ask. All questions would feel loaded. And the various modes of public transport were so crowded that any conversation would be stifled anyway. Even just asking how Callum was could be lost in translation. It had been so long since they'd seen each other that Kez had forgotten how to talk to him. Which was absurd, considering. Callum had been the one that Kez had used to confide everything to. And vice versa. But all parted childhood friends end up like this eventually, don't they?

Do they?

On the Central Line and squeezed into the carriage, Kez opened his mouth to force himself to ask something. *Anything.* Until the front page of the evening paper that all the commuters had their heads buried within were filled with the images of the burning building. He shut his mouth. He doubted Callum wanted to relive it. Kez certainly didn't. That had been his home too, once. Those pictures, and Kez's presence, would be aiding Callum with an ever-present reminder that he'd just lost everything he ever owned.

Or so Kez assumed, anyway. He didn't have the balls to ask. He was scared of the answer.

The doors dinged open, and more people shuffled on, making Kez have to squash closer to Callum. The man's subtle scent danced along Kez's nostrils. Beneath the stale smoke, Kez could make out the distinct aroma of something vaguely familiar, as if he'd just wrapped himself in the old dressing gown he'd had to leave at Eve's when the fibres had crusted.

Callum didn't look at him and instead focused on the advertising above the seats. Kez hadn't been wrong — Callum *did* look like shit. Not that he'd fared any better the last time that Kez had seen him. But Callum's appearance was to be expected after what he'd been though that day, and not, hopefully this time, down to his own reckless stupidity.

His dark blond hair, now scraped into a topknot, had flecks of black running through it and made him look less striking than he'd used to be. Never a full-on platinum, Callum had always had a bit of hazel scattered through the hair — dirty blond, he supposed — but the tousled locks looked like they hadn't been washed in a while even before gathering the remnants of smoke. His clothes were hanging off him too, as if they didn't belong to him, or he'd lost a significant amount of weight since buying the jeans and hoody. Callum had always been an avid follower of fashion back in the day. Ripped jeans, the latest trend, trainers that he'd gotten from Kez didn't want to ask where. He'd had the slender body of a clothes model and the striking face to go with it. It pained Kez to see him reduced to throwaway garments and heavy-duty work boots.

Not so much a fall from grace, as a casual decline from ground level to basement. Kez hated himself for even thinking that. He'd used to think so differently. So very differently.

Inhaling a deep breath he hoped Callum wouldn't pick up on, Kez wondered, not for the first time that afternoon, if what he had just done had been the best idea. He'd meant what he'd said, that grudges should be buried in times of true crisis. That their friendship, once so precious, was worth more than letting the man waste away in a dreary community centre after having lost his worldly possessions in a fire. Especially considering Callum had risked his life to save Kez's aunt and Callum didn't have much family to lean on. Not that he had been able to rely on his mum when she'd been in his life. It wasn't exactly a wonder how Callum had turned out. Not really. But perhaps he'd made new friends? *Better* friends? But for some reason, Kez doubted it. The fact that Callum had come with him so willingly had to mean that Kez was right —

Callum hadn't recovered the way Kez had been able to from that night five years ago.

"We getting off here?" Callum nodded toward the screeching open doors of the train.

He'd been so wrapped up in his thoughts Kez hadn't realised they'd reached their destination. He nodded and clambered off the Tube with the several other million or so people who swapped Tube lines at Stratford or used the station for the shopping centre and ample night facilities. Having moved here when he'd been a student and remained ever since as it was close enough to work, Kez still hadn't got a handle on how popular the place had become. It was nothing like where they'd grown up, on the streets of Branton. Well, certainly not now, anyway. Kez shuddered.

"Just need to stop at the twenty-four hour, grab some food," Kez said, rushing toward the exit turnstiles. "I'm not sure I have much in." He *was* sure. He didn't have much in. Living alone, he rarely worried too much about it. He had fruit for breakfast, then scoffed his lunch from the staff canteen, which usually set him up for the rest of the day, so dinners were whatever he had in the way of snacks. Or what leftovers his aunt palmed off on him after her Sunday visits.

"Listen, mate, don't go to any trouble, yeah?" Callum slotted the single ticket that Kez had purchased for him into the turnstiles and walked through. "I'll just kip on your sofa tonight. Tomorrow's a new day and all that."

Kez had so many questions to ask, but that had to wait until they were alone, or away from the crowd at least. As they emerged out of Stratford station, the usual hustle and bustle made it difficult for any conversation to take place, anyway. Hordes of people were heading up to the late-night haunts in Westfield, or coming out with bags upon bags of shopping while schoolkids, still in uniform, cluttered the bus station. Kez angled his head, taking the left turn out of the station that curved new Stratford — Stratford City as it had been renamed when it'd been designed and built to welcome the Olympic park in 2012.

"Don't 'spose you took up smoking, did ya?" Callum asked once they'd made it past the High Street and into the more subdued residential parts — where Kez always had to walk a bit quicker, just in case.

"No. But I can buy you some, if you need it?" Stopping his march, Kez nodded up to the petrol station across the road, home to the mini-convenience store with its illuminating sign an indicator that twenty-four-seven wasn't just a big three-chain supermarket concept.

"Actually, yeah. Would ya? Might take the edge off a bit." Callum shivered, his lips quivering.

Kez nodded. Things really didn't change. But cigarettes? Those he could handle. Or more that Callum could handle them. Kez had too many health worries as it was to indulge in anything more than an occasional beer every now and then. And even that was scarce these days.

"I'll pay you back." Callum's snap suggested he'd seen the look Kez must have had displayed across his face.

"No, it's fine." *Why does this feel so awkward? So forced?* Once upon a time, it had been quite the opposite for the both of them. "You just lost everything. Least I can do is spend a fiver on a pack of fags."

"They're a tenner now, mate."

"Rip-off Britain." Kez winked, attempting to lighten the mood and recapture something they'd clearly both lost. *Can't blame the fire for that, though.* Maybe just the proverbial one. "It's fine. I'll grab some now, then why don't you spark up out here while I go get some food?"

"Yeah. All right, ta."

Kez rushed into the shop, bought a twenty-pack and a lighter, just in case, and hurried outside. He held them in an outstretched hand and Callum scooped them up, his fingertips brushing Kez's palm. Even though it was Callum with the noticeably shaking fingers, it was Kez who shivered from the light tingle that unexpectedly warmed his skin.

Danger zone. Clearing his throat, Kez shuffled away.

"Cheers." Callum lit up a cigarette. "You remembered the right brand."

"It's ingrained here." Kez tapped his forehead. "From all those times I had to buy your fags 'cause you looked too young. Some things never change." He smiled.

"Some things do." Blowing out a lungful of smoke, Callum closed his eyes to wave away the trailing grey fumes.

Kez dropped his smile. He wanted to ask what had, how Callum had been doing since his release, how he'd coped inside and how he'd ended up back where it all started. But he didn't. He just rushed into the shop, biting down on his natural instincts. Because what if he heard something he didn't want to? *Or can't bear to?*

Hanging a basket on his arm, he wandered up each aisle without checking what produce was even on offer. He was too busy giving himself a stern talking-to. Had he just made the dumbest decision of his life? Well, no, that was long past. But had he just made it for a second time? He could hear Eve's animated tone bursting through his temple now as if she were his overriding conscience. And she'd be right. *Won't she?*

He peered over the shelf, out of the window where Callum stood with his back to the shop, blowing out smoke into the night sky. His head bowed, his shoulders tense, Callum appeared every bit the vulnerable yet face-value tough guy he'd always been. *So distant. So vague. So nonchalant.* If Kez had been through what Callum had, he'd be a quivering wreck, rocking back and forth in a padded room.

A banging on glass startled Kez, followed by a stern bark from the Tannoy system blasting out to the forecourt. "No smoking, please." The man behind the serving desk spoke directly into his microphone whilst glaring at Callum through the window.

Callum swivelled, eyes narrowed, then held up his middle finger.

"Move away, or put it out." The squeal of feedback from the speakers pained Kez's ears.

Drawing in a long drag, Callum stared back, unfazed. He then blew the smoke at the window, distorting the view through the glass, and strutted out of sight.

Kez sighed. *Better make this quick.* After a dash around the limited offerings, he settled on the usual snacks. Tortilla chips, frozen single pizzas with extra spicy pepperoni — *shit, is Callum a veggie?* He'd been talking about it back then, animal welfare and all that. *Helping the most vulnerable in society.* Shoving the meat option back, he settled on a plain pizza and chucked in a couple of packs of cooked meats, just in case. He paid swiftly, offering an apologetic smile to the man behind the counter then, his goods bagged, left the shop to find Callum pacing the path up ahead.

"Hey." Kez approached him with the caution of tempering a feral beast. "You all right?"

"Yeah." Callum threw the butt of his cigarette to the floor and stamped it out. "Can we get outta here?"

"Sure. Not far." Kez would have squeezed Callum's arm, but the only hand that worked currently clung on to a thin plastic bag that threatened to tear. "Come on."

Kez lived above a parade of shops a short walk from the petrol garage—a newsagents, a bookies and an electrical store. *Not the best place in the world to be housed, but beggars can't be choosers.* And in Stratford City, this was luxury living. He suspected Callum wouldn't care anyway. At least Kez had a home.

He climbed the back steps located at the side of the stretch of shops and along the concrete balcony to his gated yard. He had to drop the bag to type in the code to the lock, then shoved the gate open with his shoulder. Allowing Callum to walk in first, Kez picked up the shopping and slammed the gate shut behind him. Callum was jogging on the spot. *Antsy.* Kez couldn't expect much less, could he? What an ordeal the bloke must have been though. He doubted Callum would have expected to be here, at Kez's 'gaff' as Callum would call it, when he'd opened his eyes that morning to go—*where did he go? Work? Does he work?*

So many questions.

Callum grabbed the bag from the floor. "Sorry, should have remembered."

"I've dealt before, y'know." Kez fiddled the key into the lock and opened his front door.

"Yeah. Course. Just, well, can that thing do anything useful?" Callum nodded to the prosthetic.

"That thing?" Kez arched an amused eyebrow.

"Sorry. What do you call it?"

"My arm?"

Callum snorted a laugh. "Can your *arm* do anything? Is it, like, a robotic thing? Can you control it with your mind?"

"Nah. It's just aesthetic. All the NHS gave me at the time."

"Shame. Do you get an upgrade when your contract's up? Like a phone? Or a car?"

Kez stepped through into his house, Callum following behind a little reluctantly.

"Maybe." Kez shut the door and wandered through into the kitchen on his left. "But the working types don't look as realistic."

"You bothered by all that?" Callum dropped the bag of stuff onto the kitchen counter.

Kez knew he was asking all those questions to try to keep up a conversation that wasn't based around what had happened that morning, or what had happened five years ago. Kez didn't mind. He didn't want to relive any of those events either. Mundane chit-chat focusing on Kez's most significant change was probably better all around. *At least for this evening.*

Callum had always been Kez's biggest advocate for his disability, so Kez didn't mind him firing questions that might otherwise seem...contrite, conceited? Insensitive? Having been born without a left forearm and growing up with a residual limb—or stump as most people referred to it as—just below the elbow hadn't been easy on him. The stares, the disappointment...the *abandonment*. But Callum, at their first meeting at the tender age of seven, hadn't been fazed by it. He'd been the first one who hadn't. He'd asked a ton of questions back then, too. Then, satisfied that Kez wasn't a freak or that his congenital defect couldn't be catching, Callum had treated Kez like any of his other mates. And if anyone had had a problem with it, it'd been Callum who'd made them feel sorry for it.

"I just wanted the kids to stop gawking at me, y'know?" Kez filled the kettle. Tea, he definitely needed tea. Shit, he didn't have coffee. No one he knew drank it. *Callum had.*

"Kids?"

"I work at the children's hospital. Adults mostly ignore it, but kids, they're the ones that point and stare. This"—Kez held up his arm and rapped his knuckles on the silicone to produce a hollow tap—"is lifelike enough not to have them notice all too often."

Nodding, Callum leaned against the counter. "You'd think it wouldn't bother people anymore. What with the Paralympics and all that. Now those fellas have got it goin' on. Why didn't you get one of those blades?"

Kez laughed. "'Cause they're for legs. Not forearms."

"Right. Course."

"I only got tea. That all right?"

"Could do with something stronger, bruv. But sure. Whatevs."

"Go on, take a seat in the living room. Easily found, it's the next room along. Up the stairs is a bathroom and a bedroom. That's it, I'm afraid."

"More than I have." Callum pushed away from the counter and said the rest to the floor. "Had."

Kez watched Callum leave, then stared out of the kitchen window at his gated yard. He was doing the right thing. He was. *This time.* This was just an old friend helping out an old friend in times of need. Nothing more, nothing less.

I won't be fooled again. And repeat mantra.

The kettle choosing to reach its whistling climax at that moment was not an argument to the contrary. He hoped.

Callum relieved himself upstairs in the bathroom first, checking his reflection in the mirror of the cupboard. He really did look like crap. His face was peppered with grit and his skin was tight and crusty with bloodshot and itchy eyes. He splashed cold water over himself, wiped down his neck and redid his hair into some sort of style. Now he was here, with Kez, he thought he should at least try to show him some decency by being somewhat presentable.

Kez had changed so much. And it wasn't just the addition of the arm. He was all confident strides — a grown man now comfortable with himself. He'd always been a bit awkward, a bit cautious and a bit fearful. Callum had taken him under his wing and shown him how not to be afraid. Now here was Callum taking hand-outs. He winced, flushed the chain and slunk back down the stairs. His hoody and jeans wafted smoke, and it wasn't all from the earlier cigarette.

Shuddering, Callum coughed. The burning charcoal clung to his nostrils and scorched his throat. *Shouldn't have had that fag.* He needed a shower, and a rest. But that would have been taking things a tad too far after this cosy little reunion thing they had going on.

When he shuffled into the living room, Kez was already there, and the mug of tea on the coffee table an inviting prospect to wash out his throat and warm his insides. Kez closed the floor-length curtains, shutting out the street lamps outside, then settled down into the armchair in the corner. Callum parked his arse on the three-seater sofa to the side and had a proper look around. It was a relatively large room, considering. It managed to fit in a dining table at the back behind the sofa, the table holding an open laptop. The only other furniture was the television on a dark-oak stand. The flooring was wood, laminate probably, with a red shag-pile rug underneath the legs of the coffee table.

The mantlepiece above the mock fireplace housed an array of framed photographs, the people within them Callum just about recognised. Except the one of Kez in a graduation outfit, clutching a scroll. So the geezer had made it through university. *Wow.* Eve stood behind him, hand on his shoulder, beaming like a proud parent should. Or how Callum would expect a parent should. He wasn't exactly an expert on happy families, having been brought up without a dad, and by a mum who hadn't been any sort of a modern-day Mary Poppins when she'd been around at all. The spoonful of white stuff to get her going hadn't been sugar.

"So you went to uni?" Callum pointed up at the photo, leaning forward to grab his mug and swallowing down an invigorating amount.

"Yeah."

"And you work with kids? At the hospital?"

A vibrating bleep from within Kez's pocket captured Kez's attention for a brief moment, but he ignored it to sip from his mug. "That's right."

"Are you a doctor?" Callum widened scratchy eyes, the air having dried them out completely. Rubbing them again, he yawned.

Kez laughed. "No."

"Oh, right. Nurse, then?" Yeah, Kez could be a nurse. He had that soft, nurturing side. Look at what he was doing now. *The fool.*

"No. I'm admin. Support staff. I'm a secretary—assistant—for a couple of cardiology paediatricians."

"Right." Callum nodded, like he understood. He didn't really. He could hardly focus on anything as it was and every word Kez spoke felt as if Kez was calling to him through a tunnel. Maybe it was just the weirdness of this whole situation. Of being here. *Fuck, I'm tired.*

"I write up notes, take calls from irate parents, schedule appointments and generally act as a buffer for anyone who wants a bit of the doctor. Which, recently, has become more the job than anything else."

Callum must have given him a confused look.

Kez chuckled. "Sorry. Office gossip. One of my doctors got himself into a bit of bother and has been avoiding people. It's getting difficult to schedule his appointments at times when others aren't in."

"Right."

"Are you working?"

And there was the inevitable question. *Why did I have to start all this shit?* He shook his head. "Not really."

Kez nodded into his mug, disapproval written all over his face. Normally, Callum wouldn't have cared all that much. He'd have blamed the state of the government—not that he even knew who was ruling the country, but he'd heard the word Brexit branded around for so long now it had to mean something. Or he'd complain about the run-down London borough that couldn't provide jobs for the most educated of its residents, let alone an ex-con. But it was about time he faced facts. Not everything was always someone else's fault.

"I was. For a bit." Callum didn't miss the disappointment on Kez's face. "As a brickie. But got laid off. Been trying to find more work, but, well, it's been shit times for labouring. Even when I offer to do it cash in hand. And finding anything else is a bit hard what with...everything." And everything meaning *him*.

Kez shuffled forward in his seat. "I can imagine. Listen, perhaps we need to talk, about stuff?"

"Do we? Right now?" Callum hacked up another cough into a balled fist, his eyes bulging and his face scorching. "Shit, Kez, I'm fucking beat. And this, I'm grateful, yeah? Really. But if I have to talk now, I might say something I don't mean. Or maybe I do mean it. Shit, maybe I should have stayed at the community centre." *Or on the streets.*

"No. No, it's okay. You're right. Not a good time. I just thought it best to address the elephant in the room, y'know?"

Elephant? More like a fucking great woolly mammoth.

"I know. But not now. I ain't got the brain capacity to talk about all that." Callum had more worrying things on his mind, like where he was going to go tomorrow to avoid...well, *everything*.

Another deep ping from Kez's pocket stifled any response and Callum was kind of grateful for it.

"Sorry." Kez stood, fishing his phone out from his trousers. "I should probably respond to this, or it might not stop."

"Oh right, sure. You meant to be somewhere? Working from home?" Callum added the quotations marks for that one.

Noticeably pausing, Kez didn't look up from his phone screen. He shuffled, his shoulders tensing. "I had a date. Which I forgot to cancel."

Callum did not expect the rapid tightness to close in around his chest. *No, it's my lungs.* He coughed to make sure. But something still lingered there, squeezing him to make it difficult to breathe, let alone form words for a nonchalant response to Kez's equally as flippant statement. Yet he had to say something. *Anything.*

"Right. Shit. Course. Sorry. I really have ruined your evening, then." Callum sniffed, squaring his shoulders. "You can still go. You can trust me here." He had to laugh after saying that, and had to clear his throat again as his voice had gone hoarse. Perhaps that fag hadn't been the best idea. "Sorry. But you can. Don't make the same mistake twice, eh?" Plus, he'd left the 'mistake' in his burning building.

"No. It's fine." Kez still didn't look at him and slid his thumb along the screen of his phone as if it were the answer to everything.

Callum swore he saw a slight tinge forming on Kez's cheeks and he tilted his head, like a bird scrutinising oncoming prey.

"The date was back near work." Kez peered up over his phone, looking Callum in the eye. Did Callum only imagine that it took all Kez's effort to do so? "Raff's a doctor. Well, just graduated PhD researcher. Works on the grants for the charity part of the hospital."

"Nice." *So Kez has a boyfriend, and one who's all types of fucking perfect.* And Kez was confident about it all. He'd just said all that as if it was the most natural thing in the world to be dating a man with no fear of repercussions. *Things do change.* "Well, don't let me stop you." He waved a hopefully dismissive hand.

Staring at him, Kez appeared to be contemplating all the options and drafting out all possible scenarios. Perhaps even one that regretted having offered up his sofa to Callum—a man he hadn't spoken to in five years. Callum found it hard to believe Kez still even knew who he was. *Course he knows. Once upon a time we was all each other had.*

"I'll take the call upstairs." Kez waggled the mobile. "There's no point heading back to Holborn now. Help yourself to anything. The food, the shower, the TV. I'll bring down some blankets and stuff in a sec."

Callum nodded his thanks and tried not to watch Kez walk around the room and rush out on excitable legs. Only once Kez was out of sight did Callum exhale a lungful of smoke-clouded breath that crackled in his knotted chest. He slammed back the rest of his tea, hoping the liquid would relieve the irritation in his throat, and cupped the mug between his legs.

Wonder what Mr. Perfect looks like? Kez's type, probably. *White, blond, pretty-boy.* Callum shook his head and scrubbed his dry hands down his face. And what might Mr. P. H. Dick think of Kez bringing home a stranger to stay in his house? Well, not so much a stranger, but he doubted Mr. Wonderful would know about his and Kez's past.

Callum sometimes had difficulty remembering.

Chapter Five

Near Miss

Kez rushed up the stairs and into his bedroom, closing the door fully behind him. His phone buzzed again, reminding him he had several missed messages. He should have remembered to at least drop Rafferty a text to call off the date, but his head had been all over the place since finding out about the Marlyte fire. *And Callum.* So much for when he'd been counting down the seconds until work finished.

Shit. Work. He'd better send Lisa a message, too, just to see if there had been any fallout from his swift exit. He rushed off a brief apology to his co-worker, assuring her he would be in tomorrow and buy her a massive donut from the bakery on the way in. Send. *Done.*

Coughing from downstairs jolted him back to the reality of what he had done. *Christ. What a day.* Should he tell Raff? Or just hope that it never came up and Callum found somewhere to go before Kez could rearrange what had meant to be his first date with the new doctor? Kez had never been very good at lying, though. Callum could corroborate that.

Shaking off the unseasoned feelings of regret, Kez slapped on his smile and settled back on his bed to hit the Call button. He held the mobile between his chin and shoulder so he could roll up his shirtsleeve. His prosthetic casing was itching and the weight dragging him down. As the phone was answered, Kez unclipped the arm and placed it on the table beside his bed.

"Kwesi? Bloody hell! Where have you been?"

Kez smiled at the plummy delivery in the man's words. Kez hadn't noticed quite how softly spoken Rafferty was. Perhaps it was now he was comparing him to Callum's rougher tones. The brash East London hadn't left Callum. In a way, it had sharpened.

"Sorry, Raff, I should have called sooner —"

"That would have been nice, yes. I stood outside for ages! I nearly went home thinking I'd been stood up but thought I'd check by your office in case you were snowed under. I was told you ran out in a blind panic. Are you okay?"

"You went to my office?" *Great.* The secret was out. Not that he was keeping his workplace flirting a secret from everyone. It was just that it wasn't quite there yet. In his experience, once everyone knew that there was a romance on the horizon then everyone expected updates. He would have preferred a little time getting to know the man before everyone else got involved. Perhaps he shouldn't have agreed to date a man from the hospital. But as that was where he spent most of his time, it was hard not to. St. Cross might as well launch its own dating app.

"Yes, I spoke to Lisa, is it? She seemed a trite put out."

"Yeah. I can imagine." Kez slipped down the bandage casing that held his prosthetic in place, then tugged it off and draped it beside the artificial limb. He flexed his elbow, the relief of losing the extra weight a welcome night-time affair. The fake limb was light enough, but not more so than when he was without it. He gave the stump a quick massage to tone down the odd feeling of his limb floating skywards. "Did you hear about the fire?"

"The one in Branton? Sure. It's been all over the news."

"My aunt lives there. Or, well, did." Kez juddered. His aunt was now homeless and his childhood possessions that she had kept safe for him now ruined. He'd been so focused on Callum that he hadn't had time to grieve his own loss.

"Kwesi, sweetheart, I'm so sorry."

Sweetheart? That sounded...odd? Nice? Kez wasn't sure.

"Is she okay? Are *you* okay?"

"Yes to both. She got out." *Won't be detailing how.* "She's in Newham, being checked. She also has a broken ankle at the moment from slipping down the stairs last month. I had to go see her and I forgot to let you know. I'm sorry."

"Hey, no, no, I am! How selfish of me. Do you need anything? I could come by..."

Kez clutched the phone to his ear and paused. He needed a lot of things. A hug wouldn't go amiss. But a loud bang from downstairs brought him back to earth with a bump.

"No." He screwed his eyes shut. This wasn't lying. Not really. Omission of details was not lying. *Tell that to a court of law.* "I'm tired. I'm just going to roll up in bed and face it all tomorrow."

"Of course. No problem at all. We can rearrange our date."

Kez winced at the regret crackling in Rafferty's voice. "Call if you need anything, though."

Smiling, Kez bit his lip. It was a crying shame that their first date had been scuppered. Rafferty seemed perfect. And he wasn't bad to look at either. The day that Kez had had to drop off a research proposal from Dr. Rawlings to the Grants Admissions Team and subsequently been unable to type in the door code and push down the handle whilst holding the thick binder had made Rafferty his knight in striking yellow Ralph Lauren polo.

Normally, Kez would have hated to be rescued like that. But that sweeping mound of wavy blond hair and soft blue eyes behind square black-rimmed glasses had captured Kez's attention. Not to mention the Oxbridge accent that had been as smooth as honey. He'd never have even entertained the thought that any attraction would be returned. But an email had dinged through later that day and the inappropriate-for-work flirty email exchange had ensued, leading to the arrangement of a date.

"Listen, Raff, I really am sorry." Kez scraped his stump along his forehead. "Not just about standing you up. This day's been a bit of a headfuck. Excuse my language."

"It's understandable. Get some rest. We'll talk again. I hope."

"We will."

After hanging up, Kez knocked his head against the wall behind until another crash from below jolted him from his self-torture. He rushed back downstairs and into the living room. Callum, head back on the sofa, snored from a wide-open mouth. His cup lay on its side on the coffee table with a dribble of tea splurging out onto the black wood. Rescuing the discarded mug, Kez gazed down at his old friend. Callum looked so vulnerable when asleep. He had a boyish charm, with some of his hair loosened from the knot and draped down one side to entangle with hazel-coloured eyelashes. The sight made Kez regret having not given him the benefit of the doubt all those year ago. At having walked away from him when he'd needed him more than anything. At having listened to his aunt rather than the man he'd... *I what? Admired? Looked up to? Thought I knew inside out?*

Who was he kidding? It would never be returned. He'd never hear those words back, so why keep trying? There were many mistakes that had led to their estrangement. None of which Callum could rectify for him. That had made it easier to move, forget and reform a new life without his best friend.

Now Callum was here, in his living room. Tomorrow would be a new day for them both. After rushing out to rinse the mug and returning with a blanket from the airing cupboard in his bedroom, Kez draped it over Callum, ruffled the strands of hair away from his face and nearly, very nearly kissed Callum's forehead. Like he used to do when Callum hadn't been conscious to notice.

And repeat mantra. I won't be fooled again.

Chapter Six

FML

Callum awoke the next morning with a stink of a headache, aching muscles and what he could only assume was a temperature. Did he have the goddamn flu? *Great.* That was the last thing he needed. He dragged himself to a sitting position from the sofa and ripped off the blanket, coughing as he bent over double on his lap.

Appearing out of nowhere, Kez held out a tissue to him with true ninja-like skill. Or maybe Callum had been a little preoccupied at not throwing up an entire lung to have heard the man's descent down the stairs. Accepting the tissue, Callum refocused his vision. Kez was wearing only a pair of boxers that stretched over his pert backside and hugged his stocky thighs. Callum averted his gaze to something else. *Anything else.* Anything that wasn't black skin shimmering against the rays of sunlight that burned through the gap of the closed curtains. It landed on the picture propped up on the mantelpiece.

"How's auntie?" Callum sounded like he'd smoked the entire pack of fags last night. He couldn't feel them shoved in his pocket and wondered if that weren't true. "I mean how was she doing? Before yesterday?"

"Good. Same as. Church, cooking."

Callum nodded, hanging his head. "Miss her dumplings."

Kez didn't say anything. It was probably a conversation best left there anyway. Callum did miss her though. Even if he had been living only a few doors down from Eve for a while now, since his release from the parole board's approved address. He'd made sure he missed her. *Avoided her, more like.*

Kez glided over to the window. For a stocky bloke, he moved with an ease and control that Callum was unfamiliar with. He'd been all out of alignment when Callum had known him. All knees and elbows. Callum smiled. Kez's strong muscles tore through his skin and Callum couldn't help but stare at him. Until Kez ripped open the heavy-duty black-out curtains and in poured the glorious sun from outside to distort Callum's vision. Lucky, 'cause Kez might have caught him gaping at him.

"Looks like a scorcher of a day." Kez span to face him. "That I'll miss being in an artificially lit hospital."

"You going in?"

"Have to really. I can probably sort out more stuff for Auntie if I do. Plus my doctor will have a shit fit if I call in."

Did that mean Callum was going to be left alone? He wasn't sure what to make of that. He wasn't sure what to make of anything. He was struggling to understand what he was even doing here at all. Yesterday was some hazy mist of strange happenings. Maybe it hadn't happened at all? Maybe this whole thing was artificial.

Speaking of artificial... "Do you not sleep with it?" Callum nodded to Kez's arm, void of the fake limb he'd had attached last night.

Kez's smile lifted his cheeks and his pink tongue poked through the gap between his lips. *What the fuck! Why am I staring at his mouth? His tongue? Look the fuck away, Wrighty, before you get a slap.*

"No," Kez replied. "It'd be like sleeping with a bag on your back, or a hat on your head. It's just an addition to my body, not actually part of it."

Callum nodded. Then exploded into another coughing fit. *What the fuck must I look like right now?* Sweat-induced clothes, wafting stale smoke from clammy, pale skin. He wanted to joke this clusterfuck away and remind Kez of how it had used to be, before everything that had torn them apart. It had once been Callum that all the girls had chased back in school. Not that Kez had wanted girls. *No, he always wanted...* Callum swallowed. The tables were well and truly turned now. It was Kez who had the blokes chasing him, and from what Callum could see, for good reason. *Give him both arms and the man wouldn't have a single thing to worry about. Things really do change though.* Once upon a time, Callum had wanted to change the world and change how people saw Kez. He'd used to be fiercely loyal.

Eyes streaming, Callum composed himself and wiped away the remnants with the grotty tissue scrunched into his hand.

"Were you checked out after the fire?" Kez drew in troubled eyebrows.

Callum did his best to focus on the eyes and not the near-naked body that had filled out in the five years since his eighteenth birthday — the last time Callum had seen that much of Kez's skin. Kez's broad chest now had a healthy scattering of curly black hair over each hard nipple, and whilst not technically a washboard stomach, it still looked like a balled fist would bounce off it and crush the knuckles in the process.

"No, why?" Callum cleared his throat.

"You don't sound too good." Kez edged nearer, his groin within Callum's line of sight.

Christ. What was this? His worst nightmare? *Keep telling yourself that, Wrighty — one day you might believe it.*

Kneeling down to look Callum in the face, Kez exhaled cool, minty breath to trickle on Callum's flushed cheeks. It was a welcome relief from the hot sweats.

"You should have been checked over by a doctor. In case you inhaled any smoke."

"Course I inhaled smoke, you prat. I had a fag last night."

"I don't mean that sort of smoke." Kez spread one hand out on his thigh, the stump resting against his other. "You should see someone today."

"I don't need it, bruv, I'm good. I just woke up, having slept on a sofa. I'm just a little frazzled." He circled his shoulders. "I'll be all right after a coffee."

Kez cocked his head, disbelief bursting from his exasperated huff. "'Fraid I don't have coffee. I can do a tea, but then I have to get to work."

"Yeah, no sweat. I'll just head back to the centre or somethin', see what they got for me?" No, he wouldn't.

He had no plans to go back there. *Ever*. He gave a winning smile to hide the lie.

"Do you have to check in with your parole officer?" Kez held Callum's gaze for as long as it took for Callum to feel shit about it. Which could have been counted in milliseconds.

Scratching his fingernails, Callum noted the dirt entrenched beneath and it was a painful reminder of who he really was. "I don't have one. Not anymore. Nose clean for the whole of my license. Signed off for a civilian life."

Kez smiled. Genuinely. "Good. Then you can stay here." He stood. "As long as you need."

Callum had no response. None that he could think to give right then. He had to keep letting the man think this could all work out. Callum knew different. Callum knew that as soon as Kez turned his back, he'd be outta there quicker than his jury's deliberation time had taken. *Five minutes.*

"Cal?"

Callum hadn't realised he'd been staring at Kez's bare feet, so dragged his gaze upward to look the man in the eye. "Yeah?"

"You got a GP you can go see?"

Callum laughed.

"Walk-in centre then?"

"Forget it, Kez. I'm all good."

"I know you, Cal. You may not be that eighteen-year-old I once knew, but I still know you. The only way you'll go see a doctor is if I make you. So, here's the deal. Stay here, get some rest, eat whatever. Then, one p.m., come meet me for lunch at the hospital."

"Kez—"

"If you don't show, I'll assume you've buggered off. That's up to you." Kez meandered to the living room door, shoving it open with his stump. He seemed to use that arm more without the artificial limb attached. It was more how Callum had remembered him, not so stiff. "If you do come meet me, I won't call the centre and tell them where you stayed last night." He widened all-knowing eyes.

Fuck.

He guessed he had no choice then. He couldn't have that trace on him. Not just for his sake. Not now Kez had got into the mix. *Again.*

Fuck this life.

* * * *

Whilst not technically fully trusting Callum, Kez had no choice but to leave the bloke in his flat while he went to work. Was it foolish to think that nothing could happen in his absence? Callum had only been there for a few hours, he'd not contacted anyone — none that Kez was aware of anyway — and he looked in a bad enough way that he'd be stupid to even entertain the thought of doing anything untoward in Kez's home.

Hasn't stopped him before.

Kez shook his aunt's voice from his mind and instead recalled what Callum had said — *nose clean for five years* — as he boarded the usual stuffy and overcrowded prime-time commuter Central Line. Lucky it was only a few stops to Holborn, so it wasn't enough time to build up a hot sweat in the soaring May temperatures that would be visible through his long-sleeved shirt. He had to go long — it covered the prosthetic enough that the hand looked natural. If he rolled up his sleeve, the lack of hair and the lighter brown colour would scream fake. And if there was anything Kez couldn't stand, it was people staring at him.

He arrived at Holborn a bit flustered, but remembered to stop at the corner bakery and grab a four-pack of their glazed donuts to soften the blow of having left Lisa in the lurch yesterday. She was nice enough, but she'd let him know if he'd pissed her off. She stood up to the doctors as well, held her own against the sky-high egos that roamed the hospital corridors and looked down on those who only did the typing, rather than the life-saving. Without them, though, the hospital wouldn't run as smoothly as it did. And Lisa took delight in making everyone aware of that fact.

St. Cross Children's Hospital stood at a crossroads tucked away from the main financial district of Holborn. *Chuck a left out of the station and there's all the high-rise offices where people make their millions.* A little farther still and the British Library came into view. But over the road and to the right, then the gleaming glass frontage with painted murals of, smiley, happy waving children welcomed Kez. The first day Kez had come for his interview here, he'd known he wouldn't ever want to work anywhere else — unless he was forced to.

Which was a touchy subject, what with all the cuts to the NHS. Rumours circling the support staff offices were that St. Cross was next on the list for an overhaul in staffing and there would be a change in management any day now. Dr. Rawlings certainly seemed on edge about it. But then the guy was always on edge. Even much more so since a few months back.

As Kez leapt over the road to the entrance, nodding to the driver of the ambulance who had let him pass, he bumped into one of the cardiology nurses waiting outside the swishing double doors.

"Hey, Kwesi." Ollie beamed at him.

Kez had used to have a crush on the newest nurse on the cardiology ward. Looks wise, he was Kez's type. Kez seemed to be attracted to blonds with bright smiles. Maybe it was an opposites-attracts thing. Or maybe it came from who he'd first fallen in love with... *Nope, not going there.* But the feelings for Ollie were totally face-value. Whilst Kez liked the view, he also had a thing for the rough and the edgy. *God help me.*

"Ollie. How's things?"

Ollie held on to two take-out coffee cups and blew into the hole of one. "Good. Night shift ran over. Tough one, but it's the last for me for a few days, which is good 'cause I'm moving house." Ollie's grin grew so wide it was hard for Kez not to match it.

"Congratulations. I take it that means he finally asked you?"

Ollie shrugged, doing his best to remain nonchalant, but his enigmatic smile told a different story. "Well, it makes sense, doesn't it? Me always travelling to his, or his to mine. First I filled up a drawer, then one side of his wardrobe. Might as well just move in together. We can even afford a house!"

Kez trailed the plastic bag of donuts to his wrist and gave Ollie's arm a squeeze. "I'm happy for you, Ollie. You deserve it."

"Thanks, Kez." A car stopped up beside the road, the window lowering and a mound of dark curly hair wafting out in the breeze. "Oh, my ride." Ollie skipped off to open the passenger door, not before turning and pointing a finger from around one of the take-out mugs. "I hear there's a new man on the horizon. Will I meet this one?"

Kez's heart leapt. It had been the flashing image of Callum crossing his mind producing that reaction. *Which is wrong on so many levels.* Then he realised Ollie hadn't been referring to Callum at all. He didn't know him for a start. Ollie and the hospital were part of Kez's new life. The one he'd forged without his best friend, and he wasn't sure the two meshed together. Should they even meet? *Would that cause the world to implode?*

"Kez?"

Snapping to, Kez shook himself out and realised that it was the usual St. Cross gossip bouncing around the sterile corridors again. *Maybe IT traced my email exchange with Raff?* He smiled to cover up the sinking feeling in his gut. Yesterday he'd had such a different reaction to thinking about Rafferty.

"I'm sure you'll meet him soon enough."

"Perfect. We can double date!" Ollie slipped into the car, offered a wave then kissed his boyfriend and the car sped off.

Kez inhaled a deep breath. A double date sounded good. Ollie would certainly get on with Rafferty. He'd be easy to take to meet colleagues, with him actually being one. He'd be perfect. Kez had had images of cooking for Raff, of exchanging cheesy gifts, of walking hand in hand through Spitalfields Market. All those things that real couples did. There'd be no complications there. *But will it ever be as strong?* Shaking his head, he rushed into work. Several winding corridors later, a lift to the second floor, and Kez slammed the bag of donuts onto his desk. Lisa was over by the water cooler, filling her usual litre bottle of the stuff.

"Peace offering." He held up the bag.

"You should probably give that to the parents. We've got a backlog." She sat and tapped away on her keyboard, not giving Kez much attention. Well, even less than she normally did. Yeah, they were busy, but a little informal chit-chat hadn't ever been frowned upon. They needed it to get through the day. "Your man came in looking for you yesterday."

"Yeah. I know. Sorry, Lisa, but it was my aunt. She was in that building." Kez wouldn't normally have cried *poor me*, but he couldn't have a whole day of Lisa being glum.

She peered over the screen with a look of both having put her foot in it and flickering concern in her green eyes. "Is she okay?"

"Yeah. They're keeping her in hospital for a couple of days, then she's being taken in by a friend of hers from church."

"I'm sorry, Kez." She did soften her severe scrutiny and Kez had to hide his small lingering feeling of triumph. Not many people got through her razor-sharp scowl. "It's just with everything here at the moment, I'm on edge. Sorry. Peace offering accepted. And if you need to go early, I'll take your patients. Although" — she pointed the tip of her pen over the desk — "you can deal with Rawlings. Bad mood does not cut this one today."

"Really?"

"He was here all night."

"Thought he wasn't due for nightshift for a couple of days?" Kez logged into his computer and checked the doctor's schedule. He was sure he wouldn't have overlapped his night shifts with day appointments. But then he had been distracted lately, what with Raffety, then what happened yesterday...

"He's taking a nap in his office and said for you to wake him when you're in."

"Great," Kez grumbled. The last thing he needed was a tired and grouchy doctor. At least he had several peace offerings he could use. Except, Rawlings was a doctor, wasn't he? A cardiologist at that. Did he partake in things that weren't particularly good for him? Kez realised just then that he didn't really know an awful lot about the man he serviced every day — other than the fact that he looked good in a pair of chinos.

After a few email checks, a few schedule reshuffles and a call to the hospital to check on his aunt — who was apparently doing well, all things considered — Kez made the daunting walk to Dr. Rawlings' office to wake him up for clinic. Rawlings had his own hideaway that he often used to lock himself away from patients and staff. It wasn't his examination room that was situated next to the main ward offices, but farther down the corridor and out of view of the general public, behind the staff nurses' quarters and changing rooms. It was where he did his 'thinking' and whatever else it was that doctors did when they weren't saving lives. Of course, Kez knew there was a hell of a lot of admin in saving children's lives. Kez was the one who had to compile it after Rawlings threw the files at him, after all.

Balancing the box of donuts on his prosthetic, he tapped his knuckles on the door. Yes, he was meant to wake the bloke up, but he also didn't want to get his head bitten off whilst doing it. When no reply came his way, he peered in through the gaps left by the various notices and whatnot stuck on the door from behind to distort the glass window. *Movement. Definite movement.*

Kez stood back and waited.

"Yes." Dr. Rawlings' tired bark came through the wood.

"It's Kwesi, Doctor. With...supplies." He winced at the sheer awkwardness.

Shuffling came from behind the door, followed by a cough, and Kez seriously hadn't wanted to catch the view of Rawlings' ever-so-toned torso. Luckily it was covered up just as quickly when the doctor flung on a chequered shirt and buttoned it together before yanking open the door. Kez didn't have time to compose himself, or adjust himself, or at least attempt to move the box of donuts to a location better suited to cover up his instinctive reaction to the sight.

"Am I late?" Dr. Rawlings looked whacked. Tired. And much older than he usually did. Always so well presented, so debonair, the doctor was the most eligible bachelor on the ward. It was quite a shock to see him so dishevelled. He flattened his dark hair back into his accustomed slide-over and scrubbed a hand over his salt-and-pepper stubble. Kez had just witnessed the man's vulnerable side seep out and he wasn't sure he liked it.

"Not yet." Kez smiled. "I thought you might want a little time to prepare. And perhaps, one of these?" He lifted the box.

"Sugary treats first thing, eh? Who told you my secret?" Dr. Rawlings opened the door wider and ushered Kez inside.

Kez walked through, placing the box down on the desk, and cast a glance around. Books were piled up from the floor, mostly medical journals to do with the cardiovascular system, paediatric medicine and various other professional standards of controlled medicines. A few files littered the surface of the desk along with his stethoscope and examination equipment. Nothing much out of the ordinary, except the open suitcase piled high with clothes and the sofa that was made up like a bed.

"Are you sleeping here?" Kez couldn't get the surprise out of his voice. The office looked like it had housed the doctor for a week, not just overnight.

"Sometimes." Dr. Rawlings washed his hands at the sink, splashing cold water over his face and neck. He held Kez's gaze through the reflection in the mirror. "It's been a busy time."

Kez knew liars. He currently had a pathological liar staying in his maisonette and Kez had spent the best part of his life having ignored the tell-tale signs. So he wasn't surprised that he'd picked up on the doctor's shifty eye flicker and rapid blinking. *Classic sign.* Rawlings ripped the green paper towel from the holder, turned from the sink and dried his hands all the while counteracting his previous body language signals by not faltering his gaze from its tight fix on Kez.

"Listen, Doctor, I should apologise." Kez hung his head, not through shame but more to take another sheepish gander around the room to decipher how long the doctor had been camping out in his office rather than going home. Kez was well aware he had a home. He often had to send letters and paperwork there and, as it was situated in one of the more affluent areas of North West London, Kez had to wonder why the doctor would prefer to be cramped on a double-seater sofa in a poky NHS office. Maybe he was redecorating?

*Or, maybe, you should mind your own damn business.
He's a grown man and can do what he wants. Want him
snooping around in your life? Noooo.*

"I rushed out yesterday without cancelling the
appointments."

"Yes, you did." And there was that sternness the
doctor was famed for, back again. It felt a little like
home.

Kez quickly replaced his creeping smile with a more
accustomed solemn frown. "The fire. In Branton. That
was my aunt's building."

The way Dr. Rawlings eased away from the sink and
his entire being seemed to droop gave Kez an
unexpected warm and fuzzy feeling. He'd never had a
father figure, but he'd just had an inkling to what it
might be like for a protective alpha male to care for him.

"My sympathies, Kwesi. Is she okay?"

"Thankfully, yes. She managed to get out. She's at
Newham. They're checking her over before discharge.
She'll stay with a friend."

The doctor nodded. "Do you need time to be with
her? I can put in a recommendation to the support team
that you need some compassionate leave and have a
temporary secretary put in your place. *Agency* staff."
Dr. Rawlings gave the faintest of eye rolls. "They do
seem to like agency staff around here."

"No, no, it's fine. She's safe and they'll no doubt
rehouse her soon. She's elderly, and has a broken ankle,
brittle bones, so they won't leave her long, I'm sure. So
I'll be back to vetting parents for you right from today."
Kez smiled. He liked to be busy and useful. Having felt
like a spare part for most of his childhood, working in
such an important role now gave him a sense of
purpose and a reason to have gone through all he had.

"Good. If you need anything, just ask." The doctor went to his desk and reshuffled a few files. "Has she been checked over for smoke inhalation? Sometimes that can lay dormant for a while."

"Oh, right. Yes, I'm sure they have." It was Callum who hadn't been checked. Kez had taken him straight to his house and let him fall asleep on the sofa.

"Actually, Doctor, I know this is a real big ask…"

Dr. Rawlings, now straightened and appearing back to normal, raised a dark eyebrow.

"My friend. Well, an old friend. An acquaintance. Someone I used to know…" *Why am I babbling so much?* "He lived there too and, well, he had nowhere to go, so I took him back to mine and…he's been coughing. Lots. Eyes red."

"Get him to his GP."

"That's the thing. He doesn't have one."

"Then he should get one" — Dr. Rawlings tucked a file under his arm—"and go to a walk-in surgery right now. I am sure he would be fast-tracked through to see someone."

"Yes. Thing is, well, he's not much of a people person. He doesn't like being poked and prodded." *For good reason,* Kez didn't add. "I thought that perhaps if I got him here, on the pretence of a paid lunch, that maybe he'd let you check him over?"

"I'm a paediatric cardiology consultant. I work with children. And hearts. Not adults and lungs."

"But you're a doctor. You'd know if he needs help, right?" Kez widened hopeful eyes. Whilst he was fairly certain he'd never get Callum through a hospital door, St. Cross was a different story. He'd never even know he was being examined here. And it wouldn't go down in any file that Callum avoided like he did authority figures.

Dr. Rawlings sighed. "Do I even have a gap in my schedule today?"

"There's a fifteen-minute window after your management meeting at one."

"Shit." Dr. Rawlings hung his head and he may have even added a brief foot stamp, but Kez wouldn't like to presume. Maybe he was adjusting his feet within his tan brown pointed Oxfords?

Kez jolted at the curse word too. He'd never heard Rawlings swear before. It somehow made him more human. Things like that had been seeping out the last few months — mannerisms and quirks that filtered out from the once-tense consultant and displaying a real person beneath the professional guise. It was as if someone had popped his soul and it was slowly oozing out. Kez wasn't sure if that was a good thing or not.

"I can't bear all these meetings." The doctor gathered up more of his stuff and headed toward the door. "Bleep me. I can't promise anything. But one look should tell me if he needs a thorough check-up."

"Thank you, Doctor."

Rawlings smiled. With his eyes. *Shocker.* "First appointment?"

"Jessie Cummings. Lisa booked them down to Echo."

"Ah. She'll require a play nurse. Anyone available?"

"I'll go check."

"Thank you. Bubbles."

"Sorry? Bubbles?"

"Jessie's a sucker for bubbles."

Rawlings clomped out of the room, leaving Kez staring after him. Amazing the information that man retained. And he had compassion too. *Who knew?*

Kez left the donuts on the desk. If Rawlings didn't get home to eat, then at least there was something here that was edible. *Right, back to desk work and to convince Callum to get here for lunch.* Which, to be honest, was probably going to be as difficult a task as getting five-year-old Jessie Cummings to stay still for her echocardiogram.

Perhaps Rawlings could sedate Callum, too?

Chapter Seven

Back to Work

After Kez had left, Callum remained behind, riddled with unease. It was all sorts of bizarre being surrounded by Kez's things. Some of them he remembered from back when Kez had lived five doors down from him on the Marlyte Estate, but most were new additions. *Shiny* new additions. Things that neither he, nor Kez, had had growing up in poor town. African-style ornaments that Callum hadn't noticed last night and emphasised Kez's origins were dotted around the flat. Some, Callum hadn't seen before. Some he recognised from having decorated Eve's place at the Marlyte and had obviously been given as a gift to make Kez feel at home in his new place. The flat-screen TV mounted to the wall must have cost a fair few ton, and the soft furnishings screamed of a home well-kept. Kez had clearly been doing well for himself. He had a home, not just an accommodation unit.

Leafing through the magazines in the basket beside the sofa, Callum took in what Kez now consumed. Kez had always been a reader, mostly of books that their mates wouldn't even have heard of let alone borrowed from the library or picked up in charity shops the way Kez had. Kez had tried convincing Callum to read a few, but words had never been Callum's strong point. It wasn't that he didn't want to read, or that he couldn't—it was just the letters sometimes jumbled up and he got confused where the line ended and the next one began. No one had ever picked up on it. Not his mum, nor his teachers. He was labelled lazy, or trouble. And if he was honest, he'd become both over time.

It was Kez who had known different.

Sighing, Callum pushed back the matted pages of NHS corporate magazine amongst the glossy covers of *Enable*—the magazine supporting disabled people— and fell back against the sofa, his gaze falling to a mounted certificate of thanks for Kwesi Zakari's donation to Afrikids hung on the wall. *So the bloke still gets himself involved in charity work, huh?* And one that appeared to be close to Kez's heart. Callum smiled, but the mere act made his skull hurt. He felt all sorts of shit. Fuzzy head, itchy eyes, scratchy throat. He didn't need a doctor to tell him he'd inhaled a bit of smoke. He knew that. He'd been there.

He shuddered.

Stomach growling, he thought he'd better try to eat something and settle the mush curdling at the pit of his gut. So he hefted up and meandered through to the kitchen. It was unexpectedly clean and tidy. Not like Kez's room had been back at the Marlyte that he'd moaned about having to clean every Sunday. Maybe Eve came round to offer her services once in a while? He always wondered where she went after her Sunday church visits. Not that he kept an eye on her. Bit hard not to notice when she lived five doors down, even if they hadn't exactly crossed paths, or stairwells, or landings, for quite some time. Callum had always made sure that wouldn't happen. He couldn't bear to see her disappointed face. Not after that time when he'd come back to live with his mum and Eve had been there, probably campaigning for him to return to the probation-led housing unit.

He settled on bread and butter. Bland enough to not throw up and sustaining enough to give him the much-needed energy to flee. 'Cause that was what he had to do. Leave. He could not stay here, regardless of what Kez had done for him last night. Who knew doing one good thing in his entire life would lead to so much head-fuckery? The last thing he needed was to bring Kez back into his fucked-up life, especially now he was all graduated, holding down a decent job that provided more than the essentials for him, and had a boyfriend to share his success with. Kez was the exception to the Marlyte Estate rule—he'd got out, he was clean as a whistle and had climbed his way up to his own gaff, regardless that it was situated in Dodge-ville and above a betting shop. It was more than Callum had ever had. Callum had had more possessions when he'd been on the inside.

After shoving down the last bite, he wiped his hands on his jeans and made the decision to run. As he brought his hands to his face, he noted the black dirt under the fingernails and checked out his clothes. He sniffed himself. All right, shower first, nab some gear from Kez's wardrobe—*please have something that don't scream office worker*—then make it somewhere else.

With what, Cal? He had no cash. No possessions. No phone, and no Oyster Card. Kez had bought him a single to Stratford last night, which now felt like a one-way ticket to the past. *Fuck! Right, calm.* He needed calm. And money. *Yeah, that's what got me into this fucking mess in the first place.* Well, not exactly this. He glanced around at Kez's kitchen and read the inscription on the cork plaque hanging by a golden hook: *Strength of character means the ability to overcome resentment, to hide hurt feelings and to forgive.*

Callum hung his head. He wasn't conceited enough to think that was up there because of him, but it shanked him right where it hurt—his smoke-induced lungs. He erupted into a coughing fit, eyes streaming with mucus seeping out from everywhere. He scrabbled around the kitchen for something to wipe himself up with and found a tea towel.

If nothing else had convinced him he had to leave right now, that quote had. He'd never wanted to hurt Kez. *Ever.* It had never been his intention. But he'd also never had enough foresight to know who he was dragging down into the shit pit with him. Like when he'd agreed to come back here last night. He'd let Kez walk straight into his barrel of crap because the alternative was what? Going it alone?

Man up!

He pushed away from the counter and ran up the stairs, two at a time, heading straight for the bathroom, where he stripped off his clothes. There was an already overflowing washing basket popped up behind the door. Callum was not that much of a bastard. He screwed his ruined jumper, jeans and boxers into a heap and dropped them onto the floor—he'd throw them in the nearest bin on the way out—scraped out his hair from its topknot and stepped into the bath.

The shower wasn't particularly powerful, more just pissed-out lukewarm water, but it was doable. As

Callum scratched the curtain closed, he got a sudden whiff of Kez—his shampoo, his shower gel, his spray-on deodorant. They were all the same brands Kez had used in his teens. But mostly the lingering aroma was all Kez—his skin and his familiar earthy, grounding scent.

Shit. Callum closed his eyes, unwilling to acknowledge how stiff his dick was. He slapped his hand to the tiles, rocking the pole that held all the toiletries, and they all fell into the porcelain bath with a clang. The industrial-sized shampoo landed on Callum's bare foot, and he sucked in a wince through gritted teeth.

It was a morning thing. *Everyone gets a stiffy in the morning, right? Treat it like any other boner.* Callum wrapped his fingers around the flesh and pumped with the mechanics of experience—hard. *Fast.* Needing the release. He closed his eyes, unwilling to acknowledge whatever it was that was helping him get the necessity done, as he'd had to during his incarceration. He'd never got any privacy to drag these things out in there. Everyone did it, and everyone who was half-decent, for a crimmie, that was, turned a blind eye when their cell-mate bashed one out. Callum had learned to do it in record time and marvelled that he didn't create fires through the speed alone. *Bad choice, Wrighty. Now I'm thinking about the fucking fire!*

He peeked down, his sopping wet hair sticking to his cheeks, and slowed the movements of his hand. He focused on his prick, wrapped and hidden in the pink flesh, then when he glided his hand down, the head revealed a knowing wink.

"Traitor." Whether he was talking to himself, or his dick, he didn't know, but supposed they were one and the same.

He steadied the slide of his hand, allowing himself to at least feel something before it would all end in a splattering flash of guilt. He almost thought about fondling his balls, really going for it, giving himself a proper go — fuck knew how long it had been — but he sped up, grunting, and his arm ached. With a chesty groan, he released his orgasm into his hand and the waves of pleasure broke the droplets of now-cold water slapping over his back.

The moment passed. Callum shivered. Shaking out his hair, he cleaned his hand of the incriminating contents, discarding them down the plug hole where he should have disposed of everything else he was guilty of. He made light work of scrubbing his hair and body after that, wanting to hurry the fuck up and get out. *Leave all this behind like some whirlwind dance into what I could have had, if I hadn't been a selfish bastard.*

Stepping out of the shower, he had to use the only towel available and wiped himself down. He scurried over to the bedroom opposite, trying to focus his attention on the wardrobe and not on Kez's bedroom belongings. Was it too much to borrow underwear? Could he get away with going commando? Might be better all-round if he did. He found a passable pair of jeans that looked way too small to be Kez's and, shaking off the creepy feeling that they were Kez's boyfriend's, he shoved them on along with a faded denim shirt. Long sleeves, but it'd have to do. As he slipped it on and buttoned it up, he realised it too was slim-fitting on him. Neither of these items could belong to Kez, not now the man was all stocky and broad.

Bollocks to it, if they did belong to Mr. P. H. Dick then he'd have to come find Callum to get them back.

Socks, done. Hair shoved up into the elastic band with nothing but a wing and a prayer, much like Callum's life at the moment, he lurched back downstairs. He didn't have a plan, just to get as far away from Kez as he could. His heart sank at the thought of not being able to see him again. He'd spent five years coming to terms with that. Now he'd been teased by the thought that their friendship could resume from its pause. This was for the best though. *For Kez.* With a deep breath, Callum yanked open the front door.

A svelte blond stared back at him, his eyes startled through the lenses of square-rimmed dark glasses. He had a finger raised to the bell on the railings of the metal gate that wrapped around the concrete yard. Callum flinched, gripping onto the door and ready to slam it shut. Could he escape through the living room window to shop level? The bloke didn't look like one of the men who did the heavy work, but maybe that was the point. *Catch me off my guard?*

"Sorry, I didn't realise Kez had a flatmate. I'm Rafferty." The man waved. "Is he in?"

Fuck a duck.

* * * *

Kez's phone buzzed on his desk and he shot an apologetic look over the barrier at Lisa. She nodded and waved him off. So he stood, meandering through the waiting area to the corridor outside, and answered the incoming with a thumping heart. "Hey."

"Hi. So, um, I'm outside your flat..." Rafferty's voice sounded a mixture between wincing admission and confused irritation. "And there's a guy here?"

Shit. "Raff—"

"I thought you said you lived alone?"

"I do." Kez sighed. "Callum's an old mate, from school. He lived in the same block as my aunt. He needed somewhere to go after the fire. I said he could stay with me for a bit. Until the council rehouse him." That was all true. *Why does it feel and sound like a lie?*

"Right. I see. Sorry, I just came over because you sounded upset and I didn't think you would have gone into work. I brought you pastries..."

"That's sweet. Thank you. But I had to come in. Rawlings would have gone spare. He's got back to back today."

"No problem. I think your friend wants to leave anyway. He's standing, quite menacingly, by the door."

"Is he?"

"Yeah, I think he was off out somewhere and I might have startled him. If looks could kill." Rafferty snorted and Kez suspected that flippant chuckle hid a pang of nerves. Kez knew Callum when he was in street-mode and it could be intimidating when witnessed by the wrong person.

Or the right one.

"Yeah. He's got that vibe about him. Sorry." Kez hung his head. Was Callum making a bolt for it? Why would he do that?

"Well, I'll just bring these pastries on into work. I'm sure my team will be salivating." Rafferty's chipper tone snapped Kez from his thoughts.

"You're headed this way?"

"No point using my time off in lieu for nothing."

"Couldn't ask a pretty huge favour of you, could I?"

"Name it."

Kez winced. "Bring Callum with you?"

"Oh." There was a pause and a shuffle. "Is he likely to not appreciate my chivalrous company?"

"Yes." Kez could bet on that, so he had to offer something. *Anything to get Callum here.* He needed to be checked over. It was simply a matter of ensuring his health. "But if you get him here, I'll make it worth your while."

"Right, well, in that case, I'll put my best manly gruff tone on."

Kez chuckled.

"Just a quick question. Does he know you're gay?" Rafferty's breath whispering down the phone indicated Callum might still be in earshot, probably glaring at him from the open doorway.

Kez sucked in a breath. Callum more than knew. He'd been the one that Kez had discovered it for. He guessed there was a time and place for that conversation, and now wasn't it. It was too long, for a start. "Yes." *Simple.* To the point.

"Good, I wouldn't want to put my foot in it."

"Thank you, Raff. I really appreciate this."

Hanging up, Kez wasn't sure what he'd let either of them in for. At least now he could relax a little and get on with all the usual tasks that a busy day at the hospital entailed. Back at his desk, his daily routine of pointing anxious parents in the right direction for their appointments, scheduling more appointments and cancelling appointments due to squeezing the doctor into his many other commitments aided the speed of the day and cleared his mind. When the third meeting request came through for Kez to find somewhere within the jam-packed and colour-coded doctor's diary, Kez paused and leaned back.

"Lisa?" He tapped his pen to his lips.

"Yes?" Lisa didn't look up over the screen, her own tapping on the keyboard suggesting she was just as behind with the overflow of paperwork.

"Do you think there's something going on that we're not in on?"

"How so?"

"Rawlings is being invited to a lot — and I mean a hell of a lot — closed management meetings."

"It's part of his job, Kez. He's senior leadership staff."

"Yeah, but normally they're one a month. It's practically one a week now. Twice in one week."

Lisa popped her head over the screen. "Are you fishing for gossip?"

"No." Kez shook his head, denying the blatant fact that he probably was. "No —" He cut himself off from mentioning what he'd seen in the doctor's office and the concern he unexpectedly felt for the man. "It's just, I'm cancelling overdue appointments for him to sit in a meeting room, sip coffee and eat pastries."

"You know that's not all they do in there."

Kez shrugged. "Yeah, they work the hospital. They change things. Or they do disciplinaries."

"You think he's on disciplinary?"

"You tell me. You're the supervisor."

"Of you, yes. Rawlings is out of my pay grade and not even on my books."

"Did you hear what happened on the ward a few months back?" It had never been spoken about in this office. How could they when Rawlings so often dipped his head in without warning?

Lisa peered over her specs. "Yes."

"You think it's true?"

"About him having slept with a junior nurse? Probably. The fact that it was a man was the shocker."

Kez nodded. The rumour mill had it that Dr. Rawlings had been having an illicit—and against policy—affair with one of his staff nurses. *Ollie to be exact.* That had all come to a head when Ollie had found someone new and broken off their relationship in full view of the night staff and those admitted to the cardiology recovery ward after surgery. Since then, Rawlings had been giving Ollie a wide berth and tasked Kez with keeping the two apart as reasonably possible. Kez had to ensure Rawlings' rounds on the ward wouldn't coincide with Ollie's shift patterns. Which he'd done quite well. Except, Rawlings had been here last night. So had Ollie. Had that been why the doctor had been in such a state this morning? Kez felt sorry for the bloke. He knew what rejection and heartache felt like, especially coming from someone a person was in love with and thought he had a relationship with...

Kez sighed, leaning forward to type. *Won't go there again.*

The following hour flew by. A busy, packed schedule of paperwork kept him busy enough not to dwell on the impending incoming. It was why Kez liked the job. It made him feel useful, like he was important and needed in the world. Maybe that had come from having been told from birth to five that he was useless, that he was taboo and had to be hidden away. It was Eve who had taught him otherwise and boosted him up when he'd been so far down. Then when there had been a chance at a graduate-level job, he'd opted for St. Cross because he knew what it was like here for the children who felt different to others. There were children like him there. And he loved being a part of making their lives better.

But right then, he had to focus his care on someone else. Someone who needed him more. And the last time that had been the case, Kez had let him down. Eve's voice still echoed in his mind. He shook it off to bundle through the reception area, tripping over the kids playing at the reflective rock pool and projected fish. He waved at the purple-T-shirt-wearing volunteers he'd come to know by name, and slipped out of the sliding doors to wait at the curb entrance.

As he stood, his mind wandered, and he shivered against the warm breeze. *Can the old ever really mix with the new?* This was Kez's new life. The one he'd built for himself. It had taken all his effort to move away from what he'd known, to leave the Marlyte and all that it stood for and had done for him behind. It had hurt to leave Eve, his one stability, but all young must fly the nest at some point and it had been long overdue. This job had allowed for him to privately rent his own flat and he wasn't living hand-to-mouth anymore. He was comfortable. He could afford things. And there was the potential to climb that corporate ladder to management level.

Callum's return had caused his two worlds to collide and it was tearing Kez in half. He was a different man to the one who had grown up on the estate and he'd left that life behind, only taking cherished memories with him, whilst burying the ones that were too painful. *The ones of Callum.*

Callum's face peeped around the far corner where Holborn station resided and Kez couldn't quash the unexpected stomach flip. *Damn.* That soon meshed uneasily with the curdled, heavy sludge stuck in his chest as he slid his gaze to the man walking beside Callum. Rafferty caught Kez's eye and offered a bright smile, one that a mere twenty-four hours ago would have ignited Kez's dreary afternoon. It wasn't the perfect that had produced Kez's excitable butterflies, it was the imperfect. The flawed. The damaged. *Callum. How can this still feel exactly the same?*

Kez hadn't ever been able to shake the man from his mind and wondered now why he'd even bothered trying. It was futile. He was destined for a life tarred with the unrequited.

Fixing his gaze on Kez, Callum didn't let it falter the closer he strode toward him, even with Rafferty's no-doubt incessant chatter beside him. Maybe it was a silent plea for help, which did tickle Kez a little, but maybe — and this was where Kez *knew* he was in for a world of pain — maybe Callum had been thinking along the same lines as Kez. That their friendship wasn't in tatters. That they could restore it somehow. Now that Callum was on the straight and narrow, with no skeletons in either closet, maybe they could just pick up where they had left off? Well, not exactly where they had left off, because Kez had vowed never to set himself up for that sort of heartache again. And, well, now there was Rafferty. And the fact that Callum wasn't gay. Wasn't even really bi.

"Package delivered." Rafferty saluted and clicked his heels together on approach.

Eyes that weren't quite brown, weren't quite green and weren't quite blue stared at Kez unflinching. Docile, lifeless. The way Kez remembered Callum had been when he'd stood in the dock. Kez had known back then that Callum had been hiding something behind the mask of indifference he so often wore. *What is he hiding now?*

"Thank you, Raff. I appreciate it." Kez fished his wallet from his pocket and slipped out a tenner, holding it out to Rafferty.

"What's that for?" he asked.

"For the cost of the Tube ride."

Rafferty smiled, wrapping his hand around Kez's fingers and gently pushing it away. "I don't want your money, honey. I just want your time."

Kez had wanted to feel that. He'd wanted the rush of adrenaline to surge through him the way it had when Callum's fingers had brushed his yesterday. He'd beg for that feeling back. He wanted it so badly.

Smiling, he flicked his gaze to Callum. He had his jaw clenched tight. *Uncomfortable.* Was it because of Rafferty flirting? Or was he mad that he was here at all? Did he want to bolt? Whatever it was, he kept his gaze fixed on Kez and didn't flicker it away. Kez found himself staring back, silently conveying everything he'd never said.

"How about rescheduling that date?" Rafferty interrupted the moment with a hopeful lilt in his voice.

Kez couldn't tear himself away from the hazel eyes that held him captive. They always had. Whether in person, or through the photograph that was stuck to his school yearbook and gazed at him with every year that had passed. Callum hadn't smiled in that picture, either. He'd been far too street for that. But when he did smile, his entire face lit up to spark the fire in Kez's gut.

I'm so fucking screwed.

"Kez?"

Kez remained fixated on Callum's soft breaths, along with the rise and fall of his chest, and the way some of the strands of his hair loosened from the knot to ruffle in the breeze. Trailing his gaze southwards, he widened his eyes. Callum was wearing Drake's clothes. An odd sight of the two people who had messed with his head most in his life were now meshed as one. Trouble was, Callum looked good. *Real* good. Better than Drake had when he'd tried to pull off that double denim look.

Stepping back, Rafferty tapped Kez on the top of his arm. "I'll catch up with you some other time."

Ripping his gaze from Callum, Kez refocused on Rafferty and guilt sliced through him as if it was Rawlings' scalpel.

"Raff, thank you. Sorry. Yes, let's do lunch. Tomorrow?" It was all Kez could think of to say.

Rafferty beamed. "Absolutely."

"What am I here for, Kez?" Folding his arms, Callum nodded at the entrance of the hospital.

Families wheeled children out in buggies and wheelchairs, or held the delicate hands of their frail offspring. Some overzealous outpatients skipped with glee at having been let out, or not having to stay longer than necessary, or having avoided the dreaded blood tests. Such was life at St. Cross Children's Hospital.

"I'll leave you both to it." Rafferty held out a hand. "Nice to meet you, Callum."

Callum glared down at the hand as if he could drill a hole right through the flesh. After a dreadful long, lingering moment, he took it and shook. Rafferty smiled, at Kez, then headed on into the hospital. Kez exhaled a lungful of relief that he hadn't realised he'd been holding in.

"How you feeling?" Kez ducked to get back into Callum's line of sight. Now that the man wasn't looking at him, Kez was desperate to get the warmth back into his veins.

"Fine."

"You all right if we get that confirmed?"

Hazel eyes narrowed in on him. "By who?"

"My doc says he'll take a look at you."

"Like, official?"

"Like, for a favour. Just to be safe." Kez prevented himself from squeezing Callum's hand. "Please?"

Callum sighed, long and deep. Then after a harrowing moment where Kez thought Callum might make a run for it, Callum finally nodded. "Let's go see what the bossman says, then."

"After you." Kez gestured Callum through the sliding entrance doors that whooshed open into the bustle of the reception area.

Digging his hands deep into his pockets—Drake's pockets—Callum meandered through the entrance and noticeably clammed up. Kez watched from behind as Callum's shoulders tensed and he flinched at every wail. Valerie, one of the purple-T-shirt-wearing volunteers, homed in on her meal ticket—a scared-shitless bloke not knowing where to go.

"Can I help you?" She repeated the lines etched across her chest.

Kez rushed up behind. "It's okay, Val. He's with me." He tapped Callum's back and pushed him toward the elevators.

"How do you do this every day?" Callum asked as he focused on the lit-up numbers detailing the lift's descent.

"What? Work?" He probably shouldn't have said that as Callum's glare gave him the shivers.

"At a hospital." Callum gritted his teeth. "With sick children."

"Most aren't infectious. Not the ones running down here, anyway."

"I didn't mean that."

The elevator doors dinged open and Callum stepped in. Kez followed and hit the required button for the Cardiology wing.

"I meant...like, don't it get to you? Seeing the suffering?" Callum's face grew paler by the second.

"They're not all suffering. Mostly, they're here to get better. And they do. It's amazing what happens here. Yeah, okay, not all of it is happy endings. But everyone here is doing their best to make it that way. From the volunteers who play with the kids, to those who show scared parents where to go, to the nurses who work twelve-hour shifts and the doctors who perform lifesaving surgery. Everyone here has a common goal. I'm part of that in my own little way."

Callum's lips curved into a brief, but noticeable, smile. "So you."

Kez cocked his head. "How so?"

"You always wanted to be part of something. You always wanted to feel important, useful. It's why you did all that extra shit at school. All that volunteering, fundraising and whatever else it was that took up all your spare time."

Kez bit his lip, bowing his head to hide the fact he wanted to grin. Callum remembered. He hadn't forgotten about him. And if he didn't know better, he'd have said there was a hint of jealousy in the way Callum had recited that last line. He'd always moaned that Kez'd had to do this, that or the other instead of hanging out with him down the playground, on the street corner…or in his room.

"I volunteered here, too, before landing the job. Probably what got me it." Kez stumbled as the lift jolted upward, making him bash his shoulder against Callum's.

Callum trailed his gaze to where their shoulders had touched. He sniffed and edged away. "You can volunteer here?"

"Yeah. Val does. She's a guide. That's what I did. But we have all sorts of volunteer opportunities — playroom workers, fundraisers, shake-a-tin stuff, staffing the gift shop." Kez tilted his head, catching the look of interest flickering across Callum's softening features. "Why? You want to volunteer?"

"Got told to, din't I? Best way for an ex-con to get on the job market. Signed up to the Prince's Trust but nothing came of it. That's how I ended up labouring for a poxy no-payer and had to find other means of making dough."

"Like how?" Kez's gut knotted.

"Cash-in-hand shit."

"Cal, you're not — " Kez didn't get a chance to ask the question that had been burning his bones since their reunion as the elevator doors whooshed open and Callum lunged toward them.

"We gettin' out here?" Callum walked out through the waiting incoming of scrubs and mothers-with-children and hurried off up the corridor, without even knowing which way to go. *What's he running from?*

Kez snaked through, saying 'hi' to those he knew and those he didn't, catching up with Callum waiting by the entrance doors to the wing. He wanted to ask again. To make the man tell him the truth, even if he wouldn't believe it. But Callum softened before him, into how Kez remembered him when it had just been the two of them. Alone. Together. *Growing up.*

"The Prince's Trust find volunteer placements for ex-crims," Callum said. "You can claim benefits while gaining experience somewhere." He shrugged. "I applied to all the places I could think of. Turns out, I ain't such a catch. Maybe it was my form-filling. You know I ain't good with writing and questions and shit."

Kez lightened. "I could help?"

Callum smiled. "Like the old days."

Kez dropped his head, staring at the gleaming cream linoleum floor. Those old days had been good. Locked in his bedroom, writing his own essays whilst aiding Callum to understand the simplest of text. Callum wasn't thick. Far from it. He just needed teaching in a different way. But a state school in Branton had never had the funds to help him. He'd been ignored, usually in a corner of the classroom where his disruptive nature had caused the teachers to just leave him to it. So Kez had taken it upon himself to help Callum achieve what Kez knew he could. And he'd loved every second of it. Especially that one night when they'd fallen asleep surrounded by books, only for Kez to wake wrapped up in a warm embrace with soft breath trickling along his neck and lips that coated his shivering skin—

"Kez?"

"Yeah?" Startled, Kez shook himself and nodded down the corridor. "The doc's office is up here. He should be there." Marching off, he told himself to get a goddamn grip.

The doctor's door was open when he arrived. Rawlings sat hunched over his desk, glasses fixed to his nose and reading through a mound of files with his computer switched on. The white coat had gone and he was back in civilian clothes, with an uneaten sandwich wrapped in the St. Cross canteen paper by his side. Kez knocked on the frame to alert him to their arrival. The doctor was so immersed in his paperwork he didn't even look up, and only hummed in response.

"Doctor, this is Callum, the one I told you about." Kez held up his prosthetic to both usher in and point Callum out to the doctor.

Ripping his attention from his books, Rawlings stared across the threshold. His gaze landed on Callum and the doctor flinched. Kez wouldn't have even noticed it if he hadn't been subjected to the doctor's vulnerability earlier. *Perhaps he's forgotten?* Callum shifted on his feet, as though he was about ready to make a bolt for it. Glancing from one to the other sent a prickling feeling grating along the nape of Kez's neck. But he didn't have time to acknowledge it as Rawlings scraped off his glasses, threw them to the desk and stood.

"Yes." He nodded. "Of course. Come in." Rawlings tucked his shirt back into his chinos, moved the piles of paperwork on his desk and flung his stethoscope around his neck.

Something he couldn't define skittered over Kez's skin. But he brushed it off and angled his head for Callum to step in. He did after a moment's hesitation that Kez couldn't blame him for. He burned his gaze into Kez, as if he were pleading with him. *For what?* Kez wasn't sure. *Perhaps this isn't the best idea.* Kez knew how much Callum hated authority figures. But Kez's research about smoke inhalation after his meet with the doctor earlier had told him that leaving it undetected and untreated could be fatal, so Kez would rather go through this than have a dead Callum on his hand.

"Close the door, Kwesi." The doctor waved and removed a mound of manila files from the plastic seat adjacent to his cluttered desk. He looked around, then obviously decided that the only place worthy to dump important documentation was on top of the ones already piled high from floor to desk surface.

Callum chuckled under his breath as Kez closed the door.

"What?" he asked, trotting back beside him.

"The way he says Kwesi sounds like when Mr. Gaffney used to call you."

"Yeah. I know. I've tried to get him to use Kez, but he seems to like being formal."

"Does he now?" Callum chewed on his bottom lip with something that Kez couldn't place flickering across his features.

Finishing his clearing up, Dr. Rawlings faced them both, hands on his hips. Kez smiled awkwardly and Callum shifted his gaze to the floor. Kez felt like he was missing out on something. He had no idea what, so he waited for instructions from his boss. The doctor inhaled, his solid chest rising to stretch the buttons on his tight-fitting shirt.

"Right. Well, Callum, is it?" Rawlings sliced his palm though the air to offer Callum the seat.

"Yeah." Callum sat, his exterior returning to its pent-up tautness. Kez wished he could massage that tension in Callum's shoulders away, but they hadn't reclaimed that part of their weird friendship. Yet. And certainly not in front of other people. *Sigh.*

"I'm Dr. Rawlings. Kwesi told me you were caught in the fire yesterday and that you weren't looked over by any medical professionals."

"They were busy with others. I feel fine."

"How about I be the judge of that?" Rawlings raised his eyebrows with a small smile curving his lips. *Typical Rawlings. Stern, firm, with a hint of affability to not come across as pompous.* At least to his patients. Colleagues might be a different story. *Lovers?* Kez would kill to know how the dynamics of a relationship between the sheets with Rawlings might go...

Rawlings looked up at the wall cluttered with the same policies that Kez's desk was and avoided looking directly at Callum. Was Rawlings checking if this came under the 'special favours' policy? The doctor's face contorted and grew paler than Kez had ever seen it before. Dropping his gaze to his dusky boots, Callum wrung his hands in his lap and Kez watched from the sidelines with a spark of irritation. *Why doesn't he just get on with it?* Rawlings blew out a breath then stepped in closer to Callum, his Adam's apple bobbing in his throat.

Then he cupped Callum's jaw and stared into the hazel eyes that Kez dreamed of far more frequently than he liked to admit. Stepping away from the wall, Kez was transfixed at the sight of both of them gazing at each other as if they were searching for something they'd both lost. Kez's nostrils flared at the force of the breath he exhaled. He'd just been transported back to a time when this overwhelming burning in his chest had been the norm. Whenever Callum had wrapped his arm around anyone else, Kez had been riddled with crushing envy. *Of which one this time?* He didn't need to admit that.

"Kwesi?"

"Yes, Doctor?" Kez's heart jolted.

Rawlings didn't look at him. "Perhaps you ought to wait outside? As much as Callum isn't my patient, there is still a duty of confidentiality."

"Doctor?" Kez was confused. He'd brought Callum here. He was, for all intents and purposes, Callum's chaperone. Callum would want him here. *Doesn't he?* "Cal?"

Hazel eyes focused in on him, but not for long. "It's all right, Kez. Wait outside."

Kez's throat closed up, making it impossible to emit words. He couldn't go against his superior's demands, nor his best friend's, especially if he wanted Callum to be checked over. He did a double take of both the doctor and Callum. Neither looked his way. Stone-cold blood rushed through his veins, reminding Kez of five years ago. The only thing he could do was the same as he had done back then. He yanked open the door, stepped out into the corridor and slammed it shut behind. Leaving Callum alone.

Lock. Bolt. Throw away the key…

What the fuck was that about?

Chapter Eight

Time and Place

"Does Kwesi know?"

The doctor's deep and penetrating voice, along with the loaded question, caused an unexpected quickening of Callum's pulse. The doctor would feel it and no doubt hear it when he put that blasted stethoscope on his skin. All Callum had was his mouth to get him out of this one.

"Does he know what?" *Insolence. Works every time.* People didn't expect any better of a bloke from a broken home on a rough East London council estate and with ex-con status to complete the package.

Rawlings stepped back, staring down at Callum in menacing threat. Callum shuddered.

"Are we pretending we both don't know who each other is?"

Callum shrugged. "Might be better to do that, right?"

"Did you know before you came here?"

"No."

"So this is a complete coincidence?"

"It would seem that way, yeah."

"All I have is the benefit of the doubt here."

Callum looked away. The memories were painful as it was and now he had them staring him in the face. It hadn't been his finest moment. Callum wondered if he'd even had any. *A long time back.* Before everything that had led him away from Kez. He sighed and faced the doctor.

"I wouldn't ever tell Kez, ever, if that helps clear this up quick and proper." He sniffed, then coughed, his throat scratching through the force. "I'm here 'cause he made me and I've always had a hard time sayin' no to the fella." *Ain't that the truth.* "Secret's safe with me, 'cause it's mine to keep too, yeah? I wouldn't want him finding out how you might recognise me."

Rawlings watched him from above, as though he was trying to hear the words that Callum hadn't said. *Is he trying to figure out if this is all a set-up, too?* Was he trying to figure out if Callum was there to blackmail him or threaten to tell his work colleagues what the doctor liked to do in his limited spare time? Cogs began to wheel around in Callum's mind. He couldn't, though. *Could I?*

"Let's just get this over with," Callum suggested, because he couldn't want anything more than that right then. "So we can both skip off and pretend this ain't as awkward as fuck, yeah?"

With a deep sigh, Rawlings agreed via actions. He flipped his stethoscope from around his neck and attached the prongs in his ears. He pointed to Callum's shirt. "Unbutton it."

"Thought we weren't going to relive it." Callum couldn't resist. He winked, sliding his tongue along his top lip. There was something uplifting about having one over on a doctor. Callum's mere presence was wreaking havoc on a man who ruled this hospital wing. And that was a shift in paradigms that Callum was all in favour for. It didn't happen often. So Callum clung on with both hands.

"You can die within three days from smoke inhalation." Rawlings delivery was deadpan. "Are we on day two?"

Aaand down to earth with a firm smack to the mouth. Back at the bottom of the pecking order, Callum unbuttoned his shirt and tugged the denim away to reveal his bare torso. Rawlings' gaze settled on his chest. Or, more accurately, the metal bolt that sliced through his left nipple. The bloke was a heart doctor, so the gaze could have been instinctive to trail to that part of Callum's anatomy but the sudden lick of his lips suggested otherwise.

"Are you feeling any pain? Fever? Coughing?" the doctor asked, his voice low. Clearing his throat, he squared his shoulders.

"Coughing, yeah. Chest feels a bit tight. This morning I was hot." He arched an eyebrow. "But that's certainly gone now."

Rawlings pursed his lips. Callum couldn't help but breathe out a laugh. Firmly back in doctor mode, Rawlings lowered into the swivel chair and wheeled it forward to get in front of Callum. Placing the disc to Callum's chest, he listened and Callum jerked at the chilling temperature of the metal, not to mention the close proximity of the doctor. It made him nervous. Not in a good way, but in a way that spelled trouble. As though he was already too close.

The doctor listened, moving the disk across his chest. "Inhale."

Callum did.

"Exhale."

Callum did.

Rawlings then shone a light in his eye, jerking his face this way and that. It felt like the medicals Callum'd had to undergo when inside and the checking-in parade where he had to leave his dignity and privacy at the entrance gates. Lucky the doctor didn't do a strip search, even if the man seemed like he might want to. He was none-too-light on his face pulling either. Wheeling himself away, Dr. Rawlings slapped his hands to his thighs and stared at Callum.

"What's my outlook, doc? Bleak?" Callum left his shirt open, waiting for instructions. *Like when we last met.*

"I'd hazard a yes." Rawlings flipped the stethoscope around his neck. "But I doubt it will be to do with the smoke. You don't appear to have a noticeable blockage. I'd say your body is acting accordingly to deal with any intrusion. A couple of days, you should be fine. However, I've only done an external examination. I should advise you, as a medical professional, to seek out a blood test and further exploratory investigation just to make sure. If you were in the building for as little as ten minutes, deadly smoke can still get into your bloodstream. What floor were you on?"

"Five." Callum focused on doing up his shirt buttons.

"The fire started on four."

"Apparently."

"Then I would urge you to your nearest A&E. I cannot perform those tests here."

Fastening the last button, Callum shrugged. "Cheers, doc. I'll keep your concern in mind." He stood. "Are we done?"

The doctor stared at him again, his dark eyes penetrating Callum's thick armour.

"Do you go there often?"

Callum belted out a laugh and had to check on the door, hoping it wasn't open and Kez had heard the outburst.

"No. Not often." He turned back to the doctor, face serious. "Like anything, I only do stupid stuff when I need cash. So if you're asking when I'm next going, I'm hoping I won't have to again."

The doctor stood. "That wasn't why I was asking. It was out of concern. As your apparent ad hoc medical advisor but also as a friend to one of my staff, I want to know that you frequent and partake there because you want to. That it is a choice. And not something that is forced upon you."

"Why? Would it make you lose your stiffy knowing that us fellas you perv over don't actually like doing those things you make us? 'Cause, sorry, Doc, but most of them are only there for the handouts. That place is a goldmine for dealing." Callum swallowed. It had been how he had discovered the place, after all. When he'd thought he could make a quick sale from his mother's leftover stash. He hadn't gone through with it. He'd chucked that shit down the toilet and discovered the backroom had offered him far more in returns. "Me? I did what you told me 'cause I was desperate. I don't plan to be again. But we'll just pretend we don't know what each other is, eh?"

"You have no idea who, or what, I am."

"A sad, desperate loner who gets off on being in control?" Callum raised his eyebrows. "You love to watch. You love to make blokes do as you say. You love to tease, to tempt, to tip fellas to the edge of their free will. And you live for that ultimate superiority because you don't get it here."

The doctor baulked.

"Yeah. I know blokes like you." Callum gave a firm nod, then marched toward the door. He'd come into contact with many a psycho and many narcissistic sociopaths. Most of them had been on the inside. And they, too, preyed on those most vulnerable to their seductions. Callum was only vulnerable to his own stupid actions. *Not anymore.*

As he yanked open the door, he narrowed his eyes when Kez, startled, leaped from against the wall. He couldn't have heard any of that awkward conversation back there, could he? *Don't acknowledge it.* There was no way he could tell Kez. No way in hell. Regardless of what the doctor might think. *Although*...the doctor didn't have to know that he'd never explain to Kez how he'd coped on no money, did he? Oily cogs squeaked in Callum's jumbled mind.

"What happened?" Kez asked, eyes so wide the white outdid the brown.

"I'm all good." He smiled. Genuinely. Because he might have just found a way to solve all this crap. He might not have to run after all. And it was only a little white lie this time. No one would get hurt. No one who mattered, anyway.

Clomping up the corridor, Callum shoved his hands into his pockets and whistled. Kez caught up to him and grabbed his elbow to shove him around.

"And what was all that in there?"

"What?" Callum played dumb because he could always get away with it.

"Don't fuck with me." Kez narrowed his eyes. "You chucked me out. What are you hiding?"

All right, he could get away with it with anyone else but Kez. He'd forgotten that. With him, he had to use a different set of skills. He hoped to God that they still worked on him. It had been a long time since he had to resort to them. He hadn't been able to get away with all that shit in the slammer. If he could have, he'd have had that extra blanket he asked for each night.

Sliding a hand up Kez's back, he stroked in small circles and enlarged his eyes to doe-like levels. *Pushing it? Maybe.* "I'm sorry, Kez. I didn't know what was for best. What if he'd had to tell me I had, like, an hour left to live? I think I'd like to tell you that news myself." He tried with a smile. "Break it to you gently."

The muscles beneath Callum's hand eased from the tension. *Triumph.*

"He's right, ain't he?" Callum nudged his head toward the closed door of Rawlings' office. "Confidentiality and all that. Was nice enough of him to check me over at all, innit?"

"I suppose." Kez didn't sound too convinced.

Callum slipped a hand on Kez's shoulder and leaned in toward him. "I'm all good. I'm okay. Looks like I got off lightly. Bit clogged up, but it's working its way out my system. Thanks, mate, for even caring enough to get me here. For even bothering to come get me in the first place. I appreciate it. Especially after everything."

Kez bit down on his bottom lip and Callum could almost taste the flesh between his teeth. And by fuck he wanted to. But he wouldn't. He *couldn't.* It wasn't fair. On either of them. All he could do was try to salvage their friendship at least.

"Listen, bruv. How about I head back to yours?" Callum suggested before talking himself out of it. "We can put those pizzas on you bought and have a proper chat tonight? Clear all this air between us as well as my lungs?"

Kez almost beamed in front of him. "Yeah. Yeah, all right. I'd like that. I've got to go see Eve after work, find out what's going on with the rehousing, but I'll be home by eight? Go get some rest or something?" Kez's fingers trembled as he handed over a key.

Callum noticed, but he wouldn't let on. There was too much awkward air between them as it was. He could tell Kez feared what would happen should Callum take up that offer of access to his home with full merit. The last time hadn't fared too well for either of them. But Callum was a changed man. The fire had changed him. He gripped the metal hanging on a silver keychain, squeezing Kez's fingertips and hoping to convey the trust through touch alone. He knew it wouldn't. He knew it would take more than a cheeky glint in his eye and a promise of pizza to regain Kez's trust.

But Callum had now found a way out of his mess, and once that was sorted maybe he could tell Kez everything and start over. Maybe pick up where they'd left off?

Yeah, right. You can't compete with a fucking doctor! Medical or otherwise.

* * * *

"I'm sorry, Ms. Marsh, but the doctor isn't available to take your call today... Yes, yes, I completely understand..." Kez scraped the tip of his pen across his forehead as he clutched the office phone between his chin and shoulder. He checked on the time and the urge to cut the call was overwhelming. "She hasn't slept? At all? As in nothing?" He listened to the irate and frantic mother on the other end and knew he couldn't shrug her off. Nor could he put her through to the doctor as he was doing his last rounds on the ward. But the time was ticking to five p.m., clinic closure, and although it wasn't a hot date waiting for him at the end of today, he was still antsy to get home.

"A few hours constitutes sleep, Ms. Marsh — I know it might not seem that way to you which is why Dr. Rawlings suggested the sleep diary for her, which I have here. You emailed it last night and your daughter slept four hours — " The squeal from the other end made Kez drop the phone from his shoulder.

Lisa peeped over the border and mouthed something at him. He nodded, confirming he could handle it. This wasn't the first panic-stricken mother calling up after her child had been sent home from the hospital following heart surgery. He scrabbled for the phone receiver and held it to his ear this time. She was still talking. Babbling really. And the sobs had started.

"Ms. Marsh, I will ensure the doctor calls you first thing tomorrow when he's back in clinic." That also wasn't the first time he'd said something so bold without knowing if it could be done. Rawlings had a ton of calls to make in the morning. "Sleep is one of the hardest things after heart surgery. Keep her comfortable and ride it out. Of course, if there are any physical signs of deterioration in her health then please take her to your nearest A&E who will call on Dr. Rawlings should he be required."

Kez glanced at the clock above Lisa's head. It was ticking by faster than ever now. He still needed to visit his aunt and ensure she was okay before getting home. *To Callum.* His heart leapt at the thought. But he was determined to. He had to clear the air. Having Callum back in his life for the mere twenty-four hours he'd had confirmed that he had to fix what had gone wrong between them. He had to help him. He had to forgive. Callum *and* himself.

"Yes, she has a check-up here in three months and that will be with Dr. Rawlings unless he is called away, in which case Dr. Khan is up to speed on all Rawlings' patients. Any questions, please bring them to clinic. For medical prescriptions, your GP should be able to prescribe these as I sent the letter to your GP surgery with Dr. Rawlings' consent."

The mother seemed calmer, less sniffling anyhow. Sometimes Kez's voice on the other end of a telephone could do that. Firm but empathetic was how he had to deal with those who called in. When he'd first been on the job, the mere hint of a cry and Kez had been bleeping the doctor out of surgery to take a call. Dr. Rawlings hadn't taken too kindly to being called mid-open-heart to answer a question about a child's faeces' colour. So Kez had learned to deal with the most of it himself. He was the barrier between patient and consultant. And he took it seriously. As long as he gave the advice that any medical problems were to be dealt with at A&E, then his back was covered. It might have seemed cruel, but it was the right thing to do. Rawlings' patient load was his current lot. Anyone discharged were back to their local hospital and GP service. Such was how things worked. Dr. Rawlings never wanted to be disturbed for anything other than complete emergencies. And Kez never wanted to be on the receiving end of Rawlings' wrath.

As Kez hung up, he caught Lisa's gape over the barrier. "What?"

Lisa nodded toward the door. Kez span and there was Rawlings, slipping on his fitted blazer and with his tie firmly knotted.

"Who was that?" he asked.

"Ms. Marsh. Penelope Marsh's mother. Had surgery last month. Discharged within five days. She's not sleeping."

"The mother or the child?"

"I'd hazard a guess that it's both."

"Indeed. Give me the number. I'll call her on the way home."

Kez twisted back around in his seat, exchanging a brief look of surprise over the barrier at Lisa. Rawlings never normally hung around after surgery rounds. He never normally offered to call a discharged patient over something so trivial. In fact, he never normally asked who had called in at all. Kez wrote down the number from the file onto a sticky note, stood and handed it over.

"Thank you." Dr. Rawlings pocketed the note, hovering at the door.

"Anything else, Doctor?" *Please do not give me more work!* was what he actually wanted to say. But he needed this job.

"Are you heading out?"

"Erm...yes. Just logging off now."

"Good. I'll wait."

Surprised, Kez fumbled through his daily ritual of locking the filing cabinets and switching his PC off. Something done so effortlessly of a five p.m. most nights, but with the doctor lingering over him and *waiting* for him brought forth the bumbling fool he hadn't been in a long while. What could the man possibly want that couldn't be discussed in the office in front of Lisa? *Callum. Shit.* This had to be where he was reprimanded for having wasted Rawlings' precious time. Maybe there was a policy that forbade private use of NHS staff and Kez was about to find himself in one of those disciplinary meetings.

"Night, Lisa." Kez offered an awkward wave to his supervisor, ignoring the silent plea from her to explain what the hell was going on. If only he could.

If he had a scooby.

Once out in the corridor, Kez checked his phone for any incoming messages which gave him both distraction from his companion and to see if any news had come through about his aunt's building.

"How long have you known Callum?" The doctor's voice broke the silence after he'd pressed the button for the lift.

Kez tucked his phone away. *And here it is.* "Years. Since school. Well, on and off."

"And is he your...*boyfriend*?" Rawlings stumbled on the word like he wasn't used to saying it.

"No. No, he's not." Stepping into the lift, Kez paused the conversation as a couple of nurses said their hellos to the doctor. Kez guessed the bloke didn't want to talk whilst in polite company. So Kez kept schtum. So did the doctor. It took until they were outside the entire hospital before he spoke again.

"Are you in a sexual relationship with him?" Rawlings didn't look Kez in the eye and instead focused on adjusting the bursting-at-the-seams satchel on his shoulder.

Kez baulked at the question. Not only was it completely over the line and the doctor had never feigned any interest in his partners before, but it also wasn't any of the man's goddamn business who he slept with! Was he asking because the doctor wanted a bit of Callum? A few months back, Kez would never have believed that. But now...after all the rumours about Rawlings and Ollie and their illicit 'relationship'. After all the office gossip that said the doctor preyed on the young and vulnerable...

Kez felt sick. "I don't see how that's any of your business." That was rather brave, and foolish.

"The reason I ask," Dr. Rawlings continued, clearly cottoning on to Kez's hesitancy to negate the question or offer the confirmatory, "is that I have a concern for him. And, therefore, to you."

"A concern? What type of concern? Is he okay? Lungs-wise?"

"Oh, yes, that. He's all clear on that front. This is more of a personal concern." Rawlings tugged down his jacket sleeves, lowering his voice so those passing couldn't eavesdrop. "To do with his sexual activity."

"What?" Kez forced out a laugh. Was he hearing right? What the hell did the doctor know about Callum's sex life? Kez didn't even know about Callum's sex life. Not anymore anyway. And if he was honest, he could never have known the whole truth even when he'd thought they told each other everything.

"Please don't take this the wrong way —"

"Did you do an STD check on him as well?" Kez's voice bubbled with irritation. "'Cause he shouldn't have agreed to that. Is that why you sent me out?" Kez shook his head. "Doctor, Callum's an ex-criminal. He's been on the inside a while and, yeah, he's done some stupid shit. I don't doubt he's still doing stupid shit. Whether or not I'm sleeping with him doesn't matter here anyway. *I'm* sensible. I won't be fooled again. I know who he is and what he's done. Who he's sleeping with is also none of mine, or your, concern."

"I understand that, but if you'd let me interject here for one sec—"

"Whatever you think of him, he's still my friend. He needs my support. Those two things I can, and will, give him." Kez's rage wasn't simmering and he was in danger of shouting. To hell with all those who were walking past their loitering on the hospital door step. He was so fed up of people's judgements. One look at Callum and the doctor had suspected the worst of him. The very worst. That he was some sort of...*what*? What had he implied? Why had sex even come into it?

Kez's head hurt.

"I can see he means a lot to you." The doctor looked away, holding up a hand to an oncoming taxi.

"He does." More than a lot, but that didn't need saying. Kez was sure it would be noted in the way he'd reacted. "So, with all due respect, Doctor, I'd ask you to leave him alone. Thank you for your help today. I appreciate it. But I would urge you not to pursue anything with him."

"Kwesi—"

"Thank you, Doctor, and good evening." With that, Kez rushed across the road, narrowly missing a black cab leaping over the crossroads toward Dr. Rawlings' outstretched hand. His blood boiled and his chest ached. He'd just stood up to the doctor. First time ever.

It had been for Callum. Even if he had no idea what it had been in reference to.

Chapter Nine

Forgive and Remember

Telling himself to forget Dr. Rawlings and his blatant disregard for workplace ethics, Kez made it to Newham Hospital in record time. He must have been on autopilot, as he barely remembered the Tube ride, or the walk through the bustling streets, or passing the Marlyte Estate at all. Maybe he'd closed himself off for a reason. It would have been hard to gaze upon that place in its current state. He'd seen it on the internet news reports, in the evening commuter newspapers, and it was shredding the fond childhood memories he had of growing up surrounded by such diversity.

He knew what society thought of people brought up in council-run stacked housing. But if there was ever a place with a community feel, it was the Marlyte. They all looked out for each other there, like a huge family. That had included Callum at one point. Having lived five doors down from each other during their teens, they'd become like brothers, with Callum having spent more time at his and Eve's than his own place. There had always been enough dinner cooked and a place set at the table for when he popped by. Callum's mum hadn't been particularly maternal, or of sound mind or present for much of Callum's adolescence. So much like how Eve had taken Kez under her wing, she'd done the same for Callum. Callum had even taken to calling her Auntie. It had been the perfect family set-up. *For a while.* Until the boundaries had been overstepped. Until adolescence had sparked all those simmering feelings.

Approaching his aunt's cubical on the ward, Kez braced for what was behind the blue curtain and how he was going to explain to her that Callum was now in his house. She'd be okay. She would. She had to be. Callum had saved her and, albeit implicitly, she had encouraged Kez to seek him out. And she preached the gospel of forgiving others. That had to account for something. Right? *Right?*

As he scraped the circle rods along the rickety pole, he was startled to find the bed empty and made to exacting nurse standards that Ollie would be jealous of. The guest chair, however, wasn't vacant.

"Kwesi!" Grace was an elderly woman herself, and a fierce one. She had to be nearing seventy, but it would take a heavy-duty truck to knock her off her feet. She and Eve were best friends, having met at Our Lady of La Sallette community church and become each other's confidante. Grace's husband had been lost to cancer several years back and Eve's eternal spinster status had meant they'd needed each other, with Grace becoming Kez's second aunt.

"Grace." He scooted around the bed to kiss the woman's cheek.

"Oh, Kwesi. How are you, my dear?"

"I'm good. Where's Auntie?"

"She's being taken to the little girls' room. Then, she's discharged and coming back to mine. All airways clear. She's still in shock, understandably, and her ankle needed recasting. But other than that, she's good to go."

Kez breathed a sigh of relief. Ever since he'd done the research on smoke inhalation because of Callum, he couldn't help fearing that he hadn't even asked about that of his aunt. He'd been concerned about where she went from here, yeah, but he hadn't even worried about her health. She was always so tough, so strong. She had to be. Bringing up a disabled child who wasn't her own had given her a body and soul of steel.

"I can take her." Kez dumped his bag on the floor. "You don't have to take her in. She's my responsibility now. I can return the favour for what she did to me."

"Nonsense. She's better off at my house. I've got the room. I'm all alone there in my big old place. I'll be glad of the company. Just you come and visit, yes?"

"Of course." Kez was a little relieved he didn't have to find space to house his aunt, especially considering the sofa was currently occupied and there was no chance of sharing that or his bed, with either Eve or Callum. But he meant what he'd said. He *would* return the favour. That was what families did. Whether flesh and blood or not. It was why he was doing it for Callum. They'd been brothers from other mothers for a while.

Sinking down to perch on the end of the bed, he rested his arm on his knee and stroked the smooth plastic.

"You okay, love?" Grace shuffled to the end of the seat and placed a wrinkled hand on Kez's knee. "Eve told me about Callum."

Kez shot his head up, staring into wise grey eyes. "That he saved her?"

"Yes. That was brave. And showed he has a moral side."

"He does." Kez strangled that out. "He's good underneath it all. He wants to do better."

Grace sat back and didn't do a particularly great job of hiding her look of scepticism. Forgiveness could be preached in the gospel, but Kez guessed it was harder to put into practise when the stupid actions of others affected *their* loved ones.

"It's brought it all back, hasn't it?" Grace at least tried to keep the disapproving *tutt* out of her voice.

Kez didn't get a chance to answer as the curtain swished along the metal pole and opened. A nurse clutched Eve as she hobbled on one crutch into the cubical. Kez launched off the bed and threw his arm around her. She toppled back, chuckling as Kez squeezed her close and inhaled her familiar scent. Beneath the distinct hospital-grade sanitizer, he could still breathe her in and it felt like coming home. Of being safe and warm and *loved*.

"Well, Eve." The nurse snaked her arm free of Eve's. "Looks like you've been missed."

Kez stepped back and gave a lopsided smile. Relief wasn't the only reason he'd launched himself on her. It was everything that had happened within twenty-four hours and the inability to talk to his one confidante about it whilst she cooked him his favourite stew. The image of Eve slaving over a hotpot in the poky kitchen at the Marlyte stabbed him in the chest. She'd never be there again. Neither would he. The whole dynamics of their relationship had been altered indefinitely. What would become of them now?

"We'll call you a taxi, Eve, and it'll take you where you need to go," the nurse said, cutting through the silence.

Grace nodded. "Thank you, nurse. She'll be coming with me."

Eve ran a hand over Kez's hair. "See. Told you I'd be fine. Take more than a fire to put this old girl out."

Kez smiled. He bloody well hoped so. He had so much to tell her. He wanted to blurt it all out, but fear of her reaction kept his lips sealed.

"I'll leave you to get sorted." The nurse backed out of the cubicle. "Take care, Eve. If you need anything at all, please call the hospital."

As she left, it shunted the small space into an awkward silence.

"What's happening with the council?" Kez asked to get some conversation going that wasn't him having to address the news of Callum. "The Marlyte?"

"We've had notice that they're able to get in the building today and will be salvaging what's left." Eve allowed Grace to wriggle her into a long woollen coat that Grace had bought for her. The tags were still on it and Kez ripped them off. Why hadn't he thought to bring his aunt clothes, or something? *Anything*. Flowers would have been a nice touch. *Fuck, I've become useless again!* "Refurbishment will take place. In the meantime, alternate housing will be issued to all. But as I'm with Grace, I've told them they don't need to hurry." She gave Kez a pained look and squeezed his arm. "I am sorry about all your old things."

"It's just stuff, Auntie. What's important is you." Kez grabbed the plastic bag filled with clothes and whatnot that Grace had clearly thought to pack and held out his prosthetic for Eve to grip. She did.

"Have you heard from Callum?" She asked the inevitable with concern. "I've been thinking about him this whole time. How he came to me. He didn't have to, y'know. He didn't have to carry Thomas out. I hope he's found somewhere to go."

Kez bit down on his lip, ignoring the sharp inhalation from Grace behind.

"Best he's gone, I say!" she snapped. "That boy was nothing but trouble. For both of you. And for the estate. They should have rehoused him somewhere else!"

"If they had done that, Grace, I might not be here at all." Eve's fingers tightened around Kez's arm and she threw a pleading look over her shoulder. "Please. I know how you feel about him. But he was a boy. And now a confused young man who has lost what little he had. Let's offer some compassion and pray that he does not resort to his old ways."

Chastised, Grace scoffed. Kez offered her a brief smile. She wasn't saying it all to be nasty. It came from knowing what Kez and Eve had had to go through all those years ago. Before the fire, Eve might have been saying the exact same thing, although the subject of Callum had been off-limits for quite some time. It had been easier for them to never address it. Kez had found it difficult to talk about him without tearing up, yet he knew Eve prayed for him most nights. She'd hoped he'd find a different path, preferably one as far away from them as possible. Instead, it had paved right back to Kez. And he knew he had to tell her the truth.

"He's staying with me." Kez attempted some sort of finality, but he knew it was futile.

"What!" Grace spat.

Eve waved a hand to silence her then turned to Kez, drawing her eyebrows in. "How did that happen?"

"I went to see him. At the community centre. He had nothing, Auntie. I couldn't leave him there." He appealed to Eve through his glistening eyes, begging her to understand. To not make a fuss. To accept that Kez could never have walked away from Callum. *Not again.* He sighed. "Matthew 6: 14–15. 'If you forgive other people when they sin against you, your heavenly Father will also forgive you.'"

"If we do not forgive others their sins, our Father will not forgive us." Eve nodded. "Yes, Kwesi. I know." She tapped his arm. "I hope you know what you are doing."

"So do I, Auntie. So do I." The tightness across his chest was hopefully not a sign that he didn't. "I have to help him, don't I? If I don't, who will? It's what you did for me."

"That was different!" Grace piped up from behind. "Eve was saving you."

"And now I'm saving Callum." Kez hung his head. "From himself, at least."

Nothing more was said as Kez helped Eve away from the cubicle and out of the emergency ward, through the bustle of the hospital. Outside, the sun was settling against the concrete backdrop and the tailed-back cars heading out from the multi-storey car park caused an oppressive drone over the three of them. Kez hoped it was that anyway, and not his announcement that he planned to have Callum back in his life. *As a friend. As only a friend.* Because Callum needed one.

So do I.

At the taxi rank, a driver rushed out of his car and confirmed he would be their cab home. He opened the door and Grace lowered herself into the back, with the man taking Eve's crutch and popping it into the passenger side. Eve twisted to face Kez and took his hand, holding it between her cold, dry fingertips.

"I can't say I won't worry. I know how you felt about him."

"Auntie—"

She gripped his hand tighter. "'For as the rain and the snow come down from heaven and do not return to it without watering the earth and making it bud and flourish, so that it yields seed for the sower and bread for the eater, so is my word that goes out from my mouth. It will not return to me empty, but will accomplish what I deserve and achieve the purpose for which I sent it.'"

"Isaiah 55:10-13. I don't understand." He'd been a churchgoer when he'd lived with his aunt, but that had fallen by the wayside. After Callum. After everything. It wasn't that he didn't believe. It was that he couldn't forgive as easily as he was meant to.

"When you give your love to someone and they don't deserve it, you can feel completely deflated. You'll wonder why you cared in the first place. Isaiah reminds us that nothing happens without a reason, including all the people that come into our lives. There is a reason why we meet them and a particular purpose to serve." She tapped his hand. "It may not be what you expect or want, but there will be a reason." She lifted a hand to his cheek and he slid to the side to press his lips to her dainty palm. "Just remember that, if nothing else."

Nodding, Kez helped his aunt into the car and closed the door behind her. As he waved her off, the heaviness in his stomach didn't feel like it was made from iron anymore. It was much more fragile than that.

* * * *

It was a stroke of luck that Callum managed to find his way back to Kez's place. He'd not paid that much attention the previous night and Rafferty's incessant chatter on the way to the hospital had prevented him from mentally mapping the way. But he found it without too much of a faff. Even though he'd promised himself he wouldn't be here again, that he wouldn't rain on Kez's parade, that it wasn't fair on him, he now believed that he could find a way out of his mess. Staying put, regardless of the risks, was currently his only choice.

And maybe, just maybe, I can get Kez back. 'Cause fuck knows how much I need him.

Clapping around in the kitchen, he made a start on preparing a dinner of reconciliation. Kez was more than likely due home any minute and Callum was taking step one to rebuilding the foundations of a new life, starting with salvaging his friendship with Kez. He needed to prove — not to Kez as such, more to himself — that he could be a decent bloke. Bunging a pizza in the oven wasn't exactly culinary expertise, but it was a goddamn start. Familiarising himself with the contents of Kez's place had been like getting to know the bloke all over again and he now realised how much he'd taken him for granted back then. He'd never paid Kez back for anything. Not so much money-wise — although he was sure Kez had spent a fair bit of cash on him over the years — but more returning the favour of Kez's unbridled care and friendship. He had to rectify that. *Asap.*

It was as if the fire had ignited something in him. *Gave me a starting point, perhaps?* He wanted to become a better person. Saving Eve from a potential fatality and coming face-to-face with Dr. Rawlings — a man who had seen him at rock bottom and commanded he tumble down even farther — Callum knew he couldn't continue on his path of self-destruction. He had to leave the old Callum behind. He'd been given a second chance. Not that he believed in fate, or God, or any divine being, but something had driven this chain of events. And that had brought Kez back into his life. Now he intended to hold on to him. Because he couldn't go back to who he'd almost become. He couldn't be one of those geezers at the club. He couldn't have the same fate as his mum had. And he couldn't run. He couldn't leave Kez 'cause Kez was all he had. So the new Callum would begin by offering Kez himself in the form of a tasty after-work snack made by his fair hands. Not *him* being the snack, exactly. *Although...*

Shaking his head to rid it of the absurd thought, he squinted to read the instructions on the back of the box andsighed. The words were jumbled again, bouncing across the box as if they were attempting to flee. He slapped it down on the surface and set the oven to his fail-safe two-hundred degrees. That seemed to cook most stuff, right? His search in the fridge found a few bottles of beer shoved at the back among plastic boxes filled with meals. It was obscure, never-heard-of lager, but it was beer nonetheless and Callum could use a drink if he was going to sit Kez down and explain...what exactly, he wasn't sure. *But it's long overdue.*

He'd penned many a letter to the man when he'd been on the inside. He'd never sent them. Mostly because he didn't have anyone to check over that they had made any sense. So he'd torn them into pieces and had settled on a postcard with the word *sorry* written on it. He wasn't sure if it had ever reached Kez. He'd never gotten a reply.

As he cracked open the first bottle, he peered out of the kitchen window and caught sight of Kez fiddling with the gate. He lurched forward to help him before he remembered how much Kez hated that. So he stood and watched through the window as Kez closed the gate and meandered up to the front door. He looked weary. Tense shoulders, trudging strides.

Shit.

Callum strode to the front door to allow the man access to his own home.

"All right?" Callum asked. It was meant to have been a welcome, a greeting, a flippant, nonchalant 'how's tricks'. But the question felt loaded.

Kez stepped in. "Yeah." The word didn't match his mood, but when Kez laid his gaze on Callum, he shook his head and the tension eased from his shoulders. "Yeah. Eve's been released. She's okay. Staying with a friend from the church. Hopefully she'll get re-homed quick."

"Yeah. She should." Callum gulped from the beer, giving him something to do to quash the nerves. "I mean, she's what, sixty-odd now?"

"Yeah. But there's a lot of people to be re-homed. Including you."

"I'll be so far down on their list, they'll have run out of paper." Callum chuckled to lighten the mood. "I'm making that pizza. Go do what you gotta do and I'll bring it through when ready. Confessions time — I stole a beer. Don't tell the parole officer." He smiled, hiding his nerves that were bubbling to the surface. Whether it was for the awkward exchange or for what he knew had to come next, he wasn't sure. *Perhaps both.*

"Thought you didn't have one anymore?"

"I don't. It was a joke. Poor taste, granted. But you can have it back minus two sips if you want?" He tilted the neck of the bottle Kez-ward.

"Keep it. I'll have one with the pizza." Kez slammed his bag on the floor. "I'll shower and change, then I'm all yours."

Callum couldn't prevent the snort, nor the rush of heat that flamed his skin. Even Kez drew in a breath, but he shook it off and clambered past and up the stairs. *Not a bad start.* Now to not fuck up the food and get the words out he'd been trying to say for five years. *Sorry is so much easier to write down than it is to say.*

A while later, Kez came back into the living room, dressed down in loose jogging bottoms and a T-shirt. He'd taken his prosthetic off too. Fully shedding his layers and laying himself bare. *For me?* Callum smiled as he settled the crisp pizza on the coffee table and handed over a chilled bottle of the lager. They clinked before tucking in, sitting beside each other on the three-seater sofa.

Callum was aware of his own chewing, it was so quiet. Now he was here, he didn't know how to start. Or what to say first. Where should he begin in all the things that needed to get out? He sneaked a peep at Kez and could read the same things written all over his clenched jawline. He didn't need to worry about the jumbled-up letters on Kez.

"Kez —"

"Cal —"

They both laughed.

"You go," Kez offered, waggling the beer bottle and settling back after having endured two slices of the burnt pizza.

Callum nodded. He knew he had to. "I'm sorry."

Kez didn't say anything, waiting for more, Callum suspected. He deserved it.

"I was a prick. I fucked up. And I should never have done it."

"Yeah. Understatement." Kez sipped from the bottle, staring at the mantelpiece.

"If I knew how to make it up to you, I would. So, I'm starting now. You didn't need to come get me. You should have left me to rot in that building. I should have let myself rot."

"Cal—" Kez leaned forward, clapping the bottle to the table.

"No, Kez, it's true. I'm a waste of space. Or, well, I was. That fire, I think it saved me, y'know? Made me think. I've been given a second chance. I want to start fresh."

"Good." Kez bore his gaze at Callum, drilling a hole through his temple. "So, that life's over? For good? Nothing for me to be, say, worried about? Prepared for?"

Callum heaved a deep breath. It wouldn't exactly be lying. Not really. Because that life *was* over. He'd left it at the Marlyte to hopefully singe into ashes. *No traces.* "No," was all his croaked voice managed to get out. He coughed. "Sorry, the doc said I might still have some mucus to get up." He downed some beer to prove it.

"Okay…" Kez swiped his bare foot against the fluffy fibres of the rug beneath the coffee table. It was as though his mind was mulling over how far he could accept Callum's words. Could he trust him? Did he want to? Could a friendship that had been separated for five years really be restored with a flippant apology? "I want to help you, Cal. I do. But I can't be sucked into all that again. It isn't fair on me. It isn't fair on Eve. She's been through enough."

"I know. I know. You won't be."

Kez nodded. "Where's your mum?"

"Fuck knows, mate. And honestly, I ain't sure I give a fuck. I know I can't blame other people for my wrong choices, but we both know it was her who started it. When I got released and went back home, she was still using and owed a ton to some dealer. I told her she should quit, pay up or leave." Callum downed the rest in his bottle. "Next day, she was gone."

"Fuck, Cal, I'm sorry."

"I still worry I'll find her in some ditch somewhere." Callum sniffed, slamming back against the seat. "I'm pretty sure it's meant to be the other way around."

"We can't choose our parents, I suppose."

"No. But we can choose our mates. And I'm sorry I fucked that up for us. You were good to me. *Too* good. You deserved better."

Kez stared at him and Callum feared that Kez might have come to his senses. That he was going to agree and say this was all a mistake. That Callum wasn't worthy of him. That a friendship, a brotherhood, an unconditional love did have conditions after all.

Bashing his knee to Callum's, Kez smiled. "Glad we agree on something."

"We've always agreed. That's what made us a perfect combo. Like bacon and eggs."

"Who's scrambled?"

"Me, mate. My head's been scrambled since birth. More so on the inside."

Kez's smile faded. "What was it like?"

"Much as you'd expect. Keep yourself to yourself and you can get by. Did the rehabilitation programme. Got myself a trade. Head down and waited it out."

"I should have come visited you."

"To be honest, mate, I'm glad you didn't. For a while I was mad at you. Then I got over it. Realised it was my fault I was there, not yours. I wrote you, though."

"You did?" Kez shuffled forward.

Callum shrugged. "Maybe the address was wrong. Maybe it got lost in the post."

"Maybe Eve hid it."

"It don't matter now. But I have to say, when I went back to the Marlyte I went to knock on Eve's door more times than I should admit. Then I thought it was best to avoid her altogether. Lucky I was opposite the lift and stairs, I could see who was coming and going."

"How did we — *us* — ever get to that, eh?"

Callum agreed. Wholeheartedly. Once they'd been thick as thieves. Once they'd been joined at the hip. Once they'd been as tight as arseholes. Funny how each of those sayings held so much meaning for their relationship.

"Anyone come visit you?" Kez broke the silence.

"Stacy once or twice. Fuck knows why."

"'Cause she fancied you. Big-time. Used to wait on those swings for you to walk by. Mokira told me." Kez reached for his bottle and downed the lot, exposing that thick neck. Callum tried not to stare, or focus on the movements of muscles as Kez swallowed. "She told me I was getting in the way. That I should stop hanging around you."

"Bitch."

Kez snorted. "She was right, though."

"If I'd wanted to fuck her, I would have done it with you in the room. So, no, she weren't right."

Kez slammed his eyes closed. Then shook his head and opened them to laugh at Callum. "So you didn't start anything up with her then. If she was visiting?"

"Nah. Ain't exactly top-notch dating fodder, am I? As much as those grey trackies and plain tee can work wonders on some, I reckon she'd want a man who could at least choose his own gear. She stopped coming by after the first few months." Callum stood. "Want another tin?"

"Sure. Why not?"

Why not indeed. The first bottle had relaxed Callum enough to open up a bit. The second might get him over the hurdle that held him back from admitting everything. He took a deep breath in the kitchen, telling himself to get a grip. This was Kez. This was just Kez. *His* Kez. So there'd been changes. So there'd been a massive gap in their friendship, but that was nothing compared to the gaping hole that had been in his life without Kez in it. Kez had filled it in one night.

As he handed down the second bottle and Kez held it within his knees, they screwed off the tops in unison, sparking a crack and fizz in the muted air. Callum smiled and his limbs tingled with a hopefulness he hadn't had in forever. Until Kez's phone buzzed and Callum had to watch him take it out from his pocket, read the incoming, compose a reply with one thumb and whoosh it off.

Callum had an inkling who the message had been from. He'd endured a whole Tube ride with the bloke that morning when all he'd wanted to do was cut and run.

"So this Rafferty bloke…" Callum needed to know where he stood, even if it was going to stab him in the place where his heart should be.

Throwing the phone to the table, Kez met Callum's gaze. "What about him?"

"What's going on there?"

There was a definite sigh and Kez looked away from him. "We were meant to have our first date last night. He seems like a nice bloke. Auntie would love him. But then she liked Drake, so…"

"Who's Drake?"

"The man whose clothes you're wearing."

Callum wriggled in his seat, the denim shirt suddenly too tight and scratchy. He had an urge to rip it off and piss all over it. But that might not go down so well. So he drank beer, curtailing his response to want to punch something. Mainly a stranger named Drake.

"An ex," Kez confirmed, staring at Callum with amusement. "He stayed here a few times and left those. I was meant to take them to the charity shop but looks like they fit you pretty good, so lucky I didn't."

"Right. Yeah. Cheers. Sorry for going through your stuff, but it was this or come meet you in my birthday suit. I figured this would be more appropriate for your place of employment."

"I don't know, mate. If anyone's unfazed by nudity, it'd be in a hospital, right?"

Callum snorted, twisting the bottle around in his hands and cooling his palms. "Why'd you split?"

"Usual shit." Kez lifted his arm. "Freaked him out. Didn't say that, but the flinching whenever I touched him with it was a giveaway."

"Tosser."

Kez shrugged. "He wasn't the first. Probably won't be the last. It was him that made me try out for the prosthetic. He said it might stop people staring at me. And by me, he meant him."

"Honestly, mate, I don't think you need it. You seem more relaxed with it off. Like it drags you down. You seemed stiff on one side. Without it, you're you."

Smiling, Kez wrapped his lips around the bottle and shook his head before slamming some back. Callum returned the grin and tapped his knee to Kez's which helped him slide along the dipped sofa cushion closer and he could breathe that familiar scent in. That buttery aroma made from the cream Kez used on his dry skin. That spicy scent from the deodorant he sprayed over himself. And the sweetness from thecoconut oil he used on his hair.

"Anyway, what about you?" Kez dropped the bottle between his spread legs and scraped the label with his thumb. "Any dating? Girlfriends? Fuck buddies?" He closed his eyes on saying the last one, but opened them just as quick to centre in on Callum. "Bet there are a ton of women who love an ex-con, right? That's gotta work your swipe right."

Callum breathed out a lungful of air. If he was honest, he'd discovered that to be true. There were some on the estate who'd known him before being banged up and had all but offered themselves on a plate to him. Course, there were those who'd grown out of those circles and gave him a wide berth. But if he wanted to get laid, he knew those who wouldn't tell him to go fuck himself. And it wasn't like he wanted anything long term, 'cause what did he offer? No real job, a criminal background, no money and his mum's council flat that he couldn't afford to live in.

Still, bold use of wording from Kez.

"Why did you say women?" Callum asked, taking a shot from the beer.

Kez shifted. "Because that's what you wanted. Wasn't it? The normal stuff? Everything we did was you experimenting. And you humouring me."

Callum laughed. At least the ice had been broken. Smashed and now melting into the river of no return. "That what you think, is it?"

"That's what happened, Cal."

"Is it." Callum bit down hard on his bottom lip. He couldn't think of a single thing he could say to make the man see. To understand. To believe. To trust. Because he'd never given Kez any reason to before. Shit, he'd been a messed-up eighteen-year-old kid with no one to help guide him into being an adult and what that all meant. He could blame everyone and everything else until the fucking cows came home. Truth was, it was all his fault. He'd never shown Kez how he really felt before. He'd had words. Tons of them. He'd brandished those clichés around like they were a blessing from God. 'Gift of the gab' was the old Callum.

Not anymore. Now he had nothing but the clothes on his back. And they weren't his, either.

Actions speak louder than words. Yet another cliché that worked. He leaned forward, focussing on the outline of Kez's lips. Without thinking, he lunged forward and, sliding his hand around Kez's neck, kissed him. His chest rippled at the power of it all. At the taste. At having those lips compressed against his own. Kez's freshly washed scent shot up his nostrils to make his stomach leap and, when he trailed his hand along the back of Kez's head to hold him in place, his fingertips tingled against the tight waves. Fuck, he'd missed this. Missed kissing. Missed Kez.

Missed kissing Kez.

A sharp slap to his chest shoved him off. Kez leapt up from the sofa and Callum fell against the back, his breathing laboured and his hair falling from the topknot to drape into his eyes. He gaped up at Kez through the locks. "K—"

"Don't, Cal. Please. Just don't."

Words were caught in his clogged throat. Kez marched around the coffee table and Callum watched every move with an ache in his chest that couldn't be shifted with coughing this time.

"Don't do that, Cal. We can salvage this car-crash friendship of ours, but anything else…I can't go there again."

Callum couldn't speak. He didn't have the words. They were jumbled in his mashed-up mind as though they were the letters on a job application form. So he sat frozen to the spot, unable to reach out for the one thing that made him a better person, and had to witness Kez flee from the room and up the stairs, then flinched at the slam of a bedroom door.

Chapter Ten

Truth or Dare

Kez hadn't slept much. He'd tossed and turned, thrown the covers off, enveloped himself within them, got up and stood at the top of the stairs for a while — where he'd called himself a dick — gone back to bed and repeated the whole scenario several times. By morning, he was a mess. He stared up at the ceiling, waiting for the alarm to shrill a start to a day where he'd have no choice but to go downstairs and face everything.

And by everything, he meant Callum.

He'd thought he'd got over it all. It had been five years. He and Callum had been *eighteen*. Well, seventeen when it had all started and eighteen when it had ended with a guilty verdict. But now Callum was back. Kez had *brought* him back. *Willingly*. He'd welcomed him into his life without assessing what that would mean, what that could spell and what that would dredge up. For him. For Callum. For all those suppressed feelings that he'd pushed down into his gut and quashed with date after disastrous date.

Kez had been getting on with his life. He'd been happy. As happy as he could be. He'd come out. His aunt had reacted better than he'd expected. He'd had boyfriends. *Lovers*. One-night stands. He'd moved on and embraced his sexuality. He'd learned to love himself, putting the past firmly behind him. There had been a few bastards in his time, Drake being one. There'd been some others who, as soon as they'd noticed he was without a forearm and left hand, had made their excuses and vamoosed faster than he was able to reply with his name. There'd also been the ones who were curious enough for the short-term, but he'd shrugged their ignorance off and carried on.

Then he'd met Rafferty, who had noticed the prosthetic straight off. It hadn't deterred him from indulging in unprofessional flirtatious email exchanges, which had led to him asking Kez out. That first date could have been the start of something new. Something great.

Except now, Callum had kissed him. And Kez couldn't deny that he'd wanted him to. He couldn't pretend that he hadn't been thinking, as he'd sat a mere inch away from the man who had been his first—in both the physical and emotional sense—what it would be like now they were both grown men. He'd itched to find out if Callum could still ignite those long-forgotten fireworks that he'd planted in Kez's stomach. No one had even gotten close to sparking them, let alone produce the full-on explosions that Callum had been able to with one sly touch. Would Callum's lips still taste as sweet? Would he rage his hands over Kez with the same desperation? Would they both roll and fumble and squeal, then shush each other in fear of being walked in on? Or would they fuck like adults, set free to be as loud as they wanted without the worry of Eve being in the next room?

He'd thought about it all while resisting the urge to edge closer to him, to have their thighs touching. He'd attempted to steer the conversation to something else. He'd asked about the women Callum must have been with, because he'd thought that was what Callum would have done. Now he wasn't so sure. And it was fucking with his head. Callum did things. Did stupid things. He did them because he thought he had to. That was what Kez had thought back then. That Callum only did what he did with him because he was bored and the alternative was to ruin their friendship. Because he must have known how Kez had felt about him? And all the while he'd also been messing around with the girls on the estate.

Or he'd thought Callum had. He'd been told. And he might as well have ripped out his heart and replaced that with an artificial organ too, because he'd never thought he'd have a use for it again. He'd never had time to ask of course, to get Callum to confirm that Kez wasn't the only one he fumbled beneath bedsheets with. Why? *Because Callum had to be so fucking stupid!*

Bleep bleep bleep. Kez slammed his stump down on the alarm and shut his eyes.

He showered with little enthusiasm, dressed with less care and stabbed a comb through his hair with nothing but a laissez-faire attitude. He couldn't even muster the energy to put on his prosthesis, so he rolled his shirtsleeve up to his elbow and ambled down the stairs.

In the kitchen, he stuttered to a stop when he banged into Callum at the counter, pouring tea into two mugs. He was still in Drake's jeans, but he'd discarded the top and Kez couldn't help the mental comparison. Callum had filled out since Kez'd last seen that much of his flesh—his stints of manual labouring had obviously had an effect on his scrawny physique. He was still lean, wiry, but with added grooves of muscles honed from hefting bricks, rather than agonised over in a gym. A few additions of scratches and scars were dotted over the tight skin along his slender back and a scattering of light brown hair trailed from his stomach to beneath the flies that had been left to drape open. *No underwear to speak of.* He hadn't swiped any of those from his rummage through Kez's wardrobe. Which was a crying shame. Kez'd had dreams of Callum wearing his underwear.

As he swivelled to face Kez, the low sun rays beamed in through the window and bounced off the bolt piercing through Callum's left nipple. Kez blinked then couldn't help but stare at it while he attempted to moisten his dry lips.

"Tea?" Callum held out a mug. If he'd caught onto Kez's unease, he didn't show it.

Dragging his gaze upward, Kez accepted the drink with gratitude. When he sipped straight off, he scalded his tongue. He wouldn't be able to taste anything for a good long while now, which was another crying shame as the sudden urge for a metallic taste in his mouth all but consumed him.

"Listen, Kez." Callum rested his hip against the counter and blew into his own mug. Those jeans were in danger of trailing down his hips and Kez wasn't sure he could handle himself if they did. "I'm sorry. About last night. That was a dick move."

Kez stared at him, mulling over what that might mean. Was it that Callum hadn't meant to kiss him? That it had been nothing but Callum doing his usual failsafe method to keep himself housed and clothed? That he hadn't realised that their kissing had actually meant something to Kez, because it was nothing more than Callum passing the time away, like they'd used to as kids? That *he* was a dick for doing all that?

"I mean, I know you got this bloke…" Callum spoke to the floor, scraping his thumb along the handle of his mug. He then tried to get into Kez's line of sight. Kez hadn't realised he'd been staring southward.

"Rafferty." Kez half mumbled and half said the name like he'd just remembered what it was. *Shit, I am a horrible, horrible person.*

"Yeah. Him." Callum slurped from his mug. "I get that. So, look, if this is awkward or whatever, I'll just fuck off. I'll go back to the centre and find out what's going on. I'm sure they'll house me somewhere."

"Is your mum on the tenancy or you?" Kez wasn't sure why that was the first thing out of his mouth. It was as though he couldn't address the rest of it.

"Mum." Callum sniffed. "But I'm sure if I explain shit, they'll find me somewhere. The rent ain't too much in arrears, so —"

"Stay here." Kez clanged the mug on the surface and caught a whiff of salty residue when his shoulder brushed against Callum's bare skin. It took all his effort not to lick him. "It's fine. I said it's fine. So it's fine. We'll go through the options later. After I get in." Kez went to walk away, but Callum grabbed his arm, wrapping his fingers around the stump. Kez met his gaze, holding on to it like Callum was his flesh.

"I've done some stupid shit in my life, Kez. You know that. I know that. I can't erase it. I can't take it away. All I can do is promise you that I'll change. You meant everything to me. *Everything*. And I know I fucked it up with you. The moment that door slammed shut of a night, it was you who kept me sane. Your voice in my head. I need you to know that."

He let go of Kez's arm and Kez wished that he hadn't as he was in danger of collapsing to the floor. Callum had been holding him up and keeping him level. Like when Callum had disappeared from his life all those years ago, him stepping away now had left Kez unbalanced.

"I…I…shit, Cal, I have no idea what to say or do right now!" He rubbed his forehead, sliding his fingers across his temple to invigorate something. *Rationality. Reasoning. Hell, even recklessness will do!* "I have to go to work. Either wash those clothes or go buy new ones. I can't have you look like him." He dug into his back pocket and pulled out a card, slapping it on the surface. "It's contactless, so go to Primark."

Callum darted his gaze from the card to Kez, like he didn't know which had the greater pull. For a moment, Kez thought he might reject it. Hand it back saying he wasn't a charity case. But he didn't. Instead, he nodded and slipped the card from the surface into his back pocket.

"I'll be shiny new when you get home."

Kez smiled, albeit weakly, then said nothing more, to escape the past and head toward the present.

He travelled to work in some sort of bubble, cocooned from the world and the surroundings with nothing but his mushed mind to get him to where he had to be. He didn't even offer his usual cheery hello to the volunteers on duty, or high-five the cleaning staff, or acknowledge when children pointed at him. He slumped onto his desk and into his work in a daze of indifference. Lisa didn't seem to notice. And Dr.

Rawlings' brief "Good morning" to them both didn't even spark a dot of bother for Kez. He'd all but forgotten the words they'd had yesterday. Too much had happened. Far too much.

The tap on the office door made both Kez and Lisa look up toward the noise after having been working in silence for…who even knew how long?

Kez's chest tightened when he saw Rafferty fiddling with the brown satchel slung over his shoulder. He hovered by the open door, dressed in tan chinos and a multicoloured polo shirt—another Ralph Lauren special—and when he pushed his glasses up his nose, he offered up a timid smile.

"Hi, sorry to intrude, but I was passing and we'd said something about lunch…"

Passing? Cardiology Ward? When he worked in Grants, the other side of the hospital and then some? *Shit.*

Kez checked the time on the computer. He'd been so preoccupied he hadn't given the clock a second glance. Nor a first one, if he was honest. Had they said they'd do lunch? Was this the date rearranged? *Fuck, I did!*

"Right. Of course. We did." He ruffled the papers on his desk, not to get them in any order as such, but more to show willing. "Sorry, it's been a full-on morning."

"We can postpone, if you're busy." Rafferty backed away from the office, narrowly missing a mother passing by with buggy and child. He apologised, glowed red then shook his head when meeting Kez's gaze.

Kez caught Lisa's amused smile over the barrier. She nodded and waved him off with pointy nails. That meant he had her permission to take a break. It was lunchtime, after all. For a brief moment, Kez hated himself for wishing she'd say their busy schedule wouldn't allow for such indulgences as food. But when could anyone rely on someone else for help getting them out of sticky situations? *Truth bomb right there.*

Kez stood. "No, no. I can do lunch." He slapped the files in his locked drawer and closed down his PC, safeguarding confidential information ingrained even in a hasty departure from the office. "Although, we might have to make it the canteen. I have to be back by two for the next appointment onslaught." He nodded up to the clock and winced. A forty-five-minute gap for a date wasn't exactly romance and flowers.

"Of course." Rafferty's whole demeanour seemed to shine, though. "No problem. NHS-grade sustenance coming up!"

Kez snorted. "You know we changed from NHS and outsourced to a real catering company a few months back. I've had a three-course meal down there that's been better than anything you can get at Ronaldo's at the crossroads."

"Really?" Rafferty widened his eyes behind his lenses as Kez approached him at the door.

Laughing, Kez looped his bag over his arm. "No. That was a joke."

"Oh." Rafferty blushed. "Of course. Here —" He held out his hand. "I can take that for you?"

Kez drew in his eyebrows, then shuffled his bag across his shoulder. "I'm good."

"Right. Of course. It's just, you have no prosthetic today. Is everything okay?"

"Ever run out of time to do your hair?"

Rafferty stroked a hand through his blond waves and breathed out a laugh. "Yes."

"Same as." He angled his head. "Come on."

They made their way to the canteen, filling the awkwardness with general chitchat about the hospital. Kez pointed out the units and wards that Rafferty hadn't been shown yet. The hospital was large enough that not everyone knew everything that went on. Rafferty, mostly locked away in an office working through proposals for medical grants and funding opportunities, didn't get out in to the real workings of the children's hospital as often as he should. Kez found that walking the corridors of a daily basis gave him a renewed sense of why they were all there. *For the children.*

The canteen was busy, but not more so than any usual mid-week lunch time. A few tables were being vacated so there was still a chance they could grab a table for two. They ambled up to the serving hatch and, before Kez could grab a tray, Rafferty picked up two. Kez didn't say anything. The man was obviously awkward enough for Kez to not want to make him feel any worse. He might as well not mention that he was perfectly capable of sliding his own tray along the runway. He put his palm on it as a way to show it, instead.

Kez went for the fish option of curry and rice, and Rafferty went all Brit with his battered pollock, chips and peas. After paying, Kez noticed that Rafferty was hovering and fighting with himself about whether Kez could manage to hold a full tray with plate, cutlery and a bottle of juice across the busy canteen. He could. So he proved it by doing it without a fuss.

Once seated, Kez tucked into his food. Rafferty opened his can of fizzy pop, then leaned over with a smile, picked up Kez's bottle and screwed off the top for him, setting it back down on the table after. Kez held his exasperation within. It wasn't worth the fight. He'd had many dates where he'd been treated like an invalid. The best option was to prove he wasn't by doing stuff and not snapping at those who thought they were being helpful.

"How's your aunt?" Rafferty asked, obviously hoping to move the date along from general mundane conversation.

"She's okay. As expected." Kez swallowed down his rice. "Discharged yesterday. Staying with a friend. They should be letting them know whether anything is salvageable. I doubt it though."

"No. I guess not. I've seen the images on the news. It's such a tragedy."

"It's not so much the stuff. It's more that the place was her home for so long. Thirty years at a guess. Mine too, for a while."

"You lived with her?" Rafferty washed down his calorific lunch with the diet drink option and furrowed his brow.

"Yeah. From about seven."

"Wow. I see now why she's so important to you."

"She was my guardian. Still is, I guess. Just not in legal terms anymore." Kez shrugged. "She saved me."

"Saved you from what?"

"An orphanage. Or, well, who knows, really." Kez stabbed at the fish in the mildest sauce he'd ever known to be considered a curry. "She rescued me from the potential fate of not having a life, a future."

"Where are your parents?"

"Died."

Rafferty launched his hand across the table, obviously forgetting that the one hand available to squeeze was currently stabbing through a cod.

"I'm so sorry." He left his fingers splayed on the table.

Kez stared at the hand and did think about taking it, or tapping it, acknowledging it. But for some reason, he didn't.

"Thanks. I don't really remember much of them or living over there."

"Over there?" Rafferty slipped back in his seat, picking up his fork.

"Ghana." Kez shoved in some rice. "It's where I was born. Small village. In a weird, morbid sort of way, it was lucky for me that they did die. I don't think I would have been given the same chances that Eve gave me here."

"Why's that?" Rafferty stuttered.

Kez held up his arm. "It's considered an omen."

"Oh!" Blushing, Rafferty closed his eyes.

"Some of the smaller villages still believe in that spirit-child stuff. Eve visited her family there from time to time and I guess it could have been fate that she found me and offered to take me back here. I honestly can't say what would have happened to me if she hadn't."

"Kez, I had no idea…"

Kez shrugged. "Why would you? Eve brought me to London, enrolled me in school—something that I hadn't attended before—and with her help, I caught up pretty quick. She showed me the importance of education and compassion and never let me believe my disability would hold me back."

Rafferty got a faraway look in his eyes. "She's truly an amazing woman."

"She is." Kez held on to Rafferty's gaze and allowed himself a proper look. He searched those eyes as though he was trying to find something he'd lost. He desperately willed it to come into view. He wanted to feel it. *To touch it. To taste it.*

He couldn't.

"Well, I for one am glad she rescued you. Otherwise you wouldn't be here now." Rafferty dug into his food, flicking his gaze to Kez and offering a wink.

Kez breathed out a laugh, but not in amusement as such. More doubt.

"And I know this isn't what I would have had in mind for a first date." Rafferty glanced around at the hospital canteen filling up with patients and staff of all calibre. "But I'm still very keen to have a second somewhere less...congregated."

Kez zoned out again. He was aware that Rafferty was speaking, but all he could do was stare down at his lunch and wonder why...why couldn't he just shut it off? Why did he always have to compare? Why did any of this have to happen? A few days ago, Kez would have been all grins, all bouncing energy, all sunshine and fricking roses. Now all he had was misery. Regret. And leftovers.

"Are you okay?" Rafferty lowered his head to catch Kez's eye.

Kez fell back in his seat, dropping his fork onto the plate and heaved out a sigh. He couldn't pretend. Not anymore. It wasn't fair. On anyone. Least of all Rafferty. "It's Callum."

"Your friend? From the building? Is he okay?"

Scrubbing his hand across his brow, Kez had no idea how to explain the complexities of his and Callum's past. What to say, what to omit. He just had to say it all. *Warts and all.* No matter how bad it would look. Rafferty had a right to know. *Better is a poor person who walks in his integrity than one who is crooked in speech and is a fool.*

"He wasn't just my friend." Admitting that was the first step to absolution, he supposed. He'd never said those words out loud and, now, as he did, they didn't feel as foreign on his tongue as he'd imagined they would.

"Ah." Rafferty wiped his lips on a paper napkin. "I had a hunch. He was rather...hostile."

Kez gave a half-hearted lopsided smile, full of sweetened apologies and a strange kind of beguiling fondness. "Yeah, I can imagine."

"So, an ex?"

"No. Yes. Maybe." Kez groaned from deep within his gut. He'd dipped his toe in admitting the bizarre and, frankly, random friendship he and Callum had had but detailing the whole strange scenario was going to be much harder. He'd buried the memories so deep that they had become more like recurring dreams. But he had to explain. If only to prove to himself that it hadn't been a flash in the pan, a nothing, a time easily forgotten. So he started from the beginning, "He and I were like brothers. He lived five doors down from Eve. We were friends almost instantly after I moved in. We grew up together. Went to school together. Hung out together. Inseparable."

"I think I might know this story." Rafferty folded his arms, his face gaunt.

Kez couldn't acknowedlge Rafferty's disappointment but he had to look him in the eye in order to continue.

"He didn't have a dad. Not one that was around or he knew. His mum wasn't going to win any awards for mother of the year either. She was absent a lot of the time. Drank a lot. Got involved with drugs." Speaking about those early atrocities of Callum's upbringing at least eased some of the guilt Kez had been carrying around at not admitting who Callum really was to him and why he'd been so protective of their past. They were Callum's secrets to tell, but Rafferty had to know the whole truth or this story might paint him in an even worse light than it already would.

"There was always someone coming in and out of her place. She wasn't stable. You know how people are scared of social services? Think they'll have their child taken away because they missed an appointment here?"

Rafferty didn't look as though he knew what Kez was getting at, but he nodded nonetheless.

"Well, it's bullshit." Suppressed anger spat that curse word and Kez couldn't even apologise for it. "Eve did an anonymous call. They came and vowed she was doing all right. Callum was housed. Clothed. Clean. It didn't matter that she hadn't even noticed he couldn't read! She hadn't even bothered to find out if he had dyslexia. She left it. Callum fell behind. He spent more and more time with me and Eve. Dinners at ours five nights a week. I'd help him with his homework, teach him how to focus. Eve became his surrogate mother as well as mine."

Kez folded his arms, running his hand along the flesh of his stump—something he tended to do the more agitated he was, 'cause this was the part he'd fought so hard to forget. "I think we were seventeen when it started. We'd both enrolled at the local college. I was doing A Levels, he was on a practical BTEC but had to redo his Maths and English that he failed. One night I was in my room, books spread everywhere, trying to finish an essay or something. He was meant to be

148

working on his key skills. He liked to try to distract me. Or distract himself maybe." Kez shrugged. "I don't know. One day, the tickling led to him kissing me. I think he knew it'd work to get my attention. I think he knew I liked him. I'd been struggling with my feelings for him for a while. I kinda knew I always liked boys. But Callum..." Kez shook his head, worrying his bottom lip. "Callum was my guiding light. I'd do anything for him. Anything to get a little of his attention. So when he kissed me, it was like he'd brought me alive."

Rafferty slipped back in the seat. Silent. Listening. Kez couldn't look directly at him when he recounted the rest.

"He sure found a failsafe way to get out of doing his homework. The kissing led to touching, that led to fumbling around under the sheets, that let to me discovering how much I loved his hands on me. And I loved every part of me on every part of him. Outside in the real world, we were just bros, y'know? Kez and Cal. *Mates.* We hung out with others from the block. Callum flirted with the girls and I pined over when I could be alone with him again. I always got him in the end. He always came back to mine. It went on like that for a while. He was doing all right. He'd got his key skills. He was on for an apprenticeship. I was on for all A grades." Kez's voice strangled and he gritted his teeth with the frustration of it all.

Edging forward, Rafferty focused on Kez and his eyes filled with something Kez couldn't bear to look at. Not whilst he had to relive what came next.

"What happened, Kez? What's hurting you so much?" Rafferty could read between the lines as well as he could medical theses.

"He did a spectacularly stupid thing." Kez looked away, his frown a sure giveaway. If what he'd already said had been difficult, this, this here, was going to hurt like a stab wound to the heart. "He took in some drugs from his mum's dealer. He said he'd hold on to them. Cash in hand on delivery to the next guy. I don't know why he did it. Money maybe? Maybe he was threatened? Maybe he thought he had no choice? I don't know, because he was caught. Routine search from the police discovered a grand's worth of class A gear in his bedroom."

Rafferty sucked in a fierce breath. Now Kez had said that much, he couldn't stop. He needed to get it all out, as though he was in some kind of therapy session. The counselling he should have accepted five years ago but which pride and guilt had kept him away from.

"Yeah. That's not the worst part." Kez scraped his teeth over his bottom lip, catching on the dry skin and almost making it bleed. "He was arrested. Put on trial for possession with the intent to sell. And for once in her fucking life, his mum had gone to sign on at that particular time. So defence couldn't even claim they belonged to her. There was too much for personal use anyway. Callum begged me to give him an alibi. He was looking at a custodial sentence of five to ten if found guilty. The police were cracking down hard on dealers in our area. Y'know, making a point? He'd promised me there was no fingerprints on the package. The only thing tying him to those drugs was that they were in his flat when he was. So all he needed was for me to stand up as a witness and say that he'd been with me, that the drugs couldn't be his."

"Oh, Kez." Rafferty leaned forward, reaching out for him.

Kez couldn't allow for him to get anywhere near him. He might break down if he did and a busy hospital canteen and on their supposed first date really wasn't the time to do that. If ever there was one.

"I was going to. I'd've done anything for him. I was in love with him. To prevent him from going to prison, I would have stood up and said anything." The pain in his chest crushed tighter and he could hardly breathe, let alone get the rest of the story out. After swigging from his juice bottle, he composed himself enough to keep going.

"Eve wouldn't let me. I'd been with her. At church. For me to lie, she would have to lie. There was no way she was going to allow me to stand up and swear an oath to God and then lie. I couldn't do that to her. Not after everything she had done for me. So I couldn't. At the courts, on his trial date, I told him I couldn't do it. He turned his back on me. So I did the same to him. For five years. Until the other day." Kez inhaled a deep breath. "Until that fire brought us back together."

Chapter Eleven

When All's Said and Done

Checking out his reflection in the bathroom mirror, Callum gave a brief nod of approval. He'd spruced up all right. Passable anyhow. As much as he'd hated to take up Kez's offer of the card, he didn't have much of a choice and he really couldn't stay in borrowed clothes. He had no money of his own to buy new ones, nor could he go down to the community centre and rummage through the bags upon bags of aid that the other residents were having to accept while they waited for their lives to restart.

His trip to the local shopping centre had proved pretty fruitful. Not the bright lights of Westfield, but the precinct of cheaper shops selling off even cheaper gear had had what he'd needed – pack of boxers, socks, a two-pack of trackie bottoms and a jumper all for the thirty quid Kez's contactless allowed. It wouldn't have been his first choice in get-up, but beggars couldn't be choosers. At least it meant he didn't have to be in Kez's ex's kecks and he could leave the house to find work. 'Cause he planned to pay back Kez every penny, no matter how long it took. The building firms he tended to get a days' worth of graft with must be needing people about now.

So he'd done the ring-round. On Kez's house phone, that was. Asking fella after fella if there was any work going. Bricklaying, painting, cementing—anything that would get him the cash to pay Kez back. He could earn about fifty quid for a day on a site, a ton if it was a better firm. What he needed was a chance. A firm to take him on proper. They never would. They'd see his record and would rather get in some kid on his BTEC from the local college who didn't have Callum's shifty background. That was why he'd enrolled with the Prince's Trust to get him volunteering that could lead to something decent. It hadn't as yet. And the money had dwindled… Callum hung his head with shame.

Kez was due home any minute and Callum's stomach emulated all those cement mixers he'd had to spend his days filling up. His previous idea of running away had now been thrown out with Drake's clothes. He couldn't leave Kez. He *couldn't*. Not anymore. Callum had lost so many friends since being on the inside and after his return home, the ones he'd made were all face-value. Nothing at all like how it had been with Kez. No deep and meaningful conversation. No comfortable silences. No *intimacy*.

Or was it because it was only Kez who could give all that to him? Maybe it wasn't friendship he was after. *Is it a soul mate?* Someone who got him. Someone who understood him and accepted him. The way he did Kez.

Fuck. That's it.

Callum stared at his reflection. On the inside, he'd thought about Kez. All the goddamn time. He'd missed him. As a friend. As his confident. As his go-to-guy. He'd missed the mucking around too. And missed how Kez had looked at him — like he was the most important person in the world. Like he meant something. Like he was his God. It was hard not to get wrapped up in how Kez saw him. But as the years ticked by, and Kez hadn't been there for Callum to see himself in Kez's gaze, he'd well and truly fallen off his pedestal. *And the bump hurts like hell.*

Swallowing down the agonising lump in his throat, he scraped back his hair into its topknot. His thumping heart seemed to make the mirror vibrate and distort the view of himself. *Who am I now?* On his release, he'd searched for what Kez had given him. Getting his kicks in seedy joints had served a purpose for a while. But he needed more. He needed to be looked at the way Kez had looked at him before. He needed to be picked up, dusted off and risen back up.

That's why I kissed him last night! It hadn't been to reap old times. It hadn't been to give Kez what Callum had thought he wanted in order to salvage a lost past. *It's because I want him. I need him.*

Inhaling sharply, Callum stared into his own hazel eyes that widened with every beat of his heart. He couldn't hide from himself and he gazed back through the mirror, holding his breath. *Oh, fucking God. I —*

His whole body drooped, unable to complete his own thoughts. It was as though his soul was draining away down the plug hole in the sink. Kez had batted him off last night. Kez didn't want him. Not the way he'd used to. *Not anymore.* Callum had come to terms with the fact that Kez didn't feel the same as he once had. Kez'd moved on. Quite rightly. And to a decent bloke at that. All Callum should now offer was his friendship, 'cause there was no way he could compete with P. H. Dick. He and Kez might have a past, a background filled with memories — if somewhat tainted by the epic fuck-up — but the future? That was now down to Kez.

And the hope that I can keep hiding out in this flat and not have the past slap me in the face.

After tearing away from his reflection, he trundled down the stairs and paced the front room. *Maybe I should have got a haircut. Maybe Kez hates the long look.* He shook his head. Too late now. *And what the fuck should I be doing when he gets home?* He couldn't be in front of the TV. That screamed scrounging layabout. He had no idea what food he should prepare, not knowing what Kez might want to eat of an evening except burnt pizza, which they were out of anyway. He'd done all his job hunting and left an open pad with numbers scrawled on it in plain view to prove it — talking point for when Kez got home. He was showered, clean-shaven, with a hint of Kez's aftershave splashed on. He was as presentable as he was ever going to get. But he couldn't just stare out the window for Kez's arrival.

The lightbulb moment struck when he went to flop down on the sofa and noticed the crumbs from last night's dinner efforts. After ransacking each cupboard, he located the vacuum, plugged it in and did his A-grade building site clean-up. So caught up in the moment of scraping the nozzle over every inch of the living room floor and ceiling, he didn't notice Kez arrive home until he turned from the window and there Kez stood, mouth agape. Switching off the vacuum, Callum shunned the flat into silence.

"Hi." Ignoring the jolt of fluttering in his chest, Callum offered up a winning smile. He couldn't acknowledge how fast his heart rammed against his rib cage. He couldn't acknowledge the hot sweats that flushed every inch of his skin. He couldn't acknowledge what he'd realised earlier. *Just be his Callum.* "Good day at work, honey?"

Kez breathed out a laugh. Then, grunting, he scratched his puffed-out chest. "Making millions in the office, sweetheart. You wouldn't understand. You're too pretty. Where's my dinner?"

Wrinkling his nose, Callum tilted his neck. "Aww. How about we have this for dinner?" He stuck up his middle finger.

Kez laughed, his eyes brightening to how Callum remembered him. All open, and keen and full of eager optimism. Callum couldn't help but search within them for the old Kez. For the mate he'd grown up with. For the way he'd used to look at Callum. He'd tried to hide it back then, but Callum had always been aware. And it had made him feel like nothing else mattered but the two of them.

"I'd've worn a pinny to do this if I knew you were gonna be home soon." Callum nodded to the vacuum cleaner.

"Just a pinny?"

"I ain't got no underwear, have I?"

"New clothes I see, though."

"Standard lock-up gear."

"Comfy."

For a brief moment, it felt natural. The whole exchange, the whole carefree attitude to themselves. It felt like it had used to. Then Kez's smile faded and he glanced at the floor, his gaze no longer on Callum. *He won't look at me and I can't fucking bear it!*

"You okay?" Callum bit his lip. "Did I do your cleaning wrong?"

Kez shook his head. "Not sure you can do hoovering wrong."

"Good to know, 'cause I think I sucked up something valuable. Either you're secretly into Lego, or you're hording diamonds. And if you are, can I come in on that?"

"Probably just the screws fallen out of the walls."

"Always knew you had a screw loose."

"Says you."

Chuckling, Callum dragged the vacuum over to where Kez stood by the living room door then scooted down in front of him to unplug it at the mains. Kez inhaled. *Deeply.* As Callum stood and wound the wire around the curvature under his thumb up to his elbow, he stared deep into Kez's eyes, searching for something within them. *The answers, maybe.* To what, he wasn't sure. But Kez had always given them.

"I got the gear at the precinct." Callum gestured to his clothes. "I'll pay you back."

"You don't have —"

"I do and I will. I rang around some fellas to see if they need me on any sites. No luck today, but I'll keep trying. One day's graft and I can pay it back."

"That's short-term. What we gonna do with you in the long-term?"

Callum smiled at the word 'we' in that sentence. It was as though they were a team. *Again.*

"Long-term, I'll keep applying for a permanent role. I'll sign up with the temping agencies. I'll get work. You can help me fill that volunteering form out."

Kez nodded. "Sounds good."

"I'll keep this place clean until then, and if you have any dates planned with Rafferty" —he forced the name out—"I'll find somewhere to go if you want to bring him back here." He swallowed down the queasiness of that thought with difficulty. But if he was going to rebuild a friendship, then he had to be willing to accept Kez's choice of male companion, no matter how much it stung.

"I broke up with him." Kez scrubbed his hand across his brow, the anguish evident in his rapid strokes. Like he was trying to erase something from his memory. "Well, not so much break up. I think you have to have actually gone out with someone to break up with them. But I called it off for the time being."

Callum's heart jolted and he wasn't sure if it was a good reaction or a bad one. "Why?" he asked with caution.

Kez shook his head, still not looking at him for any prolonged amount of time and it killed Callum that he couldn't see what those eyes might be telling him. "It's not really a good idea to start something new with someone at this point in my life. And no matter what the bloke says, I don't think he's going to hang around too long and wait for me to make a decision about him and…well, everything. There's too much going on with Auntie, with the fire, with…*you*."

It wasn't right to smile about this. It wasn't right to gloat. It wasn't right to feel elated that Kez had chosen him over a chance at something new. But when had Callum ever been right except in his name? A pang of guilt caught him off guard. To think that he'd fucked up Kez's chances at something good, something pure, something not shrouded in grit.

"Kez, I'm sorry. Say the word and I'm outta here. I don't want to be another problem for you. That's not what I want at all." Callum threw the folded-up vacuum wire to the floor.

"What do you want?" Kez's voice was light, almost as though he didn't want to ask the question at all.

Callum exhaled. Slamming his hands on his hips, he gazed into those dark eyes and suddenly he didn't feel afraid anymore. He didn't have to hold back. He had to say it like it was. *Is.*

"You, Kez. You. I want *us* back. Me and you. Kez and Cal. How we *were*. Maybe…" Growling, he kicked the wire and glanced up at the ceiling as if he would get his courage from the polystyrene block tiles. "Maybe I want *more*."

Callum couldn't say anything else as Kez had stepped forward, dragged his hand along Callum's neck and pulled him in for a kiss. It started as nothing more than Kez's soft lips pressing against his, but Kez's trembling sent a rush of adrenaline through Callum's whole body. Kez quaked before him, as if he wasn't sure if what he was doing was right, or even if he should.

Callum had to prove that it was.

He slipped his hand to the back of Kez's neck, splayed his fingers through the tight waves on Kez's scalp and held him in place to deepen the kiss. And by fuck it sent shivers down his spine. Kez didn't hold back and lunged at him, delving in to entwine his tongue with Callum's in a candid embrace. It was a good job there was no dinner on the cards, as Kez might well have eaten him.

Stumbling back, Callum grappled for something to keep him steady. Kez steered him sideways, slamming him up against the wall and kissed and kissed and kissed him. Callum had never been kissed so hard, so furiously, so fucking deliriously in his entire shitty life. Well, it hadn't always been shitty — Kez had been in it for a while. But Kez'd been relatively cautious back in the day, as though he'd believed Callum would eventually push him off and laugh at him.

I wouldn't have done. Not then. Not now. Not ever.

Biting down on Callum's bottom lip, Kez hummed as he sucked it out between his own. Panting, he touched his forehead to Callum's and peered southwards. Cheap trackie bottoms were never any good at hiding a twitching package. That had been discovered on the inside where grey joggers were the standard inmate clobber.

"Tell me this isn't you fucking with me." Kez didn't look up when he said that.

"To be honest with you, mate, I've always been more the bottom bunk."

Kez looked up, eyes bulging.

"Performance anxiety." Callum held his gaze and smiled. "So it'll have to be you fucking with me. If that's all right with you?"

Kez slammed his mouth back onto Callum's, the intense kissing the only sound in the room other than gasping breaths. Grabbing Kez's arse, Callum ground him closer and rubbed their groins together. *Like old times.* Except Kez's work trousers were of a better quality than his old college wear and hid what Callum knew was concealed within them. The urge to find out what Kez's dick looked like hit rocketing heights.

Kez kissed down Callum's neck, to his ear, and flicked Callum's lobe with his tongue before slipping away. Callum stayed against the wall. He needed it for support.

"Have you…" Kez paused, struggling to find the words. "Been with other men?"

"You want to talk about that now? Or do you want to take me to bed?" Callum pushed away from the wall and pecked light kisses up Kez's neck to his lips. "'Cause I know what I'd rather. Come on, Kwesi, let's see if we've still got it."

"We never full-on fucked before, Cal."

"Like I said, maybe I want more than what we had."

Kez moaned so deep that the vibrations thrummed to Callum's groin. "God, I hope you're not messing with me."

"Why would I mess with you? I want this." Callum grabbed Kez's wrist and slammed his hand to the raging cock that poked against the cheap cotton. "Feel that? Do you fucking feel that, Kez? That's me. That's all me. Waiting for you." Softening, Callum ran his other hand down Kez's left arm and lifted it to kiss the end, brushing the soft flesh against his cheek. "I'll always be waiting for you."

That seemed to work, as Kez kissed him all lust-filled again. He scrabbled with Callum's T-shirt and Callum ripped it over his head to throw it to the floor. When Kez landed his gaze on Callum's chest, he licked his lips and Callum knew this was the point of no return. It was why he'd gone topless that morning. His nipple ring had been done years back, when he'd been seventeen. That night he'd shown Kez, he'd fucking enjoyed the man's tongue swiping along it to relieve the soreness. After that, it had become Kez's obsession. And Kez had become Callum's. He'd never admitted that though. He hadn't had the vocabulary, or the balls. Spending twenty-four months in a small box and staring at four walls helped a man think. Thank fuck he'd managed to get his piercing back from custody on release as it evidently still had its hold on Kez.

Kez lapped Callum's nipple and gripped the metal between his teeth to tug just enough for Callum to gasp.

Kez glanced up, holding Callum's gaze. "I fucking missed doing that."

"Not as much as I missed you doing it."

Kez smiled as he waggled his tongue over the metal and flesh, not tearing his gaze from Callum as he did so.

Callum groaned. "You've got a filthy mouth."

"Better believe it."

"Want to make it even dirtier?" Callum shoved down his joggers and boxers, releasing his aggressive erection. Was that too much? Should he have taken this slow and easy? He'd never made love before. He'd fucked. Hard and fast to get it over with. And when he'd messed around with Kez, fear of intrusion had kept them at Olympic pace.

But the way Kez stared at his cock — *gazed* at it — as if it was his long-lost friend — a*in't no like about it* — Callum knew what Kez wanted. *Him.* That *was* his long-lost pal, and one who'd missed setting up camp in Kez's mouth for five long years. Just the very thought that he might get to experience that scalding-hot cavern and thick, luscious tongue swirling around his dick again nearly had him coming all over Kez's work gear. Kez didn't seem to mind, as he sank to his knees, wrapped his hand around Callum's erection and glided up and down.

"Fuck, Kez. That's fucking glorious." Callum's knees jolted as the sparks travelled through him. He was the one now quivering, with only the cool wall to keep him steady.

"I'm not doing much. *Yet.* I got a ton of new moves to show you." Kez grinned from below, teasing him with agonisingly slow strokes.

"You were always good at whatever you did." Callum meant it. Every damn word.

As if in a hurry to show exactly how much he'd learned, Kez opened his mouth and sucked Callum's cockhead into it. He savoured over every inch, licking around the bumps and crevice whilst holding down the foreskin. Callum's eyes rolled to the back of his head. The teasing, the tingling anticipation trickled down to make his toes curl into the fibres of the rug. Kez had always taken his time over Callum's cock. With Kez having been circumcised, he'd said it was a novelty to see Callum's cockhead wrapped in the flesh and watch it reappear on each of his downslides. Although Callum had to assume it was no longer a unique finding. Callum hadn't been Kez's only sexual partner anymore. He'd had an abundance of them, if the way he sucked on Callum's dick was anything to go by. Like a fucking expert. And Callum would know.

"Fuck, K, fuck!" Callum slammed his head back against the wall as Kez slid Callum's entire cock into his hot mouth. Kez had no gag reflex and his throat closed in around the flesh to engulf it, setting Callum's balls alight.

Kez held Callum's gaze as he sucked with an urgency Callum hadn't known before. Gripping onto the root, Kez flicked Callum's cock out from his lips and continued his rapid pumping as he lowered and slid one of Callum's balls into his mouth instead. Callum groaned and writhed and tingled, and was about ready to explode.

"Kez, I'm gonna—"

Kez slapped off, stood and kissed him. "Not yet."

Callum burned with an excitement that scored through every vein, all of them leading to his thumping heart.

"Upstairs." Kez's voice was a low gruff. *Demanding. Authoritative.*

Callum obeyed. He wanted what was about to come. He wanted it badly. And he knew how to obey an order. As they stumbled up the stairs, with Kez grabbing him every other step to slam him against the wall and kiss him, Callum's heart pounded with what was to happen. *A new experience with an old flame.* Kez pushed the door open with his elbow and forced Callum inside with his lips not leaving his. This was more kissing than Callum had done in his lifetime. They'd forgone so much kissing back in the day, due to having to get their kicks before any interruptions. There wouldn't be any this time and Callum intended on making full use of an empty house.

Staggering away from Kez's hold, Callum paused. "I'm starkers, Zakari, and you still look like you should be in Canary Wharf. Come on." He snapped his fingers. "Off."

Kez arched an eyebrow. "I only got one hand."

"Don't give me that bullshit. Off." Callum folded his arms. He wasn't going to help. He knew how much that grated on Kez. So he stood back, watching Kez unfasten each button. Slowly. Seductively. Tentatively revealing that ridiculously enticing gleaming, dark-brown skin that stretched over an unyielding body mass. Callum knew he could do that quicker. He was teasing him. And he fucking loved it. "Keep going."

Kez fluttered the shirt to the floor, then flicked open his belt, unfastened the button and pulled down the zip on his trousers. They fell to his ankles and Kez kicked them away. Callum inhaled sharply. He'd forgotten. Well, not so much forgotten as tried not to remember the sight. Kez didn't wait for the next instruction and tugged down his boxers and discarded those with his socks. Then he stepped forward with ninja-like strides and stood directly in front of Callum, his cock so hard that it raged against Callum's.

Welcome home, old friend.

"Now what?" Kez asked.

Callum smiled, then wrapped a hand around Kez's throbbing dick. It felt magnificent in his palm. Solid, strong and seeping from the head. It sent him into overdrive with how much Kez wanted him. It hadn't faded. It hadn't been replaced. They hadn't lost who they'd been. And there was so much more to discover. Callum kissed Kez's neck, stroking his cock as he nipped upwards to his jawline and across his cheek to rest his lips at Kez's ear.

"Now you fuck me." Callum felt Kez's rapid swallow, his Adam's apple bobbing up and down. Whether it was nerves or anticipation, Callum wasn't sure but from the feel of Kez's cock in his hand, it certainly wasn't fear.

Kez kissed him, all tongue, all rapid groans from within his throat as Callum slid his hand up and down in sync with each smack of their lips. With a force Callum was unaware Kez had, he was pushed down onto the bed. Kez straddled him, kissing every inch and spending his time twirling his tongue around the metal of the nipple ring. Callum raged his hands along Kez's back, forcing him down on top. He wanted Kez to crush him, to suffocate him, to consume him.

Panting, Kez lifted up on one arm and gazed down at him.

"Have you done this before?" he asked, his voice shaking.

"I thought we weren't going to talk about that right now."

Kez cocked his head. "I need to know, Cal. I need to know how easy to take it."

Callum chuckled, then lifted up to kiss him. "No need to take it easy. I know what you got and I can take it." He gripped Kez's cock, pumping it hard to prove a point. He could take that. *No problem.* Just because he'd never had Kez inside him before didn't mean he didn't know what was coming. And he ached to find out if it would feel as good as his fantasies had.

Kez kissed him back, devouring Callum as though he was on death row and Callum was his last meal. It had to be better than the slop served in the minimum-security B Wing anyway, as Kez lapped him up. *With relish.* And Callum loved every second of it. It had only ever been Kez who could do this to him. Those times he'd searched for it in those backrooms, he'd come out feeling dirty, shady and guilty. He'd always known it wouldn't have been the same, so he'd tainted every moment by convincing himself the encounters were a necessity.

This. This is what's necessary.

"Flip around, on your front." Kez shuffled back, allowing Callum to twist under him, and reached over to the bedside table to yank open the drawer.

Callum shifted beneath him, then lifted up on all fours. Kez's breath trickled along his shoulder and Callum shivered, his body erupting in goose pimples as Kez planted delicate kisses down his back. Fuck knew how he'd achieved it, but Kez had sheathed and slicked up all the while he'd licked down Callum's body. Callum would have applauded, if he weren't knee-deep in gluttony for the man's cock. He was about to beg for Kez to hurry it up when he felt something hot and wet roaming between his crevice.

"Fuck, Kez!" Callum peered over his shoulder, only just about focusing on Kez's face buried into his arse.

Kez licked and roamed and thrust his tongue in and out to make Callum's toes curl. This was new. This was fucking deliriously new. *How does this even feel so fucking good?* Babbling incoherently into the air, Callum was undecided whether to allow the man to continue or call for him to stop as it was too fucking much. Especially when a slicked-up hand ventured beneath him to fondle his balls.

"Kez, fuck, Kez! How are you doing this?"

Kez chuckled, his deep regaling tones vibrating up Callum's spine. Before Callum could compose himself, Kez gave one final lick through his crevice then slipped a finger inside him. He twisted and stroked, and Callum's head was about ready to explode along with his dick. Callum had been fucked, he'd been blown, he'd been tossed off, sometimes all three, and with people watching on. *But it was never this fucking good!*

"Get in me, Kez. I need you in me." Callum was aware of his desperation but couldn't have cared less. If he'd thought he'd needed Kez to complete him before, it was nothing compared to how much he needed Kez inside him now. *I'm a fucking junkie.*

"In good time." Kez inserted another finger and thrust in and out. "You have no idea how long I've been wanting this. You. On all fours for me. I intend to savour this."

Callum rocked back, wriggling his hips, and Kez stroked the flesh of his elbow up Callum's back. He went in with a third finger and spread Callum open. Callum held his breath, waiting for the inevitable as though it would somehow change his life forever. Then, when Kez pulled out, shuffled on his knees and poked Callum's opening with his sheathed cockhead, Callum gripped the bedsheets in sheer desperation. *Come on. I gotta know. I gotta know now.*

"Callum?" Kez paused.

"Yeah?" Callum peered around to look him in the eye.

"This is real, right?"

Callum's chest fluttered and he inhaled a liberating breath of air. "Go ahead and find out."

Without removing his gaze from Callum's, Kez eased his way into Callum's body. Callum groaned. Kez's cock stretched him apart and he felt it in his chest, in his throat, but mostly in his heart. Hesitating, Kez slid his hand onto Callum's hip and gripped him in place.

"I'm in you." Kez sounded a bit delirious, as though he couldn't quite believe it.

"Fuck, Kez, you feel so fucking good." Callum forced back, trying to get more of Kez. He didn't know if any more would even fit, or if there was any more to go in, but he'd take it all. He'd take every inch of Kez. With her Majesty's fucking pleasure.

"Oh, God," Kez breathed out, his warm breath landing on Callum's bare skin.

Callum held on to the pillows scrunched into his balled fists as Kez began fucking him with urgency. He groaned. He yelped. He demanded more with every whimper as the bed crashed against the wall and the covers entangled around their sweaty limbs. Callum's balls tightened with every intense plunge into him and sweat droplets splatted onto his back as Kez raged above him, the slapping of skin thundering over the grunts of rampant pleasure.

"Fuck, Kez, fuck! Shit, I'm —" He didn't have time to finish as Kez slipped his hand around him and grabbed his cock, pumping it along with every deep thrust.

"Wanna go together?" Kez rumbled into his ear.

"How...do...you —"

Kez paused within him, then worked on Callum. *Up, down, up, down.* Callum groaned into the vacant air. Then just as he was about to spill, Kez thrust in hard and Callum shot his load, his entire body exploding in a frenzy that rippled through every inch of his skin. Kez shuddered against him, releasing his orgasm to be captured within the latex sheath inside Callum.

Collapsing down to the mattress, Callum panted and hid his flushed face between the gap of two pillows. Kez dropped on top of him and curled his arm underneath to hold him tight. After a few moments of composure, Kez kissed Callum's shoulder blade.

"That was...new." Kez groaned as he added a light thrust, his cock still inside Callum's body. He then dragged it out, sliding it down Callum's crevice and it was fucking glorious.

"Yeah." Callum switched onto his back. "It was."

After discarding the condom, Kez lay on his back and, side by side, they both looked up at the ceiling in silence. Callum draped his knee over Kez's leg then scraped his head along the pillow to get a proper look at him. Kez gazed back, awe evident in his flushed features.

Callum smiled. "Friends reunited."

Chuckling, Kez whacked him with his elbow.

Chapter Twelve

Spin the Bottle

Kez was having trouble believing what had just happened. He lay there, staring up at the ceiling, his cock slumped against his leg in evidence that it hadn't been a dream. Not that having Callum next to him, sweating, radiating heat, and lower limbs entangled around his own wasn't a dead giveaway. Still, he struggled to accept it all. Callum had wanted him. Had begged for him. Had loved every second of Kez being inside him. To be honest, Kez hadn't had sex any better than that. He'd had some good times, for sure. He'd had some utter catastrophes too with men finding the stump too icky to get past first base. He and Callum seemed to fit. They always had. It had been so easy to let himself go and enjoy every moment without the fear.

A pang of remorse struck that he'd allowed himself to have gone that far with Callum so quickly. Yeah, they had a past. Yeah, they'd done stuff before. That hadn't been like 'first-date' sex. But it was still rushed. Especially considering he'd only broken things off with

Rafferty a few hours ago to get his head in some sort of order. Callum had scuppered all that. He always had. He always would. He was Callum. And Kez was a sucker for him.

"You hungry?" Callum asked, breaking the silence.

"Starving." He hadn't eaten all his lunch, having not had the stomach for it after listening to Raff telling him he'd back off and let Kez decide what he wanted, and hoped they could still be friends all the while. Kez winced. He'd made up his mind the moment he'd walked back to his desk. The only thing that made him not feel totally guilty about the whole thing was that Raff would be snapped up in no time, and by someone who hadn't fallen in love at sixteen with his best friend and bided his time for five years to be lying next to him, fuck-spent.

"I didn't know what you wanted. All I could see was meat in your fridge or I'd've cooked you something."

"Right little housewife, aren't you?"

"Less of the wife." Callum slapped Kez's leg.

"Do you eat meat?" Kez realised he hadn't had that confirmed. The pizza last night had been a margarita.

"Sometimes." Callum stretched out his lean body, his skin crusted with leftover semen. Callum bit his lip through a smile. "Went all veggie inside. Had a tip off you get better meals. So I put down I was vegan. You get it all cooked from scratch then." He winked. "But since release, I started up with chicken again. Cheaper than all veg, innit?"

Kez wanted to ask more questions about what it had been like locked up. He'd seen way too many documentaries detailing life on the inside to be comfortable knowing Callum had been there. How had he coped? Had he made friends? Enemies? Had he had any — god forbid — *lovers*? Which reminded him of more pressing matters…

"You want to fill me in now about how you know you can't top?" He'd always thought if they were to do this, it would be Callum wanting to top. What had just happened was as much of a headfuck as it was a grade A fuck.

Callum slid onto his side, capturing Kez with his hazel eyes. "Not sure you're ready for that."

"Try me."

Screwing his eyes shut, Callum sighed. "I got my kicks. Probably not the way you did. But I got some."

"Grindr?"

Callum laughed. "I wish." He scooted out of bed and stood. He untangled Kez's boxers from the trousers and stepped into them. They were too big on him, but Kez didn't mind. Callum looked kinda cute with them hanging off his hips and bagging around his arse. There was always something tantalising about his men wearing his clothes. Even more so that this was Callum. "Want me to go rustle something up to eat?"

"Avoiding telling me, aren't you?"

"No. I'm just famished. So are you. I can hear that rumble from here. Let's get a bit of grub inside us then maybe we'll have the energy for a second round." He winked.

All right, that works. "How about a takeaway?"

Callum's loose hair fell into tousled locks around his delicate cheekbones, but he flicked it away to glance down and Kez was hard pressed not to jump the man again. That whole act was as innocent as it was fucking desirable.

"Sure?" Callum asked. "'Cause that costs money and I already owe you."

"You owe me nothing."

"I do and I'll pay it back, but if you wanna shout me a veggie chow mein I ain't gonna argue that one."

"All right. Done." Kez smiled and rubbed his stomach. "There's a menu pinned to the wall in the kitchen. Go order it while I jump in the shower."

"Getting clean just to get dirty again?" Callum clucked his tongue. "Like it."

Sitting up against the wall, Kez shook his head through a fond chuckle. Callum sauntered to the hallway. Kez couldn't help but watch him as he went, with a strange sense of contentment. The dirty banter was new. Back in the day, it had been as if it had never happened between them. They'd never talked about it. Certainly not joked about it. This pliable Callum was definitely shiny new. And Kez liked it. *A lot.*

Shit. I really am screwed.

"Still go for your black bean shit?" Callum asked over his shoulder.

"Yeah." Kez smiled. *He remembers.* "Chicken. Then you can have some."

Kez stretched, easing his muscles back into some sort of order and listening to Callum downstairs, placing the order. It warmed his heart, not that he wasn't already super-hot from the workout. But having Callum back in his life gave him a warm glow. He hadn't realised quite how much he'd missed him. As a lover, yeah, but also as his best friend. Someone to hang out with, someone to talk to, someone to share in his life. He only really had acquaintances for that. He'd never developed anything as solid as what he'd had with Callum. He'd put it down to trust issues and to never have his heart crushed into tiny little pieces by someone who was all things to him — friend, brother, lover. He'd thrown himself into work, getting his degree and achieving something that he'd never thought possible. Friends came and went, lovers a lot quicker.

Was that all down to losing Callum?

Kez mulled it all over while rinsing himself off in the shower. He'd made a promise to himself to not get caught up in any crap again. To not be fooled. To not be taken for granted. As that was how he'd thought things had been with Callum. But the last half hour had proved that all wrong? *Hadn't it?* Callum had felt the same. *Still felt the same.*

This grin isn't ever going away.

A few minutes later, dressed in his lounging joggers and nothing else — *easy access* — he found Callum in the kitchen, getting out the plates and cutlery ready for their food's arrival. His body was a sheen of glistening skin, stretched over a slender frame. His dark blond hair had been left in a ruffled mess to dangle into his eyes and he flicked it back with every movement. He had his back to Kez, rummaging through his cupboards, and it allowed Kez to stare at him. To ogle. To gaze with his heart swelling and knocking against his ribcage. Dr. Rawlings couldn't fix this one. He wouldn't want him to. Not anymore.

Kez wrapped his arm around Callum's midsection and kissed his shoulder from behind. "I could get used to this."

Callum smiled and leaned into him. "What? Having a naked man serve you dinner?"

"'Course. Although, you could lose these." Kez slipped his fingers into the waistband of the boxers and slipped them down to reveal the curvature of Callum's arse. "Nice." He ran his fingertips along the bump, revelling in the feel of smooth, tight skin and knowing mere minutes ago his cock had been buried in that crevice.

"Didn't think that'd be a good idea when opening your gate to the delivery bloke."

"True." Kez nodded out to the kitchen window. "Speaking of which." A shadow approached from behind Kez's gated yard, searching for the bell. Which was odd. Kez had ordered many a Chinese from Wok U Like down the High Street and they knew where to buzz. "I'll go get it."

Callum nodded and Kez left the kitchen to grab his wallet from the table by the door before walking outside. It wasn't the usual delivery guy by the gate. This one was all covered up, in black puffer jacket and hood.

"All right, mate?" Kez flicked open his wallet, clutching it between his elbow and chest to rifle for the notes. "What's the damage?"

"About two grand." The man sniffed, curling a hand around one of the poles. "So you wanna let me in and tell me where I can find Callum Wright?"

Kez glanced up at that. He dropped his wallet, darting his gaze from the heavy behind the gate to Callum's shadow reflected through the kitchen window. *What the fucking hell is this?*

"Come on." The man's face, not covered by the peak of a baseball cap or his oversized hood, glared at him through the gaps in the fencing. "That lock won't hold this." Opening his jacket, he revealed a heavy-duty hammer tucked inside the pocket. He closed it up. "So either you bring him out or you let me in."

"I don't know who you are or what this is about but—"

"Callum Wright. Know him?" The man's voice wasn't a question, more of a demand. A threatening one.

Kez narrowed suspicious eyes. "Why?"

"He owes me. Now you are more than welcome to pay me and I'll be happy to leave your filthy faggot-humping selves alone, or I break this lock and come find him myself. What's it to be?"

"What does he owe you for?"

The man's deep, sinister chuckle gave Kez the shivers and displayed the man's broken teeth. "He was meant to sell some food for me. Out of town."

Kez closed his eyes, hanging his head. *No.* He couldn't. *This cannot be happening.* Not now! Not *again*.

"What's taking so lo—" Callum stopped beside him with a jolt. He was back dressed in his joggers and T-shirt, but he shuddered. Kez doubted it was due to the wind chill and more that Callum had recognised in one instant a man who had half his face covered. "Fuck." He stumbled back, then regained composure and stood steady. "Fuck off! How the fuck—"

"Callum. Nice to see you again." The man smiled and adjusted his cap. "Be a dear and open this gate so we can have a proper chat. Your boyfriend's bein' a bit hostile."

Callum swallowed but didn't look at Kez. "Fuck off."

"Now, now, Callum. Let's not get off on the wrong foot. Your bloke's already down one limb." The man let out a sinister laugh. "Not much protection that, is it?"

Kez turned to Callum, frustration and anger seeping through his resolve. "What the hell is this, Cal?"

"Nothing." Callum didn't look at him. *A tell-tale sign.* "The man's lost his way. And got the wrong bloke. Go in, Kez, I'll sort it." He shoved Kez's arm.

"That's right. Be a good little girlfriend."

"Fuck off!" Kez pointed a menacing finger to the gate. Where he got his confidence from was beyond him. Years of being called the same thing, most probably. Plus he had a cast-iron gate between him and a metal hammer.

"Kez, don't." Callum pushed him again and turned a pleading gaze on him. "Go in. Please. I'll sort it."

"What's going on?"

"How about *I* fill you in?" The man tapped the gate with the head of the hammer. "Cocksucker here owes me my 'food' back, nothing touched, or the cost of resale plus an extra for the no-delivery and interest for each day it's been missing."

It felt as if he'd been batted over the head with that hammer and Kez wanted to throw up. *Drugs. This is all about drugs. Again!*

"Kez, it ain't what you're thinking—" Callum grabbed his arm. "I was never selling. You know I wouldn't."

"What were you doing then?" Kez's voice was a crackled, floaty breath of air, as though he really didn't want to have to ask. He certainly didn't want to know the answer.

"Holding it. Passing the baton."

"Really?" Kez found his voice and stumbled back. "Like before?"

"Yes! No. Shit." Callum gripped his hair, scraping it back from his face. "I was paying off a debt."

"To me." The man ran his hammer along the railings, the clang echoing along the hostile surroundings. "We agreed, Callum. And you didn't keep up your end." He cocked his head. "Is that always a problem for you?"

"The fucking place went up in flames, Baz!" Callum screeched, almost jumping in the air. "What could I fucking do?"

"That ain't my problem." The man who Kez now guessed was called Baz—real or pseudonym, Kez couldn't have cared less—edged his face closer to the gate. "You should have taken it with you. You escaped, right? Saved your own arse, didn't you, Cal? For him, I take it?"

"There was no time! It was out then or die!"

"But you left my valuable behind," Baz snarled like a rabid dog ready to pounce. *Thank fuck there's a locked gate between us.*

Kez shot Callum a confused glance. He hadn't left straight away. Had he? He *had* gone back for something valuable. *Eve.* He sucked in a breath that he had to hold to prevent from actually throwing up.

"You left it to burn to ash or be taken by the feds." Baz tapped the gate once with the hammer. "So, you owe. I'll take five hundred quid—no less—down payment, with the other half delivered to base camp by the weekend. Or you can pay it all off now and you won't see me again. Because, Cal, you're a liability in this business. You won't get another position in our company."

"I ain't got that sorta money." Callum hung his head. "I can get it, but not today."

Kez's mouth fell open. That was some promise. *Where does he plan to get hold of a thousand quid? He can't even afford a Chinese takeaway!* "Cal—"

"I'll get it." Callum waved him off, then focused on the man behind the gate. "I'll get it."

"I want assurances, Callum. Trust is an earned thing. Wouldn't you say, girlfriend?"

"Go fuck yourself," Kez spat.

"Be better than fucking you. What do you do, stick that thing up his arse?" Baz glided the hammer between them both.

Kez looked away in disgust. And he wasn't sure who he was angrier with.

"Shut your fucking mouth!" Callum barked. "Leave him out of this. I'll get you your fucking money. All of it. With fucking interest. Tomorrow."

After a few tense moments, Baz lifted the hammer and smashed the lock several times. Kez flinched at the aggression on the man's face. Callum shoved Kez behind him, holding himself steady as if ready to take action. What Callum could do against the menacing weapon and an insane brandisher was anyone's guess, but the fact he'd put himself in front of Kez was both gallant and — not to mention — *fucking stupid!* Kez wasn't sure how to feel about it.

Baz didn't open the gate. He left it ajar with the padlock hanging on by a bent hook.

"Don't bother getting a new one. If there's no payment by tomorrow, I'll come by and smash off his other hand. Get me?"

"You touch him, I'll kill you."

Baz laughed and it echoed along the balcony of maisonettes down to ground level. "You do that, and when the bossman finds you, your own mother won't recognise you." He cocked his head. "Not that she could anyway. She barely knows her own name these days."

Callum gulped and Kez didn't know whether to wrap an arm around him in comfort or snatch Baz's hammer and smash Callum over the head with it. Rage bubbled in his chest and Kez had to take a few deep breaths to calm himself. *This is exactly the sort of shit I wanted to avoid!* And he had, since Callum had no longer been part of his life. Now Callum had brought it all back. In one fell swoop, Callum had managed to make Kez come back to him with naive open arms, then slam him back to reality with how fucking foolish it was to have ever trusted him again. He wasn't sure who he was madder at — Callum, or himself.

"Tick, tock, Wrighty-boy." Baz waggled the hammer through the bars, each ricocheting ting of the metal making Kez's gums ache.

Footsteps scraped up concrete steps and startled them all. Baz shot a look to his left. Kez cursed under his breath and Callum stepped forward. The Chinese delivery bloke grunted on reaching the balcony landing. Baz stuttered back, not before brandishing the end of the hammer toward Callum.

"Tomorrow, Cal. Tomorrow." Launching on his heel, he covered up the weapon with his jacket and skidded off, bashing into the delivery man as he approached Kez's yard.

"Mr. Zakari, sir." The bloke held up the plastic bag of piping hot food, the smell of which would have had Kez salivating if he hadn't just feared for his life.

Callum scooped up Kez's dropped wallet and slipped out the cash. He handed it to Kez with shaking fingers. After snatching it from him, Kez stomped over to open the gate and gave the man the money. "Keep the change."

"Thank you, sir." He handed over the bag.

Kez slammed the gate with his foot. Useless now the lock was broken, but it was more to make a point. He glared at Callum before angling his head to usher him indoors. In the kitchen, he dumped the food on the counter and rested on his elbows to cover his face with his hand. Callum approached, caution in every timid step. He slipped a hand up Kez's back. Kez couldn't bear it. Not then. Not after all that. He shunted him off, then swivelled and faced him.

"What the fuck, Cal? What the actual fuck?"

"I'm sorry."

"That's all you ever say!"

"'Cause I am!"

"For what? For doing it? For not telling me? Or for getting caught? *Again!*" Kez's throat scratched with the force of getting all that out.

Flinching, Callum stepped back. "All right. Calm down."

"Calm down? Calm, fucking, down? Don't you fucking dare tell me to fucking calm down! This isn't a calm fucking situation!" Kez paced the kitchen, punching various surfaces as he went. "I can't fucking believe this. How stupid are you? Do you have a fucking death wish?"

"No."

Kez stopped, facing him. All he had was one question and his entire being deflated to ask it. "Then why? Why the fuck would you do this? *Again?*"

Callum fell against the fridge door behind him, a few magnets clanging to the floor. He looked beat. And sorry. And all the things Kez remembered him feeling the first time around. It hadn't held much clout back then. The second time only made it worse to witness. Hanging his head, Callum shivered and his face contorted in pain. Kez waited. He'd wait all fucking night if he had to. He needed to know the truth. Most of all, he needed to know why.

"Are you using?" Kez forced the question out.

Callum lunged toward him, palms open. "No! No. Swear down. I'm clean. I never have. You have to know that? Seeing what that shit did to my mum? No bollocking way. I'm so fucking clean I piss detergent."

Staring at him for a few intense moments, Kez searched for the tell-tale signs of the lie. It wasn't there. Either he'd learned how to control it, or Kez had to believe him.

"It was my only option," Callum mumbled to the floor.

"I'm going to need more than that. Imagine I'm one of the twelve."

Callum peered up, his hazel eyes filled with a remorse Kez could not give in to. *Not again.*

"Mum. She owed them. A lot. Couldn't even tell you exact. It's why she did a runner. Turns out, debt don't follow the source. It gets put on the ones left behind."

Drooping his shoulders, Kez exhaled a weary puff of air. He might have known *she'd* have had something to do with this. It angered him in a way he hadn't felt in years. The unjustness of it all.

"They cornered me. As soon as I moved in from the halfway house, as soon as I was ready to pick my life back up, they cornered me. First, I got a beating. Out of nowhere. I'm lucky I weren't knifed, to be honest. They wanted to send me home and tell Mum what would happen if she didn't pay." Callum scrubbed two hands down his face. "Didn't work though, did it? 'Cause she weren't there. She didn't clean me up. I did it myself, knowing this was going to happen again and again unless I paid up. I didn't have that sorta money, Kez. I barely had enough to make ends meet. I was using the food banks most nights."

"You could have gone to the police." Kez kept his voice light, even if inside he was a ball of swirling rage.

Callum snorted. "Sure. And that would go down so well. Ex-con, two years behind for possession, gets beaten up by the local drug gang for not paying a debt. You think they'll protect me, do ya? You think that's how it works?"

Kez bit his lip. It was futile to argue the pros and cons of going to the authorities. He'd lived that life. Not outright, but indirectly. He'd seen the hurt and anguish that drugs had caused from users, to sellers, to those unfortunately surrounded by both due to their status in the social housing. *An endless cycle of pain.*

"I thought I had it all sorted." Callum dug fingers into his eyes. "All I had to do was one hold. Look after one lot. Hand it to the next bloke. It was crossing borders, OT—out of town—transferring a new order out of London. All my involvement was to keep hold of it until the sellers came by. I'd get all debt signed off. I wasn't planning to sell it. Just pass it over to those that did."

"It's still possession, Cal. You know that!"

"But it was one lot. I got given an egg filled with ready-to-go packs. Two hours tops, they said." Callum bashed his head against the fridge, the bottles of chutneys inside clanging together. "I would have been clean free. Not a trace on me. I didn't even touch the fucking egg! They brought it in. They put it down. I waited."

"What happened?"

"The fire, Kez. The fucking fire happened." Callum stood so close to Kez that Kez could smell the stagnant remnants of their earlier session and it did things to his messed-up mind he didn't have words for. As Callum rested his forehead against Kez's, his breath trickled to fizz on Kez's tongue. "I think it saved me. I thought it had anyway. It meant I didn't touch it. I didn't pass it on. And it got me back to you."

"But they found you." The voice of reason was old Kez. And reality.

"Looks like. I got no idea how. I left no trace. Why they would even think to come here..." He stepped back. "Did you tell anyone I was here?"

"Auntie."

"*Shit.*" Callum scraped his hair back. "Anyone else?"

"Grace was there. Why?"

"From the church? Oh, shit, Kez! They talk. Everyone fucking talks!"

"You don't think..." Kez couldn't finish. He couldn't bring himself to think what they might have done to his aunt and her elderly best friend.

"They wouldn't hurt her. They'd just ask her. Or Grace. And they'd do it in a way that they wouldn't even know what they were doing. Probably offering sympathy."

"Oh, Callum. This is some serious fucked-up shit." Kez grabbed Callum's T-shirt in a balled fist and didn't know whether to yank him in for a hug or launch him into the air.

Callum staggered closer, pressing his body to Kez's. "I know. I know, baby, and I'm so fucking sorry."

For a brief moment, Kez forgot it all and allowed Callum to kiss him, to melt into him, to lean on him for the support he so clearly needed. But someone had to be the bearer of bad news around here.

"How are you going to pay him off by tomorrow?"

Callum stepped back and wiped his lips. "You got a grand lying around here?"

Shaking his head, the thought of launching Callum into the air, through the kitchen window and allowing him to slide down to ground level on his head, came to Kez with full force. *Was that was this is? Was that what all this has been about?* Yet more questions he didn't want to know the answers to, but had to ask.

"Is that why you're here? Is that why you let me —"

Gripping Kez's neck, Callum kissed him. "No. All that, upstairs, that's what I want."

"Don't fool me, Callum. Don't string me along. Don't pretend. All I ask is that you don't pretend."

"I'm not and I won't. Kez, please, believe me. I'm here because when you showed up, I knew I couldn't let you go again. I was kidding about the money. I'd never ask you for a fucking thing. I don't want your money. I never wanted your money. If I could have bought my own clothes today, I would have. If I could pay Baz back and get him off our case, I would do. But I'm boracic, Kez. Nothing. Was laid off weeks ago, behind on rent, behind on bills. That money from the pass over would have got me out of debt, yeah, but it wouldn't have given me anything else."

"So what's your plan?" Kez leaned back on the counter for support. Whether it was because of what Callum had said or to prepare for what was coming next, he couldn't be sure.

Inhaling a fierce breath, Callum took another step back. Out of grabbing range. "Your doctor."

Kez burst out an involuntary laugh. *Hysterical release, maybe?* What the hell could Dr. Rawlings do? Give him a pay rise? The NHS didn't work like that. And how did he expect Kez to explain to his senior leadership team what he needed extra money for?

Callum stared at him. *Serious. Not a trace of anything than absolute, stone-cold sincerity.*

"How do you think Rawlings can help here?"

There was a flicker across Callum's features. A painful, anguish-filled sputter as though he was about to recount something that Kez didn't want to hear. It reminded Kez of how Eve had looked when she'd had to tell him that Callum had received three to five. *Guilt.*

"He's a major player at this club I know." Callum bowed his head.

"Club?"

"Gay club. Sex club. That sort of thing."

Kez's jaw dropped and he stumbled away from the counter. "*What?*"

Squeezing his eyes shut, Callum paced the tiny kitchen with agitated energy. Kez watched him, waiting, unclear what the fuck was going on anymore.

"You asked me about other men. That's the other men. I'd go to this club. It started out as just a bit of release every now and then. All legit. Nothing more. Then one day I was desperate for cash and was chatting to this bloke who said the back room might help out. It's a place where stuff happens. People pay to watch. Pay to..." Callum swallowed and avoided Kez's wide-eyed stare. "Tell you what to do to the other."

Sick to his stomach, Kez looked away and the wafting MSG from the Chinese takeaway wasn't helping him keep the nausea down. He retched, then turned to the sink. Callum rushed to him, stroking a hand along his back.

"I only did it once. I didn't know Rawlings. I didn't know who he was. They all referred to him as the Doc. He watches. And he...directs."

Kez screwed his eyes shut. Callum's voice wasn't as confident as it once was, as though retelling it had brought it all back. It clearly wasn't a fun memory.

"I swear down to you, Kez. I only did it 'cause I needed cash."

Kez twisted his neck, meeting Callum's pleading gaze. "What did he make you do?"

Shaking his head, Callum allowed his hair to cover his face and hid behind the locks. "You don't wanna know."

"Try me." For some reason, Kez did want to know. He *had* to know. Out of morbid fascination or genuine concern, he wasn't sure.

"There were three of us." Callum swallowed. "The doc wanted me in the middle…"

Kez heaved into the sink and Callum rubbed a hand up his back. It was no comfort.

"He had a thing for me. Wanted to watch them get me to the brink—"

"Stop!" Kez pleaded. "I can't unhear this!" He wished he'd never asked. He had no idea how he'd ever shake the images from his mind.

"Sorry." Callum stepped away, his voice small and tight. "The doc, he recognised me."

"No shit! He's probably seen more of you than I have!"

Callum hung his head. "Yeah and, well, that night, he asked me to go to a private room with him after. He'd pay me if I did."

Kez whipped around so fast his neck almost ripped free from its tendons. "He *what*?"

"I didn't go."

"Two in one night enough for you, is it?"

"Kez…"

"Don't. Just—don't."

Callum sighed. "I ain't proud of it. But, fuck me, Kez, it ain't like you haven't scattered yourself around."

"I beg your fucking pardon?"

Callum screwed his eyes shut. "I just meant that you knew what to do. You know I ain't good with words and shit."

"I've had boyfriends, yeah. I've been with other blokes. I've even, I'll have you know, had one-night fucking stands. No, I didn't wait for you. Did you think I would? Did you think I'd pine over you forever? Did you think I wouldn't want to at least try and move on?" Kez widened maddened eyes and he couldn't stop his mouth from spitting out the words he had never wanted to say. "I thought this, us, whatever this was, or is, meant nothing to you. That you didn't see me in that way. That you were playing me."

Callum reached for him, but Kez shook his head. He didn't want it. He couldn't take any comfort in Callum right then.

"But me trying to get over you." Kez spoke to the floor. "And to stop myself from loving you, is nothing compared to you being a puppet boy for my boss!"

Callum sucked in a shaky breath and Kez closed his eyes, wishing he'd never admitted any of that. *No going back now.*

"All right, I know. Sorry." Callum held out his hands, beckoning Kez to him. "But we can use this, Kez. We can use the doc. He was so shit scared when he recognised me. Like literally shitting his pants that I'd tell you and everyone else his sordid secret. The man's a perv. A predatory perv who likes to watch and control. We can use that."

"What the hell do you mean, *use it*? Because if you're even hinting at the thought of going back there and —"

"No. I wouldn't. It was bad enough the first time. From now on, I'm all yours." He hung his head. "If you still want me."

"Undecided." Kez snapped that out without thinking. It fell from his tongue before his brain could process it. Callum looked hurt, but that in no way compared to the pain and misery Kez was being put through at the mere thought that the doctor he serviced, the man he saw every day, his boss, the man who tended to all those little children with heart deficiencies, had paid to see Callum, the one person Kez had been in love with for years, get fucked by strangers. Kez might as well have his own heart deficiency, because it might never be mended after this.

Callum shuffled back, spreading the gap between them both. He shivered and wrapped his arms around himself. "We blackmail him." Callum mumbled that out through quivering lips, like he wasn't totally confident it would either work, or that Kez would be in on it.

"We *what*?"

"We tell him we know. We say we'll tell. He'll lose his rep. He'll pay us off to keep schtum and we pay Baz."

"Oh, Cal." Hanging his head, Kez pinched the bridge of his nose. "You want me to blackmail my boss? You want me to tell a well-respected doctor that I see every day that I know what he does of a weekend and to pay me to keep quiet about it? Then skip into work every day where I see him saving the lives of poorly children?"

"When you say it like that…"

"When you say it any way, Callum!" Kez just about prevented his foot stamp. "This is by far the stupidest thing you have ever said or done!"

"I know. I fucking know! And I have no idea how to get out of it."

Kez folded his arms and heaved out a sigh. "I'm not sure you can. Not without doing something you won't want to do."

"Right." Shuffling away, Callum hit the fridge behind him. "I do that, and I'll be back inside."

Kez wanted to reach out for him. He wanted to offer him the support he hadn't given five years ago. He wanted to wrap him up and take him upstairs, forgetting everything that had happened in the past half hour and go back to when they'd been enveloped in each other's arms. He wanted it more than anything.

But he couldn't. Callum had to step up. To show him he could fix this. So he waited.

"I guess that's it then." Callum shivered. It was like a *Silence of the Lambs* re-enactment with his lips and teeth chattering. "Best thing I can do right now is go."

"Cal—"

As if in some trance, Callum swayed over to the front door and slipped on his trainers still tatty with black smudges from the smoke. Kez marched over, watching from the doorway.

"Where are you going?"

"Don't matter, does it? As long as I'm gone. I'll figure this out. They won't come here again, I promise." Callum yanked open the front door.

"What the fuck does that mean?" Kez held the door, ready to slam it shut and keep Callum inside, no matter what the consequences.

"It means they follow till it's paid. They either want money, or me. They'll get one of them." Callum lunged forward to walk out, but Kez grabbed his arm, digging his fingertips in to the point he'd leave bruises. The door banged onto his back, shunting him forward.

"Don't. Don't you dare leave me again."

Callum offered a troubled smile. "I'm sorry." He then leaned in and kissed him, his lips brushing the following words against Kez's. "I love you too."

A heady rush of euphoria sparked through Kez's entire being, until it meshed with overriding hopelessness making his grip on Callum's arm loosen. Callum took that moment to run. Out of the open gate and away from Kez's life. *Again*.

Chapter Thirteen

Facing It

Callum hadn't ever run so fast. He didn't know if he was running to something, or from it. Nor did he really understand why. His head pounded as he thumped his tatty dust-ridden and dirt-encrusted trainers along the pavement. He had no idea where he was heading. Away. He had to get away. His eyes stung with the force of the wind smacking him in the face and he rubbed an arm over them, sniffing as he scraped his hair back.

With no Oyster Card, he had no way of travelling anywhere other than by foot. Which was okay with him as his mind couldn't process a Tube map, but his legs seemed to know where to take him. As the stitch in his side stretched and burned, he stopped and walked at a slower pace, checking behind him, which was futile. Kez would never have had enough time to run after him. And that was the only person he would have wanted following him. Anyone else, he didn't care. He'd rather they sneaked up on him and stabbed him in the back. He deserved it — he'd pretty much done the same thing to his best friend.

Not my best friend. My only friend.

Not my friend. The man I love.

Sniffing, he glided along the London streets without looking where he was going. He bumped shoulders with pedestrians walking in the opposite direction. He fell off the curb into the road. He stumbled over dogs on leads. He was going nowhere. Fast. *Like my life.*

Why? Why did this have to happen now? Why couldn't he have been given a few more minutes? He'd planned to explain it all to Kez whilst chomping down on the chow mein. He was going to be open and honest, tell him he was in trouble and that they needed a plan to get out of it. But fucking Baz and his fucking big mouth and untimely intrusion. Callum had been floating on a high for all of one hour. He was back with Kez. They'd fitted. It had been the best fucking thing. Ever. Period. Callum could see his life paving out before him. No more scrabbling around in the dark, no more scraping the barrel, no more fucking about. That fire had saved him. Kez had saved him.

Now it was over and he had nowhere to go.

Speckles of rain sprinkled over him as he paced the darkened streets. Maybe he should just toss himself in the river? Get it over and done with? The only thing that prevented him from attempting it was Kez. The debt wouldn't disappear — he'd never hated his mother more in his life. Not for bringing him into it, but for bringing Kez into it.

Grow up, Wrighty-boy. Not everything was always someone else's fault. He should have told Kez sooner. No, he shouldn't have gone with Kez from the community centre. No, he shouldn't have accepted the fucking bundle in the first place! Or ever gone back to the Marlyte. He should have stayed away and not tried to reunite with his waste-of-space mother. He should have taken the bedsit offered after release and stayed there. Or taken up their rehabilitation and re-homed in Kent, Surrey, Hertfordshire — *fuck, anywhere away from London and the shit that the place brought*. He'd never be free. Even out of prison, he'd never be free.

With no idea how long he'd been roaming, he found himself nearing a train station. *Fuck, Forest Gate*. That had to be a good few miles' canter. He'd done most of it head down and avoiding the world. His legs made the choice to board the overhead northbound platform. Subconsciously heading toward home, he suspected, but wherever the line would take him would be fine. Avoiding the glare from the security guy, he shoved his hands deep in his pockets under the pretence of searching for an Oyster Card, then mingled among a young crowd also dodging the turnstiles by going through the family gate and onto the platform. The train shunted in and he boarded, leaning against the pole in the centre. Head down, he tried to drown out the drone of chatter, the screeching of wheels and the tinny music from headphones.

He needed a plan. He had to decide what to do. He could go back to the club. One paid-for session and he'd have the money to keep Baz and his cronies at bay. It wouldn't pay it all off, but it could be enough to keep them from Kez. Slamming his eyes shut, he shook his head. He'd never be able to go through with it. Not anymore. Not now there was Kez. *Had been* Kez. 'Cause Kez wouldn't be his anymore. Not after hearing all of that. He'd burned that friendship to the ground good and fucking proper.

There was no way he could ask Dr. Rawlings. Kez had been right. It had been a stupid idea. But Callum had been desperate. He'd have said anything to get Baz the hell away from Kez. Whether the bloke was brandishing a hammer or not, the git wouldn't have got near Kez. Callum wouldn't have let him. He'd have chucked himself in the way.

Just like he had to do now.

He flinched at the raucous banter from a rowdy group jumping on the train at the next stop. Everything was putting him on edge. He gave an eyeful to one of the lads who stepped on his foot. The bloke gave him a squint back then whispered into the ears of his mates. Boisterous laughter bellowed out along the carriage. Callum turned away and looked up at the destination map above the seats and checked which way he was going.

Home.

Where the fuck even was home?

He rode the train to the end of the line—ironically, Branton—sitting on one of the tabled seats. He thought about not getting off and just sitting there until the doors slammed and the train went wherever it did when they weren't in service. No such luck as the driver stuck his head in and told him to get a move on.

Trudging up the steps, he kept his eye on the security at the top. Branton always seemed to have more of them than any other station. More so now. He waited until they'd turned their backs then, with an energy he didn't feel, he jumped the turnstiles and legged it out of the station into the street. A few twists and turns later, he was where he needed to be.

The Marlyte housing estate was still cordoned off. Yellow tape stretched out to the playpark, around the double-decker houses and over his tower block. Callum stopped on the other side of the road and hefted in a deep breath. He fell back and perched on the wooden railing aligning the houses that stared upon the tragedy. Floor four was completely caked in black, with the windows smashed out. Five, his floor, had remnants of seared flames up the sides with cut glass and broken debris hanging off the frames. The floors below and above seemed intact, but empty and inhospitable. Apart from his two years at HM Prison Chelsmford, Callum's home had been in that building. It had been Kez's for a while too. It had been Eve's. Their unconventional family had formed in there. *Why is it my floor that's in tatters?* He knew the answer to that.

He sat, shivering in the rain that now splatted against his skin, reminding him he had nothing but the clothes on his back. Whether or not the toy egg was still in there, whether it was still intact, whether it had been found and seized, there was no point risking everything to find out. He'd made a vow to start over. And that began here and now.

He stood and walked away from the building that had brought Kez into his life more than once.

* * * *

Kez paced the living room in circles. It wasn't exactly the biggest room and his strides weren't exactly small, so it was more twisting around to burn the soles of his feet. Scratching fingernails through his scalp, he was frantic with fear, with worry, with furious, fucking anger. He'd tried to run after Callum. He'd called him back, yelled his name, screamed from the balcony to no avail. When Callum had vanished from view, Kez'd had no idea which way he'd gone. It was pointless to even try to follow. He had to stay home in the hope Callum came to his senses and returned.

Two hours in and he hadn't.

Kez had to accept it was unlikely that Callum ever would return. If Kez knew one thing about him, it was that he was a stubborn bastard who made stupid mistakes and even stupider decisions. This was all so typically Callum. *Do before think.* Then when he did think, it was dangerous. How could one man mess up so many times? How could he make the same mistakes again and again? And why did Kez keep falling for it? Why couldn't he walk away from him? Why did he have to keep hoping, wishing and praying that Callum would sort himself out?

If this had all come to light twenty-four hours ago, there was no way Kez would have rushed into sleeping with him. He wouldn't have felt everything that he had when he'd been wrapped in Callum's arms, buried deep in his body and kissing that delicate porcelain skin. He would still be thinking that their brief past encounters hadn't meant the same to Callum. He would still be just a friend, like he'd promised he would. Instead, he'd thrown himself in, hook, line and sinker, and was now drowning in the aftermath. He needed a lifeline, and it didn't look like Callum was going to be providing it.

Realising he couldn't put it off any longer, he fished his phone out of his work bag and hit Call.

"Hello, yes?"

"Grace? It's Kwesi. Are you okay?" Kez had wanted to keep the concern out of his voice but on hearing the elderly crackle on the other end of the line, he couldn't have prevented it.

"I'm fine, dear. Did you want to talk to Eve?"

Kez flumped down on the sofa and the knot in his throat dug through his oesophagus as he attempted to fight back tears. At least there was a silver lining in all this and that was that neither Grace or Eve had learned of Callum's utter foolishness. He wasn't sure he could handle hearing their disappointment again. "Please."

"You wait there, dear. I'll fetch her. She's having a lie down."

Kez smiled at Grace thinking he couldn't move. She didn't have a mobile. Neither did Eve. They were too set in their ways to learn new technology every three months so they'd both stuck to landlines. Kez tapped his feet on the rug, biting his lip and wanting more than anything to hear his auntie's voice. Just knowing she was okay had relieved his anxiety. But now he needed more than that. He needed her reassurance.

"Kwesi?" Her voice made the tears tumble down his cheeks without any effort.

He sniffed and tried to compose himself. It was futile. He couldn't control it and he clutched the phone to his ear, hanging his head as he trembled and cried.

"Kwesi? Kwesi? My darling, Kwesi? Now, now, what is wrong?"

He couldn't even get the words out.

"Take a deep breath, my love. Deep, even breaths."

Kez did as she suggested and inhaled then exhaled. He wiped his arm under his nose and sniffed, wiping the tears with the flesh on his elbow.

"There, there," Eve said, her voice like a soothing lullaby. "Now you tell Auntie what's upsetting you so much. I hate to hear you like this."

He hated being like this. And he hated that he had to admit who it was who had made him like this.

"It's Callum." He croaked the name with fear and trepidation.

"I see." There was no judgement in her voice. No 'I told you so' — nothing to suggest she was doing anything other than listening and waiting. That was her way. It always had been. It had only been her praying where Kez had learned of her disgruntled dislike for what Callum had done to him, to them and to himself. Daily she had prayed for him to be saved, to find his way. Whether or not that way was back to him, Kez doubted it. Eve didn't wish Callum any ill. But if push came to shove, Kez's well-being took precedence.

It was a shame it wasn't like that for Kez.

"I love him, Auntie. I love him." His chest wanted to burst open and he quivered with the words, and the tears that wouldn't stop falling. "I always have. I can't stop it. Why can't I stop it?"

There was a brief, all-consuming silence down the phone where Kez's soft sobs would no doubt be heard by whoever might be standing close to his aunt. After a moment, Eve's voice trailed down the receiver and swathed over Kez like the fleece blanket that he'd wrapped Callum in the other night.

'"Love bears all things, believes all things, hopes all things, endures all things. Love never ends."'

Wasn't that the truth? But Kez didn't want to hear the Bible quotes. Not this time. He wanted to be resentful. He wanted to be hateful. He wanted to curse the world about the unfairness of it all.

"He lied to me." Kez hung his head in shame at having to admit how much of a fool he'd been. Again. "He said he was on the straight and narrow. He said his nose was clean. He promised he was changed."

"He told you the things you wanted to hear."

"Why?" Kez gripped the phone, his knuckles almost slicing out of his skin.

"Because he lost his way, Kwesi. And he needed you to guide him."

"I'm sick of guiding him. I'm sick of all this. I'm sick of *feeling* like this." He scrunched up his imaginary hand into a balled fist, his biceps bulging at the force. "Why me?"

"Because you love him."

"Are you saying he's using me? He's using my feelings for him?"

"I don't know about that, Kwesi. Does he love you?"

"Does that even matter?"

"Of course that matters. For that can guide you. That can be the truth of what you know. For if he doesn't love, then he can't follow your path and we must let him find his true one. We can watch. We can forgive. But we cannot go alongside him. And you must always love, from afar."

"How do I know how he feels? How do I know if what he says is true?"

"You know it. Deep down. You know it."

He'd have to dig deeper than he ever had before to find the answer. He wasn't sure he was even ready for that sort of exploration.

"What should I do?" he asked, clinging on to the guidance of his guardian.

"Exactly what you have been doing. You be there. You wait. You live and you love."

Kez had wanted more than that. He wanted actual direction. He wanted to be told what to do in practical step-by-step details. But he hadn't given his aunt much to go on. He wasn't sure he could. Or should.

"Sometimes the path of true redemption has to be walked alone. For when he is ready, when he is truly absolved, he will return."

Falling back against the sofa, Kez nodded in idle silence. His aunt didn't press for more. Her soft shallow breaths were enough to know she was still there, she would still listen and mostly that she was okay.

"How have you been?" he asked after the silence.

"I am happy. Grace is the perfect host. I'll be sad when the time comes to leave her."

"I'm glad. You take care, Auntie. I'll come by tomorrow."

"Kwesi?"

"Yes?"

"I love you with all my heart. And I know you will always do the right thing."

Kez sucked in a breath, his chest rising. "You too."

Hanging up was harder than he thought. But maybe it was for the best. Callum might try to call him. *Does he even still know my number?*

* * * *

As soon as he walked into the corner newsagents and the man behind the counter peered up from fiddling with the shattered glass on a smartphone, Callum's apprehension grew tenfold. He shouldn't be here. He shouldn't have come back to where people knew him and could trace him. But what choice did he have? The door tinkled shut and the man's gaze followed him rather than focusing on the tiny screwdriver that he twisted around the smallest hole in a broken mobile. He had a cigarette tucked behind his ear, just noticeable beneath the brown flat cap, and his distressed leather jacket gave off the stench of an ashtray. Callum had a sudden urge to ask the man for a fag, but he didn't have the money to offer for it. He didn't even have the cash to be here asking for what he needed either, but that hadn't stopped him.

Approaching the counter with his hands tucked into his jeans pockets, Callum sniffed.

"Take 'em out." The man's voice was as deep as he was dark.

Callum did as he was told, holding up his palms.

"Flick out the rest."

Pulling out his inner jeans pockets, he displayed the nothing that was within them. With a nod, the man returned his attention to fixing the phone.

"I need a throwaway." Callum tried to sound authoritative, but next to this guy he was nothing but a squeaking weasel. He felt like one as well.

"Didn't I sell you one a couple of days ago?"

"Lost it."

"In the river?"

"In a fire."

The man nodded. Then without lifting his twisting screwdriver, he reached behind him and yanked off a standard pay-as-you-go phone from the plastic casings hung on the metal hooks. He threw it to the surface. "Fifteen."

"I can't pay you."

The deep, resonating chuckle prickled Callum's skin as the man scraped back the plastic packaging, causing a grated screech against the counter surface, and returned it to hanging on the wall behind him.

"Come on, bruv," Callum pleaded with broken eyes.

The man arched an indifferent eyebrow.

"Sorry. Look, mate, I need a phone. I lost everything in that fire. Help a fella out. I have to make a call."

"I hear there were a ton of donations for your lot. Can't you get one from them?" The man returned his attention to fixing the dodgy mobile.

"No." Callum rubbed his brow. "And I think you know why."

"Exactly. So cash, or no phone."

Defeated, Callum went to walk away. The man didn't budge. Why Callum had expected him to would be his first question. Perhaps he'd thought he'd get a bit of sympathy from the guy who worked the corner store at the edge of the Marlyte Estate. Callum had spent more than his fair share of earnings in this place on various gadgets and groceries. That clearly didn't count for shit. Yanking open the door, Callum resigned himself to another long, cold and lonely walk.

"One phone call?"

Startled, Callum twisted back. The man didn't look at him, but he nodded anyway. The tip of the screwdriver pointed to the landline phone that sat next to the till. Callum swallowed. That was dangerous. That would be traced if anyone got a whiff.

What choice do I have?

He hurried back and twisted the box phone to face him. Lifting the receiver, he gave the man a second glance. He didn't look at him. That mobile was either a tricky fix or he was doing his best to avoid having to look Callum in the eye. With a deep breath, Callum dialled the number he'd somehow burned to memory. Probably for the amount of times he'd had to call it. He checked the clock on the wall. It was late. But not too late for him to think it wouldn't be answered.

It was after the third ring that Callum blew out a desperate breath. "It's Callum...can I see you? Usual place?" Relief mixed with fear rippled in Callum's chest before he hung up and nodded his thanks to the man behind the counter.

"You know they'll find you."

Callum stopped his exit from the shop. "Yeah. I know."

He left to make his way to the designated spot. On foot, it was a bastard to get to. He had to use the underpass to cross the main A13 that led into central London, and every step was as if the knife was already stuck in his back. Tension in his body pained every muscle and made it difficult for his legs to scale the derelict building sites, through the grotty industrial estate and pass the fenced-off gateway toward the riverside. With the Thames in sight, he sped up and clambered over the empty yard that was home to the Saturday Market and the occasional car boot sale pitches. The river curved at the end. Not as great a sight as it would be in Central London. Here was more like the brown sludge of the estuary, which was why it had always been the perfect secluded spot.

Leaning on the railing, he peered out over the water. Maybe he should chuck himself in. It wouldn't be the temperature that killed him, nor the current, but the toxins that he'd no doubt swallow would make for an excruciating death. It wasn't like he deserved any better. Knowing his luck, he'd be swept off and picked up by the river coppers before that happened.

"You throw yourself in and I'll kill you."

Callum shot a look over his shoulder. The man approaching was as he remembered. Tall, stocky, darker skin that even Kez had, with his dreadlocks clipped back into a tail that bounced with his energetic leap over the hill mounds. Errol had always been a comforting sight. Slapping Callum on the back, he joined him to gaze out at the brown ripples of the passing river in silence.

"Callum." His voice waded through the sloshes in a deep, resonating rumble.

"Errol."

"I've been trying to find you."

"Yeah. I'll bet." Callum hung his head. As if he could have avoided this. Why had he even tried? He wasn't sure of anything anymore.

"I know it weren't your fault." Errol twisted to face him. "The fire, that is. Where you been staying? And don't say the streets. We've checked."

Callum nodded. Of course they had. Like he could escape anything. He gazed back out at the water and shivered as a gust of riverside windchill nipped at his cheeks. Taking a deep breath, he supposed he had to lay it all on the line. Errol deserved that much.

"Remember I told you about my mate? Kwesi? Kez?" He met with Errol's gaze with a solemn smile at having to repeat the name that a mere few hours ago had tasted like sweetness on his tongue. "From the estate?"

"Oh, yeah." Errol nodded and shoved his hands in his jacket pockets. "The one-armed guy?"

Callum snorted. In the end, Kez would always be seen as that guy. Why couldn't people see beyond it, the way Callum saw him? He guessed, in some way, that was a good thing.

"Yeah. He got back in touch."

"That's great, Callum. It's always a good idea to surround yourself with friends. *Good* friends." Errol clamped him on the arm and squeezed. "So can I have his address? To follow up?"

Shameful remorse run its course and Callum dropped his gaze to the mud underneath his sodden trainers. "I left."

"Of course you did." Errol tutted. "What for this time?"

Callum swallowed and lifted his head to turn back toward the river, the sporadic sloshing against the stone wall leading out to the dock a welcome distraction from having to answer. He knew he would eventually, though. Errol would wait there forever.

"He was — *is* — a bit more than a mate." Callum flicked his hair back and wished he either had a pair of scissors to cut the whole thing off or at least a band to scrape it back as the riverside breeze was wreaking havoc on it.

"I see." Errol nodded. Just the once. And nothing showed in his expression other than that he'd heard and he understood. Callum wasn't sure why he'd worried that there might have been any other reaction. "So, a boyfriend?"

Callum shrugged. "Maybe. I dunno."

"Perhaps you need to ask him?"

Callum laughed and it released some of the tension he held within his shoulders. "Yeah. Maybe."

"Talk to me, Callum. I'm off the clock, but I'm still your parole officer."

"That the only reason you're here?" Callum sniffed, his eyes stinging. He'd never been a crier. Not even the first night when that heavy door had slammed shut and the bolt lock had echoed through the oppressing concrete walls. Not even when his bunk mate had torn up all the letters he'd tried to write. Not even when his dinner tray had been slapped out of his hands and he'd had to pick the discarded food up off the floor and eat it as a second helping hadn't been on the cards. And not even when he'd been beaten to a pulp over a debt that wasn't his.

But right then, he would have cried over Kez.

"I'm also a friend." Errol dug thick fingertips into Callum's shoulder. "And one that wants to help. You called me. You called me to here." He waved his hand to the derelict surroundings. "The last time I stopped you jumping."

"I ain't gonna jump." Callum wasn't sure who he was convincing. "I got too much to sort out." He couldn't do what his mum had. He couldn't run off, hide or even end his own life because they all now knew where Kez was. He had to settle this himself.

"Good to hear."

"I did something stupid."

Errol slipped his hand from Callum's shoulder and his chest heaved with the force of his agitated inhalation. "Go on."

"They jumped me. Few weeks ago. Mum owed them and she ran."

"Why didn't you come to me then?"

"Because I'd been released. I was out. I was free from my license to do as I fucking well pleased."

"Within reason, Callum. You still need to notify me of anything that could lead you back inside. Like a change of address. Like being compromised from those who got you there in the first place. Callum, come on. I know you're not stupid. I know you make stupid mistakes, but there's a brain in there." Errol flicked Callum's temple. "You should be using it."

"All right. I know. Don't you think I know?" Callum's head pounded. "But you know why I couldn't, right?

You know what happens to a grass, dunt'ya? They end up in there." He nodded to the river. "'Cept they're never found. In one piece, anyway."

"So what did you do instead?" Errol's scepticism spoke louder than his words.

Callum didn't blame him. Errol lived this sort of shit all the time. He spent his life trying to convince those who had been caught to rat on their mates, or even their worst enemies, in order to follow the path to the top of the organised crime chain. No one would, though. That's what petty street life was all about. *You keep schtum no matter what.*

"I fucked up," Callum admitted, screwing his eyes shut. "I took some in for them. I was meant to pass it on, but the fire happened and that stash is either burned to ashes, still in that flat or being analysed by the feds. I'll be called in soon, I know it. I was hiding out at Kez's for a while hoping it would all just disappear."

"It didn't, I take it?"

"They found me."

"Well, they have better resources than I do."

"Come on, Errol. You know people don't talk to the pigs."

"I'm not police."

"But you're with them. Round here that means you keep your mouth shut." Callum gripped the railing, the metal digging into his palm. "They know about Kez."

"So that's why you're here?"

Pursing his lips, Callum nodded. "I can't have them get to him. This ain't about me anymore. It's about him. Fuck, Errol, I can't bear it. I couldn't live with myself if they got to him. Or to Eve. I need this over. No matter what happens to me, I need him — *them* — safe."

After a tense pause, Errol nodded. "You know what you need to do then?"

"Yeah." Callum held out his hands, his wrists banging together. "It's a fair cop, guv. Rack 'em up."

Slapping Callum's arms away, Errol tutted. "You should have done this the first time round."

"I know."

Errol tugged out his mobile from his back pocket and hit the Call button, placing the phone to his ear. "Hey. Got an empty? Yeah…bringing one in."

As Errol hung up, Callum's breath was caught in his chest. For probably the first time in his life, he'd done something right. Errol held out the phone to Callum.

"Want to call him?"

Callum stared at it. What would he even say? Nothing that would make this situation any better. Nothing that would make him see that this was right, that Callum *had* to do this. Would Kez even want to hear from him at all? Maybe it was better for everyone if he remained ignorant to it all and carried on with the life he had before Callum had ruined it all for him. Maybe Rafferty would have Kez back?

The thought caused bile to lurch up into Callum's throat. He shook his head, pushed away from the barrier and headed toward the parked-up car that was to take him to where he should never have left.

Chapter Fourteen

Lost Property

For the first time in Kez didn't know how long, he didn't want to go to work. Dread loomed heavily in his stomach, swirling along with the thoughts of having to leave his house — the one place where he could expect Callum to show up, if he ever were to again, that was. But it wasn't only that he could miss the chance of knocking some sense into Callum. It was having to face reality. Callum was gone. Kez knew that deep down. He wouldn't come back. His distant memory had returned for such a brief moment, but now Kez had to shove it far away so he could resume with his life. The life he'd had to build without Callum, except it was tainted now. Callum was all over it. Callum held his breath waiting for the inevitable as though it would somehow change his life for good to the point Kez could still smell him on his skin.

And his bedsheets.

He'd shoved those in the washing machine before forcing himself to dress. He left the house, riding the Tube with a solemn undercurrent of gloom. He almost wished for a disaster to prevent him from making it to the hospital. *How ironic, that things have come full circle.* As he trudged over the crossroads toward the gleaming frontage of St. Cross, his home from home, the place that had saved him, he caught sight of Rafferty heading in. The heaviness in the pit of Kez's stomach plummeted harder, to the point Kez wasn't sure he could even walk anymore. His legs made that decision for him by stopping. Rafferty clutched a takeout coffee cup in one hand and a stack of paper folders under his arm and entered through the sliding doors. Kez hovered back, not wanting to come into direct contact with him. Another change from a mere few days ago when laying eyes on the man had made Kez erupt in a grin.

Once Rafferty was out of sight, Kez forced his feet to move closer to the doors. When they slid open, he blew out an agitated breath. Rafferty had stopped by the main reception desk and was talking to a suited woman, her severe bun scraping back her skin like a face lift. Kez checked his watch. He was in danger of being late. *Epic* late. As the conversation between Raff and the woman grew more serious, Rafferty focused his attention on her and Kez took the opportunity to sneak past without being seen, or at least under the pretence he hadn't noticed Rafferty.

Quickening his pace, Kez shuffled through those heading out of the building ending their nightshift and had just about made it through the entrance doors when a toddler running away from his mother caught under his feet. Kez tripped, his bag falling from his shoulder to spill its contents to the floor in a loud clang and bash the woman's stiletto heels. And with all that kafuffle, Raff looked his way. *Typical.*

"Kez!" Rafferty looked as startled as the toddler now being scooped up by the mother and giving a stern talking-to.

"Hi." Kez bent down to gather the crap he had no idea why he kept in his bag. He'd managed to put his prosthetic on that morning, so he couldn't even use his limb to gather the contents up and scurry off. With just the one hand, he'd never be as quick.

"I'll catch up with you later. In your office." The woman was stern in her delivery. She was clearly one of the top execs who didn't have time for such clumsy starts to her morning.

"Sure." Raff waved her off. After a brief hesitation, he eventually crouched beside Kez and aided the collection efforts along. "I'd do this for anyone." He handed Kez a notepad and several branded St. Cross pens with an arched eyebrow.

"These write so much better." Kez blushed, taking the pens and shoving them in his bag. "And I know. Thanks."

As they both stood, Kez adjusted his bag on his shoulder and the prolonged eye contact made Kez feel like he was under a microscope. As if Raff knew. As if he knew *everything*.

"How are you?" Rafferty asked, searching Kez for the answer that he hadn't found spilled on the floor.

Maybe I just look like crap? Kez hadn't checked in the mirror before he'd left, not having been able to face his own reflection, so it was a real possibility that his face gave away his internal anguish.

"Okay," Kez lied.

Raff tilted his head, drawing his eyebrows in. "Are you sure?"

Hefting out a sigh, Kez shook his head. "It's complicated." He couldn't tell Rafferty. He couldn't tell him any of it. He'd already used him yesterday to talk through things and it wasn't fair to bring him into a situation that wasn't exactly legal. Knowing about a criminal act and not reporting it was as bad as the act itself.

"So I hear." Raff offered a timid smile that broke Kez's heart. "I'm always here to talk. Like I said, I'd like us to be friends."

"So would I," Kez admitted. He did. He wanted that more than anything. A friend would definitely be welcome about now. "Trouble is, if I tell you, that might not happen."

"I doubt it." The look on Rafferty's face certainly looked genuine.

Could Kez really trust him? He hadn't known Rafferty long, but if length of time was conducive to trust given, then Kez would be waiting forever. He'd known Callum most of his life and yet here he was...*fooled again*. He was just about to open his mouth and ask to borrow the man's shoulder when a deep, demanding voice interjected.

"Kwesi." Dr Rawlings was firmly in work mode. *Suit* work mode. He didn't often don the full-on grey jacket and tie ensemble. The doctors at St. Cross tended to be more relaxed in their attire to be open and welcoming to the frightened children they looked after. A relaxed child was far more agreeable to being poked and prodded than a kid who thought they were in trouble with the headmaster. Rawlings' suit suggested he was due another leadership meeting, or had just come from one.

"Yes, Doctor?" Kez swallowed, his throat dry. Once upon a time, he would have had to hide his lustful thoughts regarding how delectable the man looked in a tailored jacket, but all Kez could see before him was a man who had watched Callum being intimate with someone who hadn't been Kez.

"Could I speak to you for a moment? Before you head to the office?"

"Of course." Kez's heart skipped several beats, punching against his chest like it wanted to escape. He kinda hoped the doctor wasn't that good a cardiologist who he could tell that by just looking at him. If Rawlings could, he'd make for a great human polygraph. Kez wished he'd used one on Callum. The mere thought of Callum whilst Kez stood next to the doctor caused him to clench his jaw.

"I need to head straight to the examination room. Could you come there?"

Rawlings peered over Kez's shoulder, his gaze landing on Rafferty who offered up a smile, one that ignited his whole being.

"I don't believe we've met." Rawlings held out his hand.

Kez scooted to the side to allow Rafferty to slip his hand into the doctor's.

"Rafferty Carmichael." Rafferty shook, pushing his glasses up his nose. "From Grants."

"Oh, yes." Rawlings nodded. "I sent you through my research proposal. Dr. Rawlings."

"Yes, I know who you are. Researching the developmental delay in neurotypical infants after heart surgery is certainly an intriguing proposal. I've been looking into possible funding avenues."

"Well, that's good to know. Perhaps we could catch up some time over coffee and talk it over?"

"I'd be delighted." Rafferty beamed and added a few inches to his height so that he towered over Kez and matched Rawlings' six feet.

The doctor nodded once, before flicking his gaze to Kez then strode off, leaving Rafferty staring after him.

"I'd heard he was all sorts of attractive, but—"

"I'd caution against that." Kez shook his head. "A long line of broken hearts."

"His or theirs?"

Kez was about to respond with the latter, until he recalled the state of Rawlings' office earlier that week. Perhaps that had been why he'd become an avid frequenter of some sex club? Loneliness? Desperation? Filling a void left by someone's departure? All the things Kez assumed Callum must have been searching for. For a smidgen of a moment, Kez felt sorry for the man. Until Callum flashed before his eyes. *Naked and being commanded to take two men at once.* The anger seeped back after that, and the nausea.

"You have my email, Kez." Rafferty tapped his arm. "If ever you want lunch. No romance involved."

Kez smiled, then nodded. Rafferty practically skipped off down the corridor. At least Raff had found a new man to swoon over. The only life Kez had ruined was clearly his own. With heavy steps he made his way to the elevator and up to Walrus Day Ward where the outpatient examination rooms were set away from the in-patient bays. It might well have been ice running through Kez's veins as he trudged closer to Rawlings' examination room. What could the doctor want with him? Had Callum gone ahead with his ridiculous plan? Instead of coming back to Kez last night, had Callum found the doctor? Had he gone back to the club? Was Rawlings about to give him a warning? An ultimatum? His P45? One word from Rawlings and most people bowed to his every whim so the idea he could be sent on his way wasn't that absurd. Rawlings would laugh in his face at the idea that he—the most influential doctor at St. Cross Children's hospital—could be blackmailed by his paper-pusher and an ex-con.

Or worse, is he here to give me the money?

The door was open when he got there and Rawlings sat behind the desk, reading through the first file on his table. Kez tapped the door frame and the doctor hummed.

"You wanted to see me?" Kez stepped in, albeit with caution. And fear. Phenomenal, overriding fear.

"Yes. Please. Come in." Rawlings kept his gaze firmly on the file. "I need your support with this first patient."

"Support? What type of support?" Kez hadn't ever been asked of that before. Nurses gave the support. Or play leaders. Not secretaries.

"I have had to take Dr. Khan's morning caseload. He's been called to a personal emergency. Too late for Lisa to have cancelled them. This first patient is..." Rawlings closed the file and twisted in his seat to face Kez. "Awkward."

"Awkward? As in the patient is awkward? Couldn't we get a play leader? Or maybe the SEN—"

"Not the patient as such. More the situation. And the parent."

"I see." Kez might as well have been blind, if he was honest.

Rawlings sighed. "Can you keep a secret, Kwesi?"

"I—Is this a test?"

"Of your loyalty? You have a loyalty to this hospital, yes. Hence I have invited you in. I need a chaperone. Or more the patient does. A third party, perhaps. That is in the hospital's interest. As for keeping secrets, I'm sure you're quite good at that?"

Kez shifted. "I wouldn't know what you mean?"

Rawlings gave him a long, hard stare. Kez might have well have been one of his medical journals — Rawlings was reading him like one.

"Your friend."

"Callum?"

"I am sure he has told you by now. I don't need you to confirm or deny. I would rather it be something that is never discussed, certainly not in the confines of these hospital walls. All I ask for is discretion. For, if you don't know, I'm sure you will soon enough."

"I don't know what this has to do with the patient?"

"Nothing." Rawlings twisted back to the file. "But maybe after you've met Daisy Monroe, you might understand a little better. This is her first check-up since her surgery a few months back and I believe she will be accompanied by her father."

Kez had vague recollections. The name certainly rang a bell. An alarm bell. One that pierced through his skull to make him wonder what the hell was going on, and what this had to do with Callum. Should he just ask outright? He had to know. He had to find out if Callum had been to the doctor last night. More than anything, he had to know if Callum was okay.

Rawlings stood, gave a curt nod to Kez then clomped along the freshly washed floor to the waiting area. A few moments later, he returned and in skipped a young girl, her mound of dark curly hair swishing with each step. She was around nine years of age and holding her hand was a man with unruly curls to match her own. His stony-faced expression wasn't usual for an accompanying parent to a heart check-up. Normally they had hope, or fear or anticipation in their eyes. His looked to be pure hatred.

Kez recognised the man instantly. *Jacob.* Ollie's boyfriend. The one who'd kick-started all the rumours about Rawlings' affair with the nurse.

"Come in. Take a seat." Rawlings scraped a chair over to beside his desk.

Jacob stood rigid. Unmoving. "We were to see Dr. Khan."

"Yes. Unfortunately, he has been called away." Rawlings sat, picked up the file and read through the notes. He didn't give Jacob a second glance. "As you know, I am familiar with Daisy's condition, what with being the one to repair her heart. I'm sure you will allow me to check all is in working order? I have Kwesi here as an independent witness."

Jacob drifted his gaze to Kez. All he could do was offer up a smile. Attention back on Rawlings, Jacob held the doctor's gaze.

"Please sit, Mr. Monroe. The sooner I check your daughter, the sooner you can leave. I hear you are quite busy at the moment, what with the move."

Daisy beamed. "We're getting a *big* house!"

"So I hear." The doctor nodded and patted to the chair. "Come sit and tell me all about it."

Slipping her hand from her father's, Daisy skipped over to the chair and jumped onto it. Jacob remained where he was, frozen, as though this was the most awkward moment of his life. It probably was—Kez could feel it scratching the air.

Rawlings popped his stethoscope into his ears and held the round metal to Daisy's chest. "How has she been?"

"Good. No problems. Not anymore," Jacob replied to the wall.

"Energy levels?"

"She still gets a little breathless with longer exercise. Running. Jumping. That sort of thing."

"Mmm-hmm." Rawlings moved the circle across Daisy's chest as she kicked her legs under the table. "Blueness?"

"When she gets out of the bath."

"But during the day?"

"Not that I know of."

Rawlings glanced up at the man.

"She's only with us half the week. The rest with her mother. Ollie would have said if there was something off."

"Oliver isn't a doctor."

"He's my daddy's boyfriend." Daisy spoke that as if filling the doctor in with the local news. "I'm getting two daddies!" She giggled, hands over her mouth.

"Well, aren't you both exceptionally lucky." Rawlings threw the stethoscope to his desk and leaned back, darting his gaze to Jacob. "Do you have any concerns?"

"No."

Rawlings smiled, tapping two fingers to his lips. "Well then, I'd say we did a good job here. The scan images show nothing out of the ordinary. We'll still keep her on yearly checks for a while. Hopefully, next time you'll see Dr. Khan." Rawlings leaned forward and prodded Daisy's nose. "You, young lady, are good to go."

Daisy jumped down from the seat and tucked her hand into Jacob's outstretched one. "What's the matter, Daddy?"

"Nothing, pumpkin." He smiled, then held Rawlings' gaze, his stiff demeanour diminishing. "Thank you, Doctor."

"You're very welcome." He span in his chair, scribbling up the notes that Kez knew would be coming his way soon enough. "Good luck with the move. Be sure to give Kwesi here your new address so we can cc you into the report."

Jacob nodded once then tugged Daisy out of the room. As soon as they left, Rawlings let out a lungful of air, threw his pen onto the desk and pinched the bridge of his nose.

"Are you okay?" Kez pushed away from the wall that had been holding him up for the entire thorny exchange.

"I think we share something, you and I." Rawlings didn't look at him when he spoke. "Unrequited love can be quite suffocating."

Kez nodded. He understood. Unrequited or unavailable was the same thing. Perhaps Rawlings had invited him here to see that exchange to garner some sympathy. *Some understanding of why he does the things he does.* To not judge so quickly, the way Callum was always judged. Without wanting or needing to say anything more, Kez walked toward the door but stopped before exiting and, with his gaze focused on the corridor, said, "He's missing."

Rawlings swivelled his chair from side to side. He didn't say anything. Kez faced him.

"He's in trouble." Kez heaved in a deep breath. "So, if you see him, anywhere, tell him to come home."

Any movement was invisible to the naked eye, but Kez swore he saw an affirmative in Rawlings somewhere. He had to hope there was anyway. They'd both been stripped bare this week. The NHS wouldn't need to send them on any teambuilding activity to strengthen their bond. He and the doctor were now forever linked by their defiant acts of desperation.

Chapter Fifteen

Home, Bittersweet Home

"It's not that bad." Kez winced through the delivery of that flippant statement as he waggled the stiff key out of the pristine new lock.

Eve gave him a long stare, before sighing and continuing farther down the corridor of the ground floor flat. Four months had passed in a heavy haze of indifference. Kez had focused on his work, his aunt and getting his shit together all in an attempt to not think about Callum and where he might have ended up. It had been a welcome distraction when the news of Eve being re-homed had come their way.

Stepping into the doorway, Kez dumped the suitcase on the frayed laminate flooring and watched his aunt. Eve, hands on hips, inspected the paint-peeling walls and damp corners of the low-level ceiling. Her face contorted into something Kez hadn't seen in a while. *Sadness.* He couldn't blame her. As he approached into the living room, furnished only with a fake-wooden coffee table and two armchairs, she stopped and Kez stepped up beside her.

It *was* that bad, certainly when compared to the place Eve had nurtured at the Marlyte Estate for twenty years. The council might have provided her with a ground-floor property in a block that stretched lengthways rather than skywards, but it wasn't exactly a new build. It was only six floors up but hundreds along and most of the Marlyte residents were getting access to the vacant housing that had been deemed as safe, but sadly lacking in aesthetics. It was a roof though. And the council had only taken four months to sort it.

Eve sighed and faced Kez. "Maybe I should have declined the offer?"

"Why would you do that?"

"I liked staying with Grace. This could be given to someone far more needy. This just doesn't feel very me."

Kez gave a half-smile. It must have been hard for her. Four months of having company every day only to leave that behind to live on her own in a bare shell of a flat. Grace often had her extended family to stay, babysitting her great grandchildren, and Eve had felt her presence there was getting in the way. So she'd accepted the re-homing offer and was moving in straight away. Although the housing association had claimed it was a fully-furnished letting, the scarce surroundings weren't as much minimalistic as non-existent. Kez made a note to buy her everything she needed. He'd max out his credit card if he had to, which he probably would.

"We'll put a few pictures up," Kez suggested, wrapping an arm around her shoulders. "I can get some of those old ones off my laptop. Get some printed onto canvas. We'll make this place yours."

Eve smiled, then kissed his cheek. "I brought some mugs and groceries from Grace's. Make this old girl a cuppa, will you?"

"Sure. Take a seat. I'll put the kettle on. After that, we'll go shopping. *Furniture* shopping."

Eve tapped his cheek, her dry hands rubbing against his growing-out stubble. He wasn't trying to grow it out. It had happened through pure laziness and no longer seeming to care about his appearance. He'd had a few jibes about it from work colleagues, mainly Raff. Maybe after moving his aunt in, he'd consider a new start for himself.

The kitchen was the size of a shoe box. It barely fit two people in. These really were single-occupancy homes. For the elderly. For the couples without children. For the *single* and alone. Kez wished he could have convinced his aunt to move into his maisonette. He would have given her his room and bought himself a sofa bed to sleep on downstairs. It wasn't as though he had any guests of a night. Not anymore. Not since Callum had left a gaping hole in that area of his life.

But the flight of steps up to the back would have been a struggle for Eve, so she'd kept declining his offers. He'd even looked into moving and getting a two-bed somewhere, but his searches only served to prove his NHS support staff wages wouldn't stretch to anywhere other than out of the borders of London which would be a ball ache with commuting, not to mention taking Eve farther away from Grace, her friends and her church. So the ground-floor single-occupancy the council had found was the only option.

Flicking on the limescale-filled kettle and adding another piece of equipment to his 'to-get' list, he leaned against the tiny counter to wait. It wasn't that bad. Lick of paint here and there, few soft furnishings, few pictures on the wall and it could be considered a home. He'd have to come round every weekend to get all that done. Especially the decorating. DIY wasn't exactly his forte.

A sharp knock against wood caught his attention and he dipped forward to watch his aunt limp out to answer the front door. Kez couldn't see beyond her. Eve's whole frame was taking over the entranceway and her wrapped-on-top cornrows prevented any view from above. But his heart pounded hard nonetheless.

"Hello, Eve."

Gulping, Kez stepped out of the box kitchen and into the corridor. He edged closer to the door on tiptoes, all while his mind told him he was wrong. *I'm hearing things. It can't be who I think it is.* His mind was clearly playing tricks on him. He'd been hearing that voice in his head for so long, that he was now listening to it in daylight. *It's driving me fucking crazy!* Now that voice was seeping into his reality to seal the deal and exposing his insanity.

"I'm part of the welcome committee." The voice spoke again and it drove through Kez's chest to capture his heart, pausing the essential beats that had been the only thing to keep him going these past four months. It took all Kez's will to keep moving toward that door.

"Me and a few lads are offering our services to those moving in. We'll paint what needs doing, or put up wallpaper, fix the mould spots. Any DIY. Anything you want. Name it and we'll do it. Free of charge."

As Kez slipped in beside Eve, his lips parted. She reached for his hand and gripped the plastic with desperation. Holding on to a bunch of brightly coloured flowers wrapped in a crunchy paper that screamed *independent florist* and not picked up on a whim at a supermarket, Callum stood, eyes wide, behind the door. Focussing his gaze on Kez made Callum swallow and step back, his startled expression showing he hadn't expected Kez to be there. *Well, fucking ditto!*

"Callum," Kez breathed out the name that had been on the tip of his tongue for months.

"Kez." Callum cleared his crackling throat. "I thought you'd be at work."

"I took the day off."

"Right."

"What are you—"

"Come in, Callum." Taking hold of Callum's arm, Eve tugged him in.

Callum staggered over the threshold, hazel eyes staring at Kez as he did so. Eve shut the door behind him and Callum held out the flowers to her, finally tearing his gaze away from searing into Kez's soul. "For you."

Smiling, Eve took them and sniffed. "Thank you."

"Housewarming." Callum shrugged, shoving his hands deep in his jeans pocket. "As I know these flats ain't exactly welcoming."

"You can say that again." Eve angled her head toward the living room. "Go sit your behind in there and I'll make the tea."

Callum darted his gaze to Kez, probably checking to see if that would be okay with him. Kez wasn't sure. He was numbed to the bone. He could barely think through the pounding of his heart and the consistent ringing in his ears. There was Callum. In the flesh. Not only was he alive, he was a radiating glow of health. His hair had been cut, the blond strands back to their dusky golden flecks that he'd chopped into a side brush over. Kez missed the long topknot, but Callum appeared more respectable this way. More appealing. And it was doing things to Kez's stomach he couldn't control, not to mention his aching groin.

"I can't stay long." Callum's shoulders drooped.

Perhaps Kez's mute status indicated that he wasn't as welcome in the flat as the flowers were. If only Kez could get any words out, but he was too preoccupied with taming his reaction to the man before him.

"I'm over at number ten, painting Mr Aksu's hallway."

That was when Kez noticed the clothes Callum wore. His white overalls were splattered with all colours of paint and unbuttoned to drape open, revealing the tight-fitting T-shirt underneath. The V-neck accentuated his protruding collarbone and Kez's fingers itched to trace that slender chest to find the metal hidden behind the thin cotton. He licked his lips.

"I'm sure you can squeeze in a little break." Eve trotted off, sniffing the flowers again as she went.

Callum gave Kez an awkward-as-hell smile, lingering near the front door as if ready to bolt. Snapping to, Kez strode through to the living room and—*miracles do happen*—Callum followed and sat on the edge of one of the armchairs.

Kez paced. He had no idea what to say. There was too much to ask and he hadn't a clue where or how to begin. Having spent the best part of four months trying to track the man down, he'd come up a blank. No one seemed to know—it was as if he'd disappeared into thin air. Kez's fear that Callum had become another unidentified body floating in the Thames had steadily become the most logical, because someone had to have known something. Kez had risked his own life trying to find out. No one had been back to his place either. The new lock remained intact, as did the newly fitted security light.

Hanging his head, Callum stifled a chuckle. Pausing his erratic pacing, Kez stared down at him and curled his fingers around the back of the armchair facing Callum.

"What the fuck, Cal?" Kez gritted his teeth to utter the curse word as under his breath as he could whilst still allowing Callum to hear him. It was an ingrained habit from having been clipped around the ear too many times by Eve when swearing or saying the Lord's name in vain. It wasn't the best way to start, but what could Callum really expect?

"Sorry, but you're real fucking sexy when you're angry." Callum didn't even flinch when he said that.

Kez did. But Eve shuffled in, holding a tray that carried three piping hot mugs, a glass pot of sugar and a side plate of custard creams, to intrude on whatever that moment was. No matter how dishevelled the surroundings, Eve would always be the best hostess she could. Sliding the tray onto the coffee table, she then lowered herself into the armchair in front of Kez and nodded to the mug.

"Get some of that inside you." Eve stirred one sugar into her tea.

Callum took one of the mugs and settled back in the seat. Realising he looked like a pillock just standing there, Kez plonked down on the arm of Eve's chair and joined them in their cosy tea party. His jaw clenched — he wasn't going to take a biscuit as he'd break some enamel with how hard he'd chew.

"We're neighbours again, Aun — Eve." Callum sipped from his mug, eyes fixed on Eve and not Kez. "I got re-homed here too. A couple days back." He flicked his gaze to Kez. "Number twelve."

"Oh really?" Eve tapped Kez's knee, whether for comfort or a warning, Kez wasn't sure. "That is good news. Be nice to have a familiar face around here, won't it, Kwesi?"

Kez's reply was stuck in his throat. Callum smiled, those hazel eyes sparkling with something Kez hadn't seen in them for a long time. Perhaps there had been a brief flickering of it when they'd had that one time together back in Kez's bedroom. Kez's cheeks heatedand held his breath as his chest rippled. Shuffling on the armrest, he scratched at the plastic on his arm.

"I'm part of this rehabilitation group," Callum said, breaking the silence. "It's a charity thing. We all get a mentor." He snorted, waving it off as if it were ridiculous. In a way, it kind of was, but Kez leaned forward and waited for the rest nonetheless. "The charity gets kids off the street, away from gangs, prevent prison sentences, y'know? Education, apprenticeships, volunteering stuff. I got shoved into this social enterprise of theirs 'cause of the qualifications I got in the construction and trowel trades when I was inside. Me and the lads do painting, decorating, DIY for social housing that ain't getting the love from the council. The borough funds most of it. And the charity puts in the rest. Run by some entrepreneur fella. Businessman. Bossman."

"That's great, Callum." Eve beamed, sipping from her mug. "How did that come about?"

Callum flicked his gaze up at Kez, his cup at his lips. "I turned myself in."

Startled, Kez bolted forward, but Eve steadied him on the seat by tapping his knee again. "You what?"

"I went to the police," Callum replied, darting his gaze from Kez to Eve. "Well, to my parole officer. Told him what happened. With the drugs. My mum. Baz."

Kez winced. He couldn't look at Eve then. She hadn't moved or offered up any expression other than that of someone listening, the way she always did in front of people. Kez hadn't told her about Callum's second lot of drugs. All she'd known was that Callum had disappeared. Again. *Guess she knows now.* Kez feared her reaction. All that stuff about forgiveness might be a distant memory, the reason he'd kept it from her. She'd only be disappointed and Kez had enough of that within himself for the both of them.

"I was taken in. Couple of weeks' lock-up while they did the investigation." Callum gulped down the rest of his tea. "Baz got arrested, no parole while they waited the court case. Then I got offered a deal. I give them names, they'd give me a way out." He shrugged. "Grassing is dangerous, I know that. But it weren't more dangerous than being dumped back out on the street, or to let them find you." Callum hung his head. "So I did it. I gave them what they wanted in return for me to get taken on by the rehab charity. I gave evidence and after the court case, I got re-homed here as part of the deal."

Kez's mouth hung open. He couldn't believe Callum had done all that by himself. Kez would have been there for him. He would have stood by him. He would have been the friend that Callum had needed the first time around. Had he not proved that? Had he really made Callum feel as though he was alone?

"I managed to get a job on a building site, thanks to my mentor." Callum clapped the mug back on the tray and wiped his hands down his jeans. "Fully employed brickie now an' all. I'm doing this as a side. To prove I'm making a change." He glanced around the room, ready to heft himself up. "Give us a colour, Eve, and we'll get this sorted tomorrow for you. If you don't mind a bunch of rowdy lads stepping in your flat, that is."

"I'm used to it." Eve smiled.

Callum chuckled. "Yeah. Well, they're harmless really. They want to do a good job as it'll give 'em the possibility of an apprenticeship."

"Yellow." Eve patted Kez's knee. "That would look nice in here, wouldn't it, love? Like sunshine?"

"Yes, Auntie. That'll brighten up the place." Kez leaned back, watching Callum's every move. He feared if he looked away, Callum wouldn't be there anymore.

Callum stood. "Thanks for the tea, Aun—Eve."

"You can still call me Auntie, Callum. I'd like it if you did."

Nodding, Callum scooted around the coffee table and launched himself at Eve. He clung, hugging her tightly and Kez slipped off the armrest, the lump in his throat unbearable.

"Come on, now, Callum." Eve tapped his arms. "You're welcome here, anytime. Right, Kwesi?"

Callum stepped away, sniffing as his eyes glistened. All Kez could do was nod.

"I'll be done today pretty late. Eightish probably." Callum rubbed under his nose, his fingers trembling then shrugged. "But as I'm only a few doors away, number twelve, I can come by early tomorrow. Yellow paint." He hesitated for a moment but all words were stuck in Kez's throat. Then with a resigned nod, Callum turned on his heel and headed out to the hallway.

Kez watched him go, listening out for the closing of the front door before peering down at Eve. She ruffled out her skirt, then picked up a custard cream and nibbled the end.

"When we stray from His presence, He longs for you to come back."

She didn't need to say anymore. Kez knew what she was getting at. But he had his own mantra to repeat. Reaching for a biscuit, he recited it over and over in the hope that, this time, he might follow his own advice.

Won't be fooled again.

* * * *

Shutting the front door behind, Kez breathed in the late-night air. The only light in the yard came from the residences that had their curtains open and their lamps shone through the windows to brighten the communal gardens. Not all the flats were occupied, so the darkened path wasn't easy to follow. The chill in the air bit Kez's cheeks and he zipped up his jacket to saunter up the gravel, away from his aunt's new building.

He'd stayed for dinner and had helped her spruce the place up enough to make it more hospitable than the vacant shell they'd walked into. It would look better after the damp and mould spots were painted over. He drew in a breath at that. It was Callum who planned on painting it. Reaching the fence that led onto the main street, he glanced back to the block. Counting the windows along from Eve's, he then paused at number twelve. The blinds were drawn, but the distorted light behind formed a shadow from within.

Callum.

He couldn't. He shouldn't. For his own sanity and self-preservation, Kez had to walk away. Whatever improvements Callum had made for himself in the short time since he'd run from Kez's flat, it couldn't fix everything. It wouldn't mend Kez's broken heart, or his hanging-by-a-thread trust, or his bruised and battered ego. It was better, for them both, to keep things as they were.

At a distance.

Sucking the cool night air into his lungs, Kez turned away and walked out of the new estate. The sinking in his gut wouldn't be there forever. The long, painful nights of insomnia would pass. And the empty feeling of loneliness would be filled eventually. *By who?* Kez wasn't sure. Nor did he think he should rush to fill it. *Not this time.*

The double-decker bus up ahead caught Kez's eye and he rushed toward the stop, holding up his hand for it to pull in. As it screeched into the layby and the doors shunted open, Kez rustled in his jacket for his wallet. Checking each pocket, he offered an apologising smile to the driver.

"You getting on, mate?" the driver asked, leaning forward out of his cab.

Kez stepped on. Then glanced behind him toward the block of flats. "Sorry." He tapped his pockets again. "I think I've left my wallet back at my aunt's."

"Next bus in twenty." The driver revved the engine, yanking the stick in to gear.

Kez jumped back down to ground level and had to watch the bus pull away. *Typical.* Defeated, he jogged along the path toward the entrance to the building. With a sudden jolt, Kez stopped. Another man in front, clutching onto a plastic carrier bag, headed straight for the communal entrance door. He was big. *Real* big. And his dreadlocks trailed down to the middle of those broad shoulders. Kez sucked in a breath, remaining hidden in the shadows, and watched the bloke buzz the entrance bell. Within a few torturous moments, Callum opened the door, holding it wide and offering the man entrance.

Kez could have thrown up.

Muffled voices that Kez knew distinctly as Callum's talking to the deeper, vibrating tones of the man he was ushering in, caused a wrenching pain in Kez's chest. *Callum moved on quick. Too quick.* Now Kez couldn't wait to get out of here. Hanging his head, he dipped forward and was unable to look upon the scene at the entrance. He'd just have to knock on Eve's window rather than go through that door.

"Kez?"

Kez stopped, eyes focusing down as his throat closed in. He couldn't ignore the call. He couldn't be *that* bloke. He peered up to witness Callum lurching past the man stood at his open door. All Kez could do was offer a timid smile.

"Kez!" As Callum approached nearer, he smiled. As though he'd just won the lottery. Then it faded. "Are you off home?"

"Uh, yeah." Kez looked away toward the bus stop, knowing he had a twenty-minute wait until he could board the getaway train.

Callum gripped his arm. *Desperately.* "Can you spare a minute? Or two?"

Kez finally looked into those hazel eyes. *Why did I ever try denying it?* "I don't know, Cal..." He peered over at the heavy stood waiting by the door.

"That's Errol." Callum angled his head. "I want you to meet him."

Kez raised his eyebrows. "That wise?"

Laughing, Callum tugged on Kez's arm. Even though it was his arm that Callum pulled, Kez felt a hard shunt to his back. As though a hand was pushing him forward, edging him closer to the point of no return. *Is this the greater being guiding me?* Kez shook that absurdity off, even if he couldn't deny it completely.

"Kez, this is Errol." Callum motioned toward the bloke holding open the door. "He's my parole officer."

"Was." Errol's deep voice rumbled in Kez's chest. He held out a hand. "The bloke's a free citizen now. I just like to keep him in check."

Clutching Errol's hand, Kez shook as his shoulders eased out of their tension. "I'm glad to hear it. Someone's gotta."

Callum snorted.

"So, Kez, is it?" Errol smiled. "I've heard a lot about you. And don't panic, it's all been good. Honestly, if it wasn't for you, I think we both know where this one would be right now."

Hanging his head, Callum's shameful puppy-dog eyes stared at the ground.

"I don't think I did anything." Kez had to admit that. It was the truth.

"You'd be surprised. But—" Errol pushed away from the door and stepped into the yard, holding out the bag to Callum. "But don't let me be the one to tell you. Let him. Over dinner. There's enough in there for two. He made me order some black bean chicken shit just in case."

Kez darted his startled gaze to Callum. He smiled. And shrugged.

"I'll leave you two to it." Errol shoved his hands in his pockets. "Check in with me tomorrow, Callum."

"Will do."

As Errol left, Kez didn't know what to do. He was stuck. And he wasn't sure if he wanted to be or not.

"Come in." Callum stood against the door, holding it open. "Please?"

"Cal, I'm not sure I can do it."

"Do what? Talk to me? Come on, Kez. Please. I've got so much I gotta say and you know I ain't writing that shit down."

Another shove to his back made Kez glide over the threshold. He'd give him ten minutes. Then the bus would be back and he'd get on that. The door slammed behind, making Kez flinch, and Callum's lingering presence tingled on Kez's back as he walked behind him toward number twelve. Stopping at the door, Kez waited. Callum reached over him to push it open off the latch.

"Go on." Callum ushered him inside.

The flat was scarcer than Eve's. No furniture other than a double mattress laid out on the floor in the middle of the front room. At least it had a duvet and two pillows. Kez turned back to Callum and must have had sympathy written all over his face.

"It ain't much, I know," Callum said. "It's all I got for now. That and a few kitchen essentials. Which includes plates and cutlery for this." He held up the bag. "Want some?"

Kez did. He could smell the inviting aroma that only mildly masked Callum's own intoxicating scent. He shook his head though.

"Fair enough. Tastes better cold anyway. Let me dump this in the kitchen and get you a drink. Sit if you like. The mattress is comfy. Errol bought it new."

Kez hovered, undecided, and Callum ran off to the adjacent kitchen. He returned just as quick with two bottles. Feeling ridiculously uncomfortable standing, Kez sat on the edge of the mattress, knees clutched to his chest. Callum handed down a bottle.

"Cheers." Beer was also appealing right then.

Callum bit off the top to his and discarded the cap in his joggers pocket. Holding the bottle between his knees, Kez attempted to twist it open but the groves dug into his skin. Callum waited, taking a gulp of his drink.

"Would you?" Kez held out the bottle.

Smiling, Callum took it and bit the cap off. As he sat beside Kez, he handed it over and Kez took an immediate, desperate gulp.

"First lot of wages due at the end of the week. Means I can get some things on deposit." Callum waved his bottle to indicate the bare room. "Errol showed me this place that gives away donated items. Maybe I should take Eve, get her some stuff?"

Kez nodded, hovering the bottle at his lips. "Yeah. That'd be nice."

"Not sure I can afford a TV, but it ain't like I need it." Callum fished out a smartphone from his pocket. "Errol got me this. Can watch a loada shit on this thing."

"This Errol...he's being a bit..." Kez didn't know how to finish that. So he didn't.

"It's all the stuff I should have taken him up on the first time round. But I thought I could make it on me own. Turns out, I couldn't, could I? Handing Baz over to them means I get a few perks." Callum gulped from his drink. "The flat, the phone, the job."

Kez nodded and inhaled the courage to start the conversation. "I'm sorry, Cal."

"For what?"

"For not being there. For not helping. For everything."

Callum shook his head and scooted on the mattress to face him. "None of this is your fault. It's all mine. And I did the time for it. You gotta know, Kez, I never wanted you involved. I never wanted to bring this all on you."

"I still should have reacted better. Twice I've done it. I'm meant to be your mate, your brother, and twice I've let you do the most difficult thing you can alone. What sort of person am I? I hid behind this moral high ground, this desperate desire to climb out of bottom of the pile, to fit myself in a world I don't come from. And in doing that, I turned my back on the one person who sees me as an equal."

Callum bit his lip. "Don't say that."

"Say what? It's all true, Cal. And I'm so sorry. I guess, in some way, it all boils down to jealousy."

"Jealous?" Callum wrinkled his brow. "Of me?"

"Not of you. Of everyone around you." Kez stared hard into confused hazel eyes and knew he had to spill everything. *Warts and all.* "Sometimes I can't bear it. I can't breathe at the thought of you with someone else. Shit, Cal, I've been in love with you since year nine! Since that day we had to squeeze on that packed bus. I was against the window and you were in the middle with Stacy practically on your lap. I knew it then. I felt you everywhere."

Gulping, Callum picked at his hands. "You should have told me."

"How could I?" Kez threw back the remnants of his beer. "You were Callum. My mate. My brother. Rejection ain't easy, doubly so if it had come from you. I walked away so I didn't have to go through the pain of losing you to someone else." He sucked in a confidence-boosting breath. "And I didn't run after you when you left my place 'cause I couldn't look you in the eye knowing if I hadn't turned my back on you the first time, then maybe you wouldn't have done what you did, with the drugs, with the doc."

Callum fell silent for a while. Then he smiled and his eyes lit up the room. "Remember that night? That first night? When you got off the bus after college and walked past me and the girls at the playground? I asked you to come join us. You said 'no', you had homework or some shit. What did I do, Kez?"

Kez bit his lip, holding Callum's intoxicating gaze. "You left them and came to mine."

"Yeah. I did. And guess what, dickhead?" Callum nudged Kez's knee with his own. "I kissed you. The only way to get you away from those fucking books and look at me was to kiss you."

Kez remembered that night as if it was yesterday. He'd never been able to shake it from his mind, his dreams, his morning fantasies.

"I kissed *you*, Kez."

"I know." Hanging his head, the remorse overwhelmed Kez to the point his chest constricted. "I thought you only did that so I'd help you pass your key skills."

"Then you're a moron."

A lighthearted chuckle escaped Kez's lips and he met Callum's wide-eyed gaze. "How could I ever believe it though? You, Callum Wright, the one all the girls wanted a piece of, the wide-boy on the estate, the man about town, would want me? This!" He held up his prosthetic, the one thing that dragged him down in his own estimations. "The disabled, black bloke that they all took the piss out of."

"Then you should add blind as one of your disabilities."

What? Kez licked his dried lips. "What?"

"I can't believe you think I would care about any of that. After everything, Kez. How could you not know?"

"Know what?"

"That I worshipped you. You fucking fool!" Callum slapped Kez's chest with the back of his hand, causing a deserved sting. "I worshipped the ground you walked on." Callum smiled. "You *walk* on."

Kez couldn't breathe. "What you saying?"

"I'm saying…" Callum plonked the empty bottle on the floor beside him. "I'm saying…actually, I ain't saying." Sliding a hand up Kez's neck, Callum tugged him toward him and pressed his lips to Kez's.

Rippling euphoria bubbled inside Kez and he allowed his body to take over. He kissed Callum back, sliding his tongue inside to lap up the words that Callum couldn't say out loud. And it tasted fucking glorious. There was no reading between the lines. There was no lost in translation. There was no jumbled-up letters to spell out nonsense. This was Callum, proving to him that he felt the same.

It got a bit heated after that, with hands roaming and lips smacking, and Kez was caught off guard when

Callum threw a leg over his lap to straddle him. Callum kissed with an urgency that only a desperate man who had to prove himself would and, falling flat into the mattress, Kez allowed Callum to smother him. For a while. Until sense took over.

"Hey, hey." Kez kept his voice light as he dipped farther into the soft cushion.

"What's wrong?" Callum panted, lifting up on his arms.

"I just think we should go slow." Kez winced. He knew how that sounded. *Ridiculous*. They'd already gone too fast. Kez had already declared his love for the man. But they needed to go backward. *For my sanity.* "I don't want to rush this. I don't want to ruin anything. I think we need to adjust to it. Me and you."

Callum breathed out a sigh. "You sayin' no fooling around?"

Drifting his hand up into Callum's top, Kez smiled. He stroked the taut flesh beneath and, for a brief moment of lunacy, he wanted to keep going. He wanted it so badly. His dick was also telling him to keep at it. *But it's not right.*

"You know I want you, Cal." He lifted up to kiss Callum's lips. "I've always wanted you. And ever since I've had a taste of you, it burns even more."

Callum furrowed his brow. "I hope that ain't a bad thing."

Kez burst out a laugh. "Me too. You know what I mean, though, right?"

Sliding off from Kez, Callum nodded and landed on his back beside him. He stretched his arms behind his head and stared up at the ceiling. "Yeah. I get it."

Kez sat. "I want to take you to dinner." He stared forward at the bare walls, unable to look at Callum and witness the flicker of disappointment, or even disgust at what Kez was going to suggest next. *But if this is going to work, it has to be done right.* "I want to walk hand-in-hand with you down the street. I want to be proud about this, not hide it behind closed doors. I want to introduce you to my friends. I want to introduce you to Auntie."

"I already know Eve."

Kez glanced back down, holding on to Callum's gaze and searching for the courage to keep going. "I want to introduce you to her as my boyfriend."

Silence stung the air. Horrid, awkward silence that wreaked havoc on Kez. *I should have got on the damn bus!* Maybe he still had time…

Callum sat with a start, glided a hand along Kez's cheek and kissed him. "All right."

Smiling, Kez rested his forehead against Callum's. "We can do this. We can. Me and you. We work. But it'll take some time to build up the trust. For both of us."

"We will."

"No more lies. No more secrets. No more fooling around."

Callum arched an eyebrow.

"We'll make love from here on in. If that's all right with you?"

"I always knew you were a sucker for love stories."

"Sue me."

"How about I just kiss you instead?"

"That'll be better. Lawyers cost shit loads and I need all my cash for that dinner I'll be taking you on."

Callum laughed. "It's a date then."

"Saturday night?"

Nodding, Callum bowed his head. "So, you off now?"

Kez thought about that. He should go. There was still time to catch the next bus, get home and sleep soundly for the first time in so long. He needed the rest. He needed the time alone – to think, to reevaluate, to plan out their new start. Not to mention he was back at work tomorrow and it was a long journey to St. Cross from here.

"You working tomorrow?" he asked.

"Told the lads we'd be painting from six a.m. then I'm on a site from nine."

"Let's eat then. And you can wake me up the morning." Kez stood and unbuttoned his shirt, wriggling it down his arms.

As Callum watched him, a smile danced across his glowing features. Kez unclipped his prosthetic from its shutter lock and handed it down. Callum took the limb, placing it on the floor beside the mattress, then stood. Callum did the rest – unravelling the silicone liner from Kez's upper arm, sliding it off and stripping Kez bare. Kissing him, Kez wrapped his arms around Callum and held him. Because he didn't want to let the man go. He didn't want to leave. He didn't want to walk away.

I won't be that *fool. Not again.*

Want to see more from this author? Here's a taster for you to enjoy!

Pink Rock: Love & Tea Bags
Author Name

Excerpt

The slurp was loud and rather obnoxious, especially when the man was sipping from one of Mark's grandmother's dainty china tea cups that Mark saved for special occasions. Since Mark hadn't had any need for the guest china in quite some time, he'd let Grammy's cardinal rule slide for the strapping workman clambering up in his loft.

"Yup, I see the problem," the workman yelled down the open hatch in Mark's landing ceiling that led to the over-cluttered store of stuff that Mark hadn't set foot in for…well, quite some time.

Mark wished he hadn't offered the man a brew. He really hadn't had the time to wait for the kettle to boil, for a start. But he'd been brought up well, and one must offer one's tradesmen a cuppa in the hope they'll knock a few quid off the call-out charge. He suspected he would have to delve deep into his already ravine-like pockets, so anything that could be considered mates-rates would really help at this point in his life. Mark wished he did have mates. Ones that were handy, anyway.

"Oh, yes?" Mark called back, his voice echoing through the square hole in his ceiling. He closed his eyes, for some reason, as if that would soften the blow of what was going to come out of the man's mouth next.

"Gonna need coupla new roof tiles, mate. A lotta this stuff is gonna get ruined."

"Bugger," Mark muttered into his own mug of piping-hot tea. Well, it was rude not to join the man in a beverage.

"What was that?" The man's round, if somewhat flushed, face appeared at the hole.

"Nothing, nothing." Mark shook his head. He didn't much fancy repeating himself. The man might take it seriously and give him a whack. Or, which would be much worse, not take the job of fixing Mark's leaking roof. "Thank you." He smiled.

Mark had been told, on occasion, that he had quite a nice smile. One that relaxed people. Mark, however, believed it to be far more useful to allow people to walk all over him. Or pass by him. *Through him...*

With a grunt, the workman set his steel-toe-capped boots on two metal rungs of the ladder, revealing the tip of his rounded behind popping out of the elastic waistband that appeared to be failing in its one basic function. Normally, on an average Saturday night, Mark wouldn't have minded the view, as his internet history would evidence. But today was a Monday and the man didn't look like he would appreciate Mark's ogling. Not that Mark was ogling. He just had nowhere else to look. *Honest.*

On reaching the landing, the workman crashed back into Mark. Stumbling, Mark gripped his cup with both hands to prevent the utter travesty of spillage onto the carpet. Not only did he not have time to clear up any stains—not that any would show on the swirling patterns of the seventies-design stitch work — but he also hated to waste a cup of the good stuff.

The workman hefted up his jogging bottoms, his hands empty of the china tea cup he had been avidly slurping from up in the loft. And that meant Mark would now either have to venture up into the space he avoided like the seaside lido on a May bank holiday afternoon, or leave it up there to breed new life. He knew which he would rather.

"Right." The man scratched his stubbled chin. "See, you're gonna need a coupla new tiles. Tha's what the leak is. The rain we been 'avin is comin' in frou ta 'ole in ya roof. Travelling daan the walls and dripping aaat ya ceiling."

"Good-oh." Mark nodded, not letting on for a single second that he had no idea what the man had just said. "Uh, can you fix it?" He mentally crossed his fingers in the hope that he hadn't just said that he could. Or couldn't.

"Yeah, no sweat. I can do two tiles at a ton."

"A what now?"

"A ton."

"A ton of what? *Tiles*?"

"No. A hundred smackers."

Mark blanked, shaking his head.

"Paand?"

"Oh, I see. Well, that's not too bad then." Mark smiled. And phewed. Mentally.

"But that won't fix ya problem."

"Oh dear." Mark furrowed his brow, which he didn't like to do all that often as the lines weren't smoothing out after so much anymore.

"Dunno which bleedin' cowboy did ya roof last, but they didn't felt it." The man tucked a tiny pencil behind his ear. Where he'd got the pencil from was Mark's first question. Quickly followed by, *do I really want to know?*

"That cowboy would be my grandfather." Mark attempted to add a hint of pride to his voice, but the vacant expression of the workman before him just made him slink into a guilty, wincing admission. "He built the house."

"Ah. Right. 'Nover 'and-me-down was it?"

"Hand-me-down?" More deep-set wrinkles formed on Mark's brow. He must remember to use that skincare range for men he'd got as a Secret Santa present at work last year, the one that claimed to defy even the deepest-set wrinkles. He had a hunch who'd been bold enough to buy that for him. *Bloody Yvonne.*

The man waved, indicating Mark's attire. "The clothes."

Mark held out his arms, still clutching his mug of tea, and peered down at himself. Trusty grey corduroy trousers, wonderful and comfy, and rather warm considering the current climate, matched with a white button-down shirt. The vest underneath was simply due to the fact that his dark nipples tended to show through the thin material of cheap cotton. He'd discovered that tidbit of information back at secondary school when the popular boys used to poke his nipples through his school shirt, many twisting for added effect. *And people say all-boy grammar schools are a safe haven from bullying.*

Mark ran a hand through his thick dark hair, sliding it across his forehead in a floppy fringe, ignoring the jibe at his attire and moving on to the pressing transaction at hand. "So you were saying about the roof?"

"Yeah. Gonna need ta replace it." The man sniffed, his chest rising with the inhale of breath, then shrugged. "Set ya back 'bout five grand."

The fact that Mark had chosen the man's pause to take a sip of tea probably summed up his entire existence. It had been, of course, the wrong decision. He spat the tea out, liquid escaping from his nose, and coughed, gasping to get air, rather than the delightful Twinings English Breakfast, into his lungs.

The workman slapped him on the back. Perhaps he thought that would help the situation. It didn't. It only exacerbated it, knocking Mark off his feet and forcing him to grapple for the banister to prevent a rather tragic tumble down the stairs.

"Better out than in, I say." The workman *did* say.

Mark blanked. If only the boys at his delightful modern secondary grammar had believed in that statement back when Mark had been in year ten and announcing to the world he was gay. Not that any of his peers had had any doubt before Mark had made his fabulous speech. But Mark presumed they would have preferred him to stay in on that day, considering many had received detention for the words of "encouragement" they had called out in a perfect display of teenage camaraderie.

"Well, I can do the tiles tomorra," the man carried on, oblivious to Mark's inner turmoil. "Fink about the rest of da roof, though. You don't want it cavin' in on ya."

Mark nodded, although, right then the thought of paying out five thousand pounds that he didn't have made him consider the alternative option.

"Righty-oh. Thank you very much for coming out on such short notice." Mark ushered him down the stairs.

"No probs. Give me card your granddad, then." The man handed over a bent business card, a mobile phone number scrawled on the back with black pen along with the words *The Man With The Van Who Can*. Mark pondered if there was anything that he couldn't? *Or wouldn't?*

"That would be rather futile. Grampy died quite some time ago."

"Oh." The man squinted, stepping out into the daylight and onto Mark's porch. "So you chose this?"

"Chose what?" Mark desperately tried not to furrow his brow.

The man waved his hand, indicating, Mark presumed, the entire house's internal decor.

"I like antiques." Could seventies decor be considered antique? He supposed it could.

"You get antique wallpaper these days then?"

Bastard. "Oh, indeed." Mark nodded. "Worth a fortune."

Mark slammed the door shut and rested his back against the wall, glancing around at the house he'd lived in coming along ten years now. It was falling apart and no redecoration had been done since probably the last time he'd been up in the loft. He sighed, slammed his mug down on the windowsill and decided now was the time for a decent cup of the good stuff.

Grabbing his black Barbour jacket from the coat hooks, he slipped his feet into the black loafers by the door then ventured out into the morning sun. And what a glorious day it was, perfect to be beside the seaside. And Mark was. He lived directly opposite the pebble beach of Marsby in the south east, a quaint little seaside town that homed more retirees than tourists. Not that Mark was retired. He could only wish for that, although he was leaning nearer to the end of his career than the start. Mid-career, perhaps? *Christ, maybe I should think about actually having a career rather than simply a job that barely pays the bills?*

Trying to forget that he had left a gaping hole in his roof — and now his ceiling having forgotten to shut the loft hatch — Mark rammed his hands into his jacket pockets and thanked whomever above for the abnormal radiant sun. And that was when the inevitable dark clouds glided overhead and droplets landed with splats on his cheeks. Such was Mark's luck. So he trotted that bit faster along the pathway beside the beach and into the main High Street, stopping at the welcoming sign of Macy's Ye Olde Style Tea Shoppe on the corner.

The bell above the door chimed as Mark hurried into his regular haunt. He'd been going there for quite a few years now, since his move back to his home town from the mean streets of London, and still hadn't figured out why Macy added the extra p and e to the shop. He shook his hair out like a wet dog and nodded at the umbrellas Macy always offered to customers on such regular occurrences as torrential rain, a quick downpour, scattered showers and that really fine light rain that has one believing they aren't getting wet until they get home and their clothes are sopping.

The shop was empty, which was rather odd. There was usually someone sipping on a decent cup of tea made from the loose leaves in a well-stewed pot. Macy made proper tea, using a strainer, and it tasted every bit of the aromatic leaves that it should. She was also a rather good baker and Mark was horrified that there were no buns, baps or any other derogatory term used for parts of the female anatomy displayed on the counter for Mark to scoff and instantly burn off the calories by breathing. He had a fast metabolism, which was both a dream and a curse.

As Mark slapped a hand down on the counter, he heard shuffling back in the kitchen area. Thank God Macy was there. He needed a chat. And a tea.

"Helloooo? Only me, love. Usual cuppa when you're ready."

Drumming his fingers on the counter, Mark swivelled a one-eighty. Vacant seats and no-one in the vicinity looking like they might want venture on in to grab a tea to go, which would be quite difficult as Macy only served tea in porcelain cups. And rightly so.

"So, Macy, love," Mark called out over his shoulder, thinking it was best to fill her in now or he might not have time to divulge all the details of his eventful morning before he had to head into work. "I've decided I'm better off if I just kill myself now."

He leaned forward over the counter, ensuring his voice would drift to the kitchen. "Turns out my roof might collapse on me anyway. And according to this rather annoyingly beefcaked member of the male species, the sight of whose perfectly rounded behind is now imprinted on me for many a future solo endeavour, and who graced me with a whole other English language making me feel every bit of my — cough — years, it's going to cost me rather more than my arm and my leg. And I'm sadly going to have to admit it, Macy love, that I'm not sure the fellow would accept an offer of my penis as monetary value. Not that I have a wealth of offers for that part of my anatomy these days anyway. Much like the pound to the euro, I swear it's shrinking in value."

He chuckled at his own joke, as he so often did, then spun around to face the seating area. A couple of joggers zoomed past the window, obviously on their beachside run rather than the mad dash for cakes and biscuits that he did.

"You okay, Mace? Need a hand?"

No reply. So Mark leafed through the selection of pre-packed biscuits crammed in the bowl by the till. Macy had one of those old-fashioned registers. No electronic buttons to press. No new-fangled tablet hooked up to the mains. It was basically a calculator with a drawer.

Choosing a packet of chocolate-dipped Viennese shortbread fingers, Mark cocked his head to peer through the open kitchen door. "I mean, Macy, what is the point in filing paperwork for a living just to earn enough money to fix a roof when I have no man to enjoy the comforts of my damp-free living space along with me? And by the time I find a willing participant to snuggle with me on my *antique* sofa looking at my *antique* wallpaper in my *antique* house, I'll be ready to pop my clogs anyway. So, death by sugar, please, Macy."

He slapped the counter to finalise his self-depreciative monologue, and nearly threw up the entire contents of his breakfast when a male vacated the back kitchen. Said man was wiping his hands on a rather beautifully stitched gingham tea towel. But that wasn't the only thing that was a delight for the eye. The man was shirtless—rippling muscles, a glowing sheen of glistening skin and white-wash jeans hanging low on his perfectly sculpted hips. Needless to say, that wasn't Macy.

"Hello," Mark said, because, it is the polite way to greet a man, regardless of the lack of shirt and the highly embarrassing fact that Mark had already told his life story, leaving out all, or indeed any, good bits.

"G'day," the man replied.

PUBLISHING

Sign up for our newsletter and find out about all our romance book releases, eBook sales and promotions, sneak peeks and FREE romance books!

About the Author

Brought up in a relatively small town in Hertfordshire, C F White managed to do what most other residents try to do and fail — leave.

Studying at a West London university, she realised there was a whole city out there waiting to be discovered, so, much like Dick Whittington before her, she never made it back home and still endlessly searches for the streets paved with gold, slowly coming to the realisation they're mostly paved with chewing gum. And the odd bit of graffiti. And those little circles of yellow spray paint where the council point out the pot holes to someone who is supposedly meant to fix them instead of staring at them vacantly whilst holding a polystyrene cup of watered-down coffee.

She eventually moved West to East along that vast District Line and settled for pie and mash, cockles and winkles and a bit of Knees Up Mother Brown to live in the East End of London; securing a job and creating a life, a home and a family.

Having worked in Higher Education for most of her career, a life-altering experience brought pen back to paper after she'd written stories as a child but never had the confidence to show them to the world. Having embarked on this writing malarkey, C F White cannot stop. So strap in, it's gonna be a bumpy ride...

C F White loves to hear from readers. You can find her contact information, website details and author profile page at https://www.pride-publishing.com